T0109520

THE CASE OF THE BAITED HOOK

ERLE STANLEY GARDNER (1889-1970) was the best-selling American author of the 20th century, mainly due to the enormous success of his Perry Mason series, which numbered more than 80 novels and inspired a half-dozen motion pictures, radio programs, and a long-running television series that starred Raymond Burr. Having begun his career as a pulp writer, Gardner brought a hard-boiled style and sensibility to the early Mason books, but gradually developed into a more classic detective story novelist, showing enough clues to allow the astute reader to solve the mystery. For more than a quarter of a century he wrote more than a million words a year under his own name and numerous pseudonyms, the most famous being A. A. Fair.

OTTO PENZLER, the creator of American Mystery Classics, is also the founder of the Mysterious Press (1975), a literary crime imprint; MysteriousPress.com (2011), an electronic-book publishing company; and New York City's Mysterious Bookshop (1979). He has won a Raven, the Ellery Queen Award, two Edgars (for the *Encyclopedia of Mystery and Detection*, 1977, and *The Lineup*, 2010), and lifetime achievement awards from NoirCon and *The Strand Magazine*. He has edited more than 70 anthologies and written extensively about mystery fiction.

THE CASE OF THE BAITED HOOK

ERLE STANLEY GARDNER

Introduction by
OTTO PENZLER

AMERICAN MYSTERY CLASSICS

Penzler Publishers
New York

Published in 2020 by Penzler Publishers
58 Warren Street, New York, NY 10007
penzlerpublishers.com

Distributed by W. W. Norton

Cover image: Andy Ross
Cover design: Mauricio Diaz

Paperback ISBN 978-1-61316-174-6
Hardcover ISBN 978-1-61316-172-2
eBook ISBN 978-1-61316-173-9

Library of Congress Control Number: 2020902252

Printed in the United States of America

9 8 7 6 5 4 3 2 1

THE CASE OF
THE BAITED HOOK

INTRODUCTION

On several occasions, Erle Stanley Gardner said, "I'm no writer."

There were numerous voices who felt differently. In 1934, only a year after his first novel, *The Case of the Velvet Claws*, was published, G.K. Chesterton wrote admiringly of his work. Sinclair Lewis, in an article on writers in 1937, wrote, ". . . the magicians are the authors of literate detective stories: Agatha Christie, Francis Iles, Erle Stanley Gardner, H.C. Bailey." The mystery aficionado W. Somerset Maugham in the early 1940s wrote that he read "Dashiell Hammett and Brett Halliday for rough stuff; Rex Stout, Ellery Queen, Gardner, Christie, and H.C. Bailey." In the same decades, the *Time* magazine reviewer of *The Case of the Cautious Coquette* quoted Evelyn Waugh, a close friend of Graham Greene, as saying he wished he could "write whodunits like Erle Stanley Gardner and Margery Allingham."

To talk about Gardner, it is inevitable that large numbers come into play. Here are a few:

- 86—Number of Perry Mason books; eighty-two novels, four short story collections.

- 130—Number of mystery novels written by Gardner.

- 1,200,000—The number of words that Gardner wrote annually during most of the 1920s and 1930s. That is a novel a month, plus a stack of short stories, for a fifteen-year stretch.

- 2,400,000—The number of words Gardner wrote in his most productive year, 1932.

- 300,000,000—The number of books Gardner has sold in the United States alone, making him the best-selling writer in the history of American literature.

What cannot be quantified is what magic resided in that indefatigable brain that made so many millions of readers come back, book after book, for more of the same. Not that it was ever actually the same.

The Perry Mason series had a template, a model, a formula, if you like. But the series changed dramatically over the years. Gardner started his career as a writer for the pulp magazines that flourished in the 1920s and 1930s. Authors were famously paid a penny a word by most of the pulps, but the top writers in the top magazines managed to get all the way up to three cents a word. This munificent fee was reserved for the best of the best of their time, some of whom remain popular and successful to the present day (Dashiell Hammett, Raymond Chandler, Cornell Woolrich), some of whom are remembered and read mostly by the modest coterie that avidly reads and collects pulp fiction (Carroll John Daly, Arthur Leo Zagat, Arthur J. Burks). One who earned the big bucks regularly, especially when he wrote for *Black Mask*, the greatest of the pulps, was Erle Stanley Gardner.

Gardner had learned and honed his craft in the pulps, so it is not surprising that the earliest Perry Mason novels were hard-boiled, tough-guy books, with Mason as a fearless, two-fisted battler, rather than the calm, self-possessed figure that most readers remember today. Reading the first Mason novels, *The Case of the Velvet Claws*, published in 1933, and *The Case of the Baited Hook*, published seven years later, it is difficult to remember that they were written by the same author. Both styles, by the way, were first-rate, just different.

Gardner was born in Malden, Massachusetts, in 1889. Because his father was a mining engineer, he traveled often as a child. As a teenager, he participated in professional boxing as well as promoting unlicensed matches, placing himself at risk of criminal prosecution, which gave him an interest in the law. He took a job as a typist at a California law firm and after reading law for fifty hours a week for three years, he was admitted to the California bar. He practiced in Oxnard from 1911 to 1918, gaining a reputation as a champion of the underdog through his defense of poor Mexican and Chinese clients.

He left to become a tire salesman in order to earn more money but he missed the courtroom and joined another law firm in 1921. It is then that he started to write fiction, hoping that he could augment his modest income. He worked a full day at court, followed that with several hours of research in the law library, then went home to write fiction into the small hours, setting a goal of at least 4,000 words a day. He sold two stories in 1921, none in 1922, and only one in 1923, but it was to the prestigious *Black Mask*. The following year, thirteen of his stories saw print, five of them in *Black Mask*. Over the next decade he wrote nearly fifteen million words and sold hundreds of stories, many pseudonymously so that he could have multiple stories in a single magazine, each under a different name.

In 1932, he finally took a vacation, an extended trip to China, since he had become so financially successful. That is also the year in which he began to submit his first novel, *The Case of the Velvet Claws*. It was rejected by several publishers before William Morrow took it, and Gardner published every mystery with that house for the rest of his life. Thayer Hobson, then the president of Morrow, suggested that the protagonist of that book, Perry Mason, should become a series character and Gardner agreed.

The Mason novels became an immediate success so Gardner resigned from his law practice to devote full time to writing. He was eager to have privacy so acquired parcels of land in the Southwest and eventually settled into the "Gardner Fiction Factory" on a thousand-acre ranch in Temecula, California. The ranch had a dozen guest cottages and trailers to house his support staff of twenty employees, all of whom are reported to have called him "Uncle Erle." Among them were six secretaries, all working full time, transcribing his dictated novels, non-fiction books and articles, and correspondence.

He was intensely interested in prison conditions and was a strong advocate of reform. In 1948, he formed the Court of Last Resort, a private organization dedicated to helping those believed to have been unfairly incarcerated. The group succeeded in freeing many unjustly convicted men and Gardner wrote a book, *The Court of Last Resort*, describing the group's work; it won an Edgar for the best fact crime book of the year.

In the 1960s, Gardner became alarmed at some changes in American literature. He told the *New York Times*, "I have always aimed my fiction at the masses who constitute the solid backbone of America, I have tried to keep faith with the American family. In a day when the prevailing mystery story trends are towards sex, sadism, and seduction, I try to base my stories on speed, situation, and suspense."

While Gardner wrote prolifically about a wide variety of characters under many pseudonyms, most notably thirty novels about Bertha Cook and Donald Lam under the nom de plume A. A. Fair, all his books give evidence of clearly identifiable characteristics. There is a minimum of description and a maximum of dialogue. This was carried to a logical conclusion in the lengthy courtroom interrogations of the Perry Mason series. Mason and Gardner's other heroes are not averse to breaking the exact letter of the law in order to secure what they consider to be justice. They share contempt for pomposity. Villains or deserving victims are often self-important, wealthy individuals who can usually be identified because Gardner has given them two last names (such as Harrington Faulkner).

Mason's clients usually have something to hide and, although they are ultimately proven innocent, their secretiveness makes them appear suspect.

Clues often take a back seat in the Perry Mason books, with crisp dialogue and hectic action taking the forefront—a structure clearly adopted from his days as a pulp writer. Crime and motivation are not paragons of originality as Gardner wanted readers to identify with his characters.

Much like the Sherlock Holmes and Nero Wolfe stories, the Perry Mason novels also feature certain other characters on a regular basis. The most prominent is Della Street, Mason's secretary and the love of his life. Knowing that Mason would not allow her to work, she has refused his marriage proposals on five separate occasions. She has, however, remained steadfastly loyal, risking her life and freedom on his behalf; she has been arrested five times while performing her job.

Also present at all times is Paul Drake, the private detective who handles the lawyer's investigative work. He is invariably at Mason's side in times of stress, though he frequently complains that the work is bad for his digestion.

Hamilton Burger is the district attorney whose office has never successfully prosecuted one of Mason's clients. In a large percentage of those cases, the client was arrested through the efforts of the attorney's implacable (albeit friendly) foe, Lieutenant Arthur Tragg.

Although Mason is invariably well-prepared, he is so skilled at courtroom procedure that he can think on his feet and ask just the right question to befuddle a witness, embarrass a prosecutor, and exonerate a client.

The staggering popularity of the Perry Mason novels inevitably led to him being portrayed in other media, including six motion pictures in the 1930s, a successful radio series in the 1940s, and a top-rated television series starring Raymond Burr that began in 1957 and ran for a decade. More than a half-century later, it is still a staple of late-night television re-runs.

—OTTO PENZLER

1.

Two persons in the city had the number of Perry Mason's private, unlisted telephone. One was Della Street, Mason's secretary, and the other Paul Drake, head of the Drake Detective Agency.

It was early in March, a blustery night with rain pelting at intervals against the windows. Wind howled around the cornices and fought its way through the narrow openings in the windows to billow the lace curtains of Mason's apartment into weird shapes which alternately blossomed into white ghosts, collapsed, and dropped limply back against the casements.

Mason fought off the heavy lethargy of that deep sleep which comes during the first part of the night, to grope for the ringing telephone.

The instrument momentarily eluded his sleep-deadened fingers.

Mason's right hand found the chain which dangled from the light over his bed. At the same time, his left, reaching for the telephone, became entangled with the cord and knocked the instrument to the floor.

Now thoroughly awake, he retrieved the telephone, placed the receiver to his ear, and said, "My gosh, Della, why don't you go to bed at a decent hour?"

A man's voice said, "Mr. Mason?"

Surprised, Mason said, "Yes. Who is it?"

The voice said crisply, "You are talking with Cash."

Mason sat up in bed, bolstering himself against the pillow. "That's nice," he said. "How's Carry?"

For a moment the voice was puzzled. "Carrie?" it asked. "I don't know to whom you refer."

"Come, come," Mason said amiably. "If you're Cash, you must know Carry."

"Oh, a pun," the voice said with the offended dignity of a man who has no sense of humor. "I didn't understand at first."

"What," Mason asked, "do you want?"

"I want to come to your office."

"And I," Mason said, "want to stay in bed."

The man at the other end of the line said, carefully clipping his words, "I have two one-thousand-dollar bills in my wallet, Mr. Mason. If you will come to your office and accept the employment I have to offer, I will give you those two one-thousand-dollar bills as a retainer. I will also arrange for a further payment of ten thousand dollars whenever you are called upon to take any action in my behalf."

"Murder?" Mason asked.

The voice hesitated for a moment, then said, "No."

"Let me have your full name."

"I'm sorry. That's impossible."

Mason said irritably, "It only costs ten cents to put through a telephone call and talk big money. Before I go to the office I want to know with whom I'm dealing."

After a moment's hesitation, the voice said, "This is John L. Cragmore."

"Where do you live?"

"5619 Union Drive."

Mason said, "Okay. It'll take me twenty minutes to get there. Can you be there by that time?"

"Yes," the man said, and added courteously, "Thank you for coming, Mr. Mason," and hung up the telephone.

Mason scrambled out of bed, closed the windows, and picked up the telephone directory. There was no Cragmore listed at the address given on Union Drive.

Mason dialed the number of the Drake Detective Agency. A night operative said in a bored monotone, "Drake Detective Agency."

"Mason talking," the lawyer said crisply. "I have an appointment in twenty minutes at my office. The man will probably drive up in a car. Put an operative at each end of the block. Check the license numbers of any cars that park anywhere in the block. Get all the dope you can, and have it ready when I call. I'll drop in at your place just before I go to my office."

Mason hung up the telephone, stripped off his pajamas, and hurriedly pulled on his clothes, noticing as he dressed that his wrist watch gave the hour as ten minutes past midnight. He ran a comb through the tangled mass of hair, struggled into a raincoat, gave a hasty look about the apartment, and paused to telephone the night clerk to have the hotel garage deliver his car. He switched off the lights, pulled the door shut, and rang for the elevator.

The Negro elevator boy looked at him curiously. "Rainin' pow'ful hard, Mista Mason."

"Cats and dogs?" Mason asked.

The boy flashed white teeth. "No, suh. Ducks and drakes. You goin' out some place, suh?"

"There is," Mason announced, "no rest for the wicked."

The boy rolled his eyes. "Meanin' you's wicked?" he asked.

"No," Mason said with a grin, as the elevator slid to a smooth stop at the lobby floor. "My clients are."

He greeted the night clerk on duty at the desk, said, "You got my message through to the garage man?"

"Yes, Mr. Mason. Your car will be waiting. Pretty wild night."

Mason nodded absently, tossed his key to the desk, and strode across to the stairway which led to the garage, the skirts of his raincoat kicked about by the long strides of his legs. The clerk watched him curiously, the extent of his interest shown by the manner in which he weighed Mason's key in his hand before placing it in the proper receptacle.

The lawyer acknowledged the greeting of the garage man, slid in behind the wheel of his big coupe, and sent it roaring up the spiral ramp of the garage. As he left the shelter of the garage, the wind swooped down upon him. Sheeted rain beat solidly on the body of the car, streamed down the windshield. Mason turned on the windshield wiper, shifted cautiously into second, and eased the wheels through the curb-high flood at the gutter.

The headlights reflected back from miniature geysers of water mushrooming up from the pavement ahead. Mason eased the car into high gear and settled down to the chore of driving through the rain-swept, all but deserted streets.

He noticed that there were no cars parked in the block in front of his office building. Over in the parking station, where Mason rented a regular stall, were two of the nondescript cars of the Drake Detective Agency, and no others. He parked and locked his automobile, and stepped out into the storm. Rain beat against his face, cascaded in rivulets from his raincoat, spattered against his ankles. Mason, who detested umbrellas, shoved his hands down deep into the pockets of his raincoat, lowered his head against the force of the storm, and sloshed through the puddles which had collected in the parking place, to push against the swinging door in the lighted lobby of his office building.

Streaks of moisture which seemed fresh indicated that others were there ahead of him. He paused at the elevator, rang the night bell which summoned the janitor, and waited for a full minute before the sleepy-eyed Swede, who had charge of the basement and night elevators, brought a cage up to the lobby floor.

"Some rain," the janitor said, and yawned.

Mason crossed over to look at the register which persons entering the building at night must sign. "Anyone for me, Ole?" he asked.

"Not yet," the janitor said. "Maybe she rain so much they don't come on schedule."

"Someone down from Drake's office a few minutes ago?" Mason asked.

"Yah."

"Still out?" Mason inquired.

"No. He comes back oop."

"No one else been in in the meantime?"

"No."

The janitor missed the floor by six inches with the elevator, and Mason said, "That's good enough, Ole."

The sliding doors rolled smoothly back, and Mason stepped out into the semi-darkness of the long corridor. He walked rapidly to where the corridor made a T, but in place of turning left to his own office, turned right toward the oblong of illumination which marked the frosted glass door of the Drake Detective Agency. He pushed open this door and crossed a small waiting room just large enough to accommodate an open bench and two straight-back chairs.

Behind an arch-shaped, grilled window marked "Information," the night switchboard operator looked up, nodded, and pressed the button which released the catch on the swinging door.

Near a radiator, an undersized man was trying to dry the bottoms of his trousers. A soggy felt hat and a glistening raincoat hung on a rack near the radiator.

"Hello, Curly," Mason said. "Did you give up?"

"Give up," the operative asked, looking ruefully down at his wet shoes. "What do you mean, give up?"

"Ole says no one came up."

"Yeah," the operative said. "What Ole doesn't know would fill a book."

"Then someone came in?"

"Yeah. Two of 'em."

"How did they get up?"

"The man," Curly said, "pulled out a key ring, unlocked the door of one of the elevators, switched on the lights, and whisked himself and the woman up here just as neat as a pin. By the time I got up, the cage was there with the door locked and the lights out."

"Did Ole notice it?" Mason asked, interested.

"No. He was too sleepy. He's having a hard time keeping his eyes open."

"Then there's a man and a woman on this floor?"

"Uh huh."

"How long ago?"

"They've been waiting about five minutes. Gosh, I wish you'd pick clear nights for your shadowing jobs. I felt like a guy trapped in a sunken submarine."

"Where did you pick them up?"

"They came in a car. The man was driving. He dropped the woman in front of the lobby. Then he drove on and turned the corner. I figured he was parking the car, so I took it easy, tailed him into the building, and up to this floor."

"How about the automobile?"

"I got the license number and checked on the registration. It's owned by Robert Peltham of 3212 Oceanic. I checked up on him in the telephone directory. He's listed as an architect."

Mason thoughtfully took a cigarette case from his pocket, scraped a match on the side of the radiator, and began smoking. "How about the girl?"

"There's something funny about her," Curly said. "I call her a girl. I don't know. She was a jane. That's all I know. She's all bundled up in a big black raincoat. She walks like her shoes were two sizes too big for her feet, and she kept a newspaper over her face."

"A newspaper?" Mason asked.

"Uh huh. When she got out of the car, she put a newspaper up over her head as though to protect her hat, but I noticed she had the newspaper held over her face when they went up in the elevator. And that's the last I've seen of them."

"They're on this floor?"

"The cage is."

Mason said, "Find out all you can about Peltham."

"I'm working on it," Curly said. "Got an operative on the job now. Do you want me to report at your office?"

"No," Mason said. "I'll get in touch with you. In about fifteen minutes you'd better come in my office and get a drink of whiskey—unless Paul keeps a bottle in *his* desk."

"Thanks a lot, Mr. Mason. I'll be in."

Mason said, "I'll do better than that. I'll put the bottle on a desk in the entrance room, and leave the door unlocked."

"Gee, that'll be swell. Thanks."

Mason's heels pounded echoes from the silent walls as he marched down the corridor toward the end of the passage where he had his office.

He saw no one, heard no sound save the pound of his own footfalls. He unlocked the door of the reception office, left it unlatched, and walked on into his private office. He opened the drawer of his desk, found a pint of whiskey, and was just placing it on the desk used by the information clerk when the door opened and a thinnish man in the late thirties said, "Mr. Mason, I presume?"

Mason nodded.

"I'm Peltham."

Mason raised his eyebrows. "I thought the name was Cragmore," he said.

"It was," Peltham observed dryly, "but several things have caused me to change it."

"May I ask what those things are?" Mason asked.

Peltham smiled, a frosty gesture of the lips. "To begin with," he said, "I was followed from the time I parked my car. It was cleverly done—but I was followed just the same. I notice that the office of the Drake Detective Agency is on this floor. After you came up in the elevator, you went down to that office and were there for some five minutes. I notice that you are now placing a bottle of whiskey on your desk where it can be picked up. Under the circumstances, Mr. Mason, we'll abandon our little subterfuge. The name is Peltham, and we won't bother beating around the bush. You've won the first trick rather neatly—but don't over-bid your hand."

Mason said, "Come in," and indicated the door to his private office. "You're alone?" he asked.

"You know I'm not."

"Who's the woman," Mason asked; "—that is, does she enter into the case?"

"We'll talk about that."

Mason indicated a chair, slipped out of his raincoat, shook drops from the brim of his hat, and settled back in the big swivel chair behind the desk.

His visitor gravely took out a wallet. "I suppose, Mr. Mason," he said, extracting two one-thousand-dollar bills, "that when I said I'd pay you two thousand dollars for taking this case, you hardly expected to see the color of my money so soon."

He didn't hand Mason the two one-thousand-dollar bills, but held them in his hand as though just ready to place them on the edge of Mason's desk.

"What," Mason asked, "is the case?"

"There isn't any."

Mason raised his eyebrows.

"I," Peltham said, "am in trouble."

"*You* are?"

"Yes."

"Exactly what is it?"

Peltham said, "I don't want you to bother about that. I have my own ways of handling those things. What I want you to do is to protect her."

"From what?" Mason asked.

"From everything."

"And who is she?"

Peltham said, "First I want to know whether you'll accept the employment."

"I'd have to know more about it," Mason told him.

"What, for instance?"

"Exactly what you think is going to happen—what you want her protected against."

Peltham lowered his eyes to study the carpet for several thoughtful seconds.

"She's here," Mason said. "Why not bring her in?"

Peltham raised his eyes to Mason. "Understand this, Mr. Mason," he said. "No one must ever know the identity of this woman."

"Why?"

"It's dynamite."

"What do you mean?"

"Simply that if it was known this woman had any connection with me, it would raise the very devil all around. It would bring about the very situation I'm trying to avoid."

"What," Mason asked, "is she to you?"

Peltham said steadily, "She's everything to me."

"Do I understand you want me to represent some woman, but I'm not to know who she is?"

"Exactly."

Mason laughed. "Good Lord, man! You seem entirely sober and in possession of your senses."

"I am."

"But you're asking the impossible. I can't represent a client unless I know who she is."

Peltham got up from the chair. He walked gravely across to the exit door which led from Mason's private office to the corridor. He said, "Pardon me, Mr. Mason, if I seem to take a liberty." He clicked back the spring lock on the door and stepped out into the corridor. Mason could hear low-voiced conversation, and a few moments later the door opened and Peltham ushered a woman into the room.

She was garbed in a dark raincoat, buttoned up around the throat, which stretched almost to the ground and concealed all of her figure. It was a voluminous coat either cut for a person several sizes larger or else it had originally been a part of a man's wardrobe. She wore a small, close-fitting hat which nestled well down on her head. The upper part of her face was concealed by a mask, through which sparkling dark eyes held a twinkle that was almost a glitter.

"Come in, dear, and sit down," Peltham said.

The woman walked calmly across the office to seat herself in the chair opposite the lawyer. Her chin, the tip of her nose, and the full-bodied crimson lips indicated youth, but there was nothing else about her to give a clue to her age or appearance. She sat motionless in the chair, her hands concealed in black gloves. She did not cross her knees, but sat with her feet flat on the floor. Those feet were encased in galoshes which were evidently a size too large.

"Good evening," Mason said.

She might not have heard him. Her eyes—dark, glittering, and restless—stared through the eyeholes in the mask.

Mason quite evidently began to enjoy the bizarre situation. Outside the dark windows of the office, wind-driven rain pelted against the glass, lending a semblance of fitting background to the situation.

Peltham was the one person in the office who seemed to see nothing unusual in the conference. He once more took from his pocket a pin-seal wallet. From it he took a bank note. "This, Mr. Mason," he said, "is a ten-thousand-dollar bill. Perhaps you would care to examine it to see that it is genuine."

He passed the bill across to the lawyer who looked it over and silently handed it back.

"Have you a pair of scissors, dear?" Peltham asked.

The woman wordlessly opened a black purse and took out a pair of curved manicure scissors. She handed these to Peltham who took them and walked over to Mason's desk. He held the bill in his left hand, the scissors in his right.

With the careful touch of a man whose hands are trained to do exactly what he wants them to do, he cut the bill in two pieces by a series of curved segments.

With the last snip of the small scissors, a piece of the bill representing about one-third of its area fluttered to Mason's desk.

Peltham returned the scissors to the masked woman. He held the two sections of the ten-thousand-dollar bill so that Mason could see they fitted perfectly, then he presented the larger portion of the bill to the woman, and dropped the smaller portion on top of the two one-thousand-dollar bills, which he shoved across the desk to Mason.

"There you are," he said. "I don't want a receipt. Your word's good. You'll never know this woman's identity unless it becomes necessary for you to know it in order to protect her interests. At that time, she'll give you the rest of this ten-thousand-dollar bill. That will be her introduction. You can paste the two halves together, take it down to your bank, and deposit it. In that way, your fee will be guaranteed, and there'll be no chance of an impostor imposing on you."

"Suppose someone else should get that other half of the bill?"

"No one will."

Mason looked across at the woman. "You understand what Mr. Peltham is asking of me?" he asked.

She nodded.

"I take it that you knew what he had in mind when he came here?"

Again she nodded.

"And you're satisfied to have me accept employment under those conditions?"

Again there was a nod.

Mason straightened in his chair, turned to Peltham, and said, "All right. Sit down. Let's get down to brass tacks. . . . You want me to represent this woman. I don't know who she is. Perhaps tomorrow morning someone will walk in and ask me to take a case. I'll accept the employment. Later on, this woman will announce that she's the adverse party in that case, and hand me the rest of this ten-thousand-dollar bill. I'd then find myself retained on both sides of the same case.

"I think that explains my position. I can't do it. What you ask is impossible. I'm interested, but I can't do it."

Peltham raised his left hand to his head. The tips of his fingers massaged the left temple. He was silent for an interval. "All right," he said at length. "Here's how we'll get around that. You're free to take any case except one that involves matters in which I am apparently directly or indirectly interested. If such a case should come to your office, you will get my permission before you accept the employment."

"How can I get that permission?" Mason asked. "In other words, how can I get in touch with you? Will you be instantly available?"

Again Peltham rubbed his temple for several seconds of thoughtful deliberation. Then he said, "No."

"All right," Mason said impatiently. "That leaves us right back where we started."

"No, it doesn't. There's another way."

"What is it?"

"You can put an ad in the *Contractor's Journal* in the personal column. You will address it simply to *P*, and sign it with the single initial, *M*. You will ask in that ad if there is any objection to your accepting employment on behalf of the person calling on you."

"That," Mason said, "wouldn't be fair to my other clients. Clients don't care to have their names broadcast in the personal columns of a newspaper."

"Don't mention that person by name," Peltham said. "Take the telephone directory, list the number of the page, the column, and the position of the name in that column. For instance, if it's a person on page 1000 of the telephone directory, the fourth name down from the top in the third column, you will simply say, 'If I accept employment for 1000-3-4, would I be in danger of handling a case against you?'"

"And you'll answer it?"

"If I don't answer it within forty-eight hours," Peltham said, "you may consider yourself free to accept the employment."

"And how," Mason asked, "will I know about your affairs? I take it, you have somewhat diversified business interests. I may not know . . ."

Peltham interrupted. For the first time, there was in his voice evidence of mental tension. "You'll know by tomorrow," he said, "—that is, if you read the newspapers."

Mason said, "It's goofy. It doesn't make sense."

Peltham indicated the two thousand dollars on the desk. "There's two thousand dollars," he said. "That money is paid over to you with no questions asked. I don't want a receipt. I'll take your word. Ninety-nine chances out of a hundred you won't have to turn a finger. That money will be velvet. But if you should become active on behalf of this woman, you will then automatically receive the additional ten thousand dollars."

Mason said, with finality, "I'll take you up on that proposition on one condition."

"What's the condition?"

"That I'll use my best efforts to be fair. I'll act in the highest good faith. If I make a mistake, and find myself involved, I have the right to return the two thousand dollars and wipe the matter off the books as effectively as though we'd never had this conversation."

Peltham glanced inquiringly at the masked woman.

She shook her head vigorously.

Mason said, "That's my proposition. Take it or leave it."

Peltham looked about him at the walls of the office. His eyes fastened on the door to the law library. "Could we," he asked, "go in there for a moment?"

"Go right ahead," Mason said, and then added, "Are you afraid to have me hear this woman's voice?"

It was Peltham who started to answer the question, but the vigorous nodding of the woman's head gave Mason his answer.

The lawyer laughed. "Go ahead," he said. "After all, it's your show. I'm just sitting in the wings."

"In a twelve-thousand-dollar seat," Peltham said with some feeling. "It's bank night as far as you're concerned, Mr. Mason, and you've won the jackpot."

Mason indicated the door of the law library with a gesture. "Go ahead," he said. "I'm going to be back in bed within thirty minutes. You have my proposition. Take it or leave it."

Peltham crossed over to her chair. "Come, dear," he said.

She arose with some reluctance. He cupped his hand under her elbow, and they walked across the office, her raincoat rustling as she walked.

The galoshes gave her a somewhat awkward gait. The raincoat, hanging loosely from her shoulders, gave no indication of the contours of her figure, but there was something in her gait which showed that she was young and lithe.

Mason pinched out his cigarette, tilted back in the chair, crossed his ankles on the corner of the desk, and waited.

They were back in less than three minutes. "Your proposition is accepted," Peltham said. "I only ask that you use the highest good faith."

"I'll do the best I can," Mason said, "and that's all I can promise."

For a moment, it seemed that Peltham was about to put more cards on the table. His face twisted with expression as he leaned forward across Mason's desk. "Look here," he said, in a voice harsh with emotion—and then caught himself.

Mason waited.

Peltham took a deep breath. "Mr. Mason," he said, "I wouldn't do this if it weren't absolutely necessary. For two hours now, I've been racking my brain trying to find some method of accomplishing what I want to accomplish without undoing everything in the process. If it were ever surmised by anyone that this woman and I had any connection, it would . . . it would . . . it would be absolutely ruinous to all concerned. I must keep her out of that at any cost—no matter *what* it costs. Do you understand?"

"I can't understand the necessity for all this hodgepodge," Mason said. "After all, you could afford to be frank with me. I don't betray the secrets of my clients. I respect them. If this young woman wants to take off her mask and . . ."

"That's impossible," Peltham snapped. "I've worked out the only scheme which will give us all protection."

"You don't trust me?" Mason asked.

"Suppose," Peltham countered, "that you happened to have information which the police considered vital evidence. Would you be justified in withholding it?"

"I'd protect the interests of a client," Mason said. "I'm a lawyer. A client's communications are confidential."

Peltham's voice was determined. "No," he said shortly. "This is the only way."

Mason looked at him curiously. "You evidently have made elaborate preparations for this interview."

"What do you mean?"

"The elevator for instance."

Peltham dismissed the matter with a gesture. "Whenever I do anything," he said, "I lay my plans carefully and well in advance. I have watched your career with interest. Months ago I decided that if I ever needed a lawyer, I'd call on you. It may interest you to know, Mr. Mason, that I drew the plans for this building when it was constructed—and that at the present time, I own a controlling stock interest in it. Come, dear."

She arose and silently started for the exit door.

Mason, thinking perhaps he could surprise her into letting him hear her voice, called banteringly, "Good night, Miss Mysterious."

She turned. He saw her lips tremble in a nervous smile. She made him a slight curtsy, and wordlessly left the office.

Mason pocketed the two one-thousand-dollar bills. He looked at the fragment of the ten-thousand-dollar bill, and chuckled. Walking over to the safe, he spun the combination, opened the door, unlocked the drawer, opened it, held his hand over it for a moment, and then noisily closed the drawer and clanged the door of the safe shut. He snapped the bolt home, and twisted the combination.

But the fragment of the ten-thousand-dollar bill had not been dropped into the drawer of the safe. Instead he had unobtrusively slipped it into his trousers pocket.

He walked over to the hat tree, put on his wet hat, got into his raincoat, looked out into the outer office, and made certain that the bottle of whiskey he had placed on the desk was no longer there. He locked the door of the reception room and switched out the lights. He returned to his private office and went to the exit door. As he had surmised, Peltham had left this door unlocked, the spring lock being held back with a catch.

Mason dropped the catch, releasing the lock, switched out the lights, and went out into the echoing corridor.

He noticed that the locked, dark elevator was still on the seventh floor. He rang the elevator bell, and after a few moments, the janitor came shooting upward in the cage.

Mason indicated the dark elevator. "One of your elevators stalled on this floor?" he asked.

The janitor stepped out of the cage to stare at the elevator. "Ay be a son of a gun," he said in an astounded voice which seemed to Mason to be thoroughly genuine.

Mason entered the lighted elevator. "Okay, Ole," he said. "Let's go."

2.

DELLA STREET was opening the morning mail when Mason came sauntering into the office.

"You're early," she said. "Didn't you remember that the Case of People vs. Smithers was dismissed by the district attorney?"

"Uh huh. I came down to study the newspaper."

She stared at him with her brows arched, laughter trembling at the corners of her lips, but her eyes grew puzzled as she saw the expression on his face. "Going in for contemporary history?" she asked.

He scaled his hat to the hat tree, pushed the mail on his blotter aside without so much as glancing through it, and spread out the newspaper on the desk. "Quite a rain we had last night."

"I'll say. What about the newspaper, Chief?"

"Shortly after midnight," Mason said, "I received a two-thousand-dollar retainer and a piece out of a ten-thousand-dollar bill. I had an interesting session with a masked woman and a man who seemed very much worried about something, who intimated that some startling news would be found in the morning newspaper."

"And you can't find it?" she asked.

"I haven't looked as yet," he said with a grin. "Sufficient for the day are the business hours thereof."

"Who were the parties?"

"The man," he said, "was Robert Peltham, an architect. He didn't seem particularly pleased when I discovered his real identity. He wanted me to believe that he was John L. Cragmore of 5619 Union Drive. That was the one slip he made. There isn't any Cragmore listed at that address in the telephone book. It was a slip which I can't understand. He had so thoroughly prepared all the other steps in his campaign that I can't imagine him falling down on such a simple matter. If he'd only given me a name that appeared in the telephone book, I'd have fallen for it—at least temporarily."

"Go on," she said.

Mason told her briefly of the mysterious caller and what had taken place at the interview.

"How did he get your unlisted telephone number, Chief?"

"That is simply another indication of the care with which he'd prepared his campaign."

"It wasn't something on the spur of the moment?"

"I think the thing that caused him to call on me was something that happened rather unexpectedly, and apparently he'd decided some time ago that if he ever needed a lawyer he'd call on me, and he blueprinted his plans for reaching me and filed them away in the back of his mind. It's indicative of the man's character."

"But how about that elevator business?" Della Street asked.

"That," Mason said, "was a case where luck played into his hands. He owns a controlling stock interest in this building. He probably has duplicate keys to everything. Just as a matter of precaution, I didn't leave that fragment of the ten-thousand-dollar bill in the office overnight. I figured a man who had a key to the elevator would very probably have a passkey to my office."

"How about the woman? Do you think he'd planned to consult you in connection with her?"

"No. I think that was something that developed rather unexpectedly," Mason said musingly. "Take that mask for instance. I'm virtually certain it had been part of a costume at a masquerade ball. It was a black mask with tinsel trimming. Evidently, it had been made to go with a masquerade costume—one of the things a woman would file away in a drawer of keepsakes."

"Couldn't you tell *anything* about her, Chief?"

"I'd say she was not over thirty," Mason said, "and that she had a good figure. Her hands were small, but she was wearing gloves much too large. There were a couple of rings on the right hand, and one on the left. You could see the outlines through the gloves. She'd turned them so that the stones were on the inside."

"Wedding ring?" she asked.

"I don't think there was a wedding ring. And she was afraid to let me hear her voice."

"Then you must know her," Della Street said. "That is, you must have already met her, and she was afraid her voice would give her away."

"Either that, or I'm going to meet her in the near future. Somehow I'm more inclined to the future theory than the past."

"Why?"

"I don't know, just a hunch."

"How do we handle it on the books?"

Mason handed her the portion of the ten-thousand-dollar

bill. "That's up to you—but that piece of ten grand you've got there is powerful bait."

Della sniffed. "You know perfectly well you're more intrigued by the Mysterious Madame X than you are by the money. Why not 'The Case of the Masked Mistress'?"

"Well, that's a thought," he said, "although you may wrong the girl's morals."

"Did she look like a moral young woman?"

Mason grinned. "As to that," he said, "it's hard to tell even when you see them in complete regalia, watch the gestures of their hands, and listen to their voices. This woman kept her hands on the arm of the chair, her feet on the floor, and her mouth shut. Open up a file on 'The Case of the Baited Hook' and you'll be right whoever or whatever she is."

"And the answer's supposed to be in the newspaper?"

"Not the answer," he said, "but a clue."

"Do you want me to look through it?"

"You take the first section," he said. "I'll take the second. Let's not overlook anything: notices of death, or intentions to wed, birth notices, and divorces—particularly divorces."

And Mason promptly turned to the sporting page.

Fifteen minutes later, Della Street looked up from the section of the newspaper she had been studying. "Find anything?" she asked.

"Nuh uh."

She said, "I thought perhaps you'd find that One-punch Peltham had been signed up with Joe Louis for a fifteen-round bout."

He grinned. "No harm killing two birds with one stone, Della."

"We've thrown all our rocks, and haven't even got a feather. I can't find a thing. Did he act as though he expected it would be something obscure?"

"No, he didn't," Mason said. "I gathered that it would be spread on page one of the newspaper—something one couldn't miss."

"Well, it hasn't broken then, that's all."

"That," Mason said, "complicates matters. I don't have any idea what it was he really wanted me to do. I might take a divorce case against Mrs. Jones and have Mrs. Jones walk in and shove the other half of this ten-thousand-dollar bill across the desk, and say, 'Is this any way to treat a client?'"

"Or," Della Street said demurely, "you might fire me for inefficiency and suddenly have me push the rest of that ten-thousand-dollar bill in front of you, and say, 'Is this any way to run a law office?'"

Mason looked at her with sudden suspicion. "By George," he said, "—now you *have* given me something to think about."

She laughed.

Gertie, the big, good-natured blonde, who presided over the information desk and switchboard in Mason's outer office, tapped on the door, then opened it, and slipped into the room. "Can you," she asked, "see A. E. Tump?"

"What does he want?" Mason asked.

She shook her head. "It isn't a he. It's a she."

"What's the name?"

"Just A. E. Tump, but she's a woman."

"What does she want?"

"She wants to see you, and she looks like a woman who has a habit of getting what she wants."

"Young?" Mason asked.

"Nope. She's around sixty-five, and she still has sex appeal, if you know what I mean."

Mason said, "Good Lord, Gertie. You don't mean she's kittenish."

"No, not kittenish, and she isn't one of those women who tries to have the figure of a young woman of twenty. But . . . well, she has personality and uses it. She puts her stuff across."

Mason said to Della Street, "Go find out what she wants, Della. Give her the once-over."

Mason returned to the newspaper, turning idly through the pages, reading the headlines, and waiting.

Della Street returned in a few moments and said to Perry Mason, "She's white-haired, smooth-skinned, broad of beam, matronly in a seductive way. She seems to have money and poise and she has character and personality. Maybe you ought to see her."

"What does she want?"

"It's over a trust fund and an illegal adoption proceedings."

Mason said, "Bring her in," and Della returned to escort the new client into the office.

"Good morning, Mrs. Tump," Mason said.

She smiled at him and walked across to seat herself in the big leather chair.

Mason, sizing her up, said laughingly, "You were announced as A. E. Tump. I thought you were a man."

The woman beamed across at him. "Well, I'm not," she said. "A is for Abigail, and E is for Esther. I hate both names. They reek with respectability and Biblical associations."

"Why didn't you change your name?" Mason asked, watching her with the shrewd, lawyer-wise eyes.

"Too much trouble in connection with property. My holdings

are in the name of Abigail E. Tump. Well, I gave my daughter a break anyway."

Mason raised his eyebrows.

Mrs. Tump needed no prompting. She went on smoothly in the effortless voice of one who is an easy, fluent talker. "I christened her Cleopatra Circe Tump. I guess it embarrassed her to death, but at least she wasn't chained to a life of mediocrity by having names that were a millstone of conventional respectability around her neck."

Mason flashed a swift glance of amusement at Della Street. "Do you then associate respectability with mediocrity?"

"Not always," she said. "I haven't any quarrel with respectability. I just hate the labels, that's all."

"Did you want to consult me about your daughter?"

"No. She married a banker in Des Moines—a stuffed shirt, if you ask me. She's a pillar of respectability, and hates her names as badly as I hated mine. None of her friends even know about the Circe part of her name."

Mason smiled. "What *was* the matter you wanted to discuss?"

She said, "It goes back to 1918 shortly before the Armistice."

"What happened?"

"I was a passenger on a British boat sailing for South Africa. On the ship were two Russian refugees—traveling incognito, of course. They had been high officials under the old regime—that is, he had. It had taken them years to escape from that awful nightmare of Bolshevism, and their little daughter had been left behind."

Mason nodded and offered Mrs. Tump a cigarette. "Not right now," she said. "Later on, I'll join you. Now I want to get this off my chest."

Mason lit a cigarette and glanced across to where Della Street was holding a pencil poised over her notebook ready to take skeleton notes on the conversation.

"The boat was torpedoed by a submarine without warning," Mrs. Tump said. "It was a horrible experience. I can see it yet whenever I close my eyes. It was night, and a heavy sea was running. The boat had a bad list almost as soon as she was struck. A lot of the lifeboats capsized. There were people in the water, only you couldn't see them—just arms and clawing hands coming up out of the dark waves to clutch at the slippery steel sides of the boat. Then the waves swept them away. You could hear screams—so many of them, it sounded just like one big scream."

Mason's eyes were sympathetic.

"This couple I was telling you about," Mrs. Tump went on, "—I'm just going to hit the high spots, Mr. Mason—they told me their history. The woman was psychic if you want to call it that, or just plain frightened and worried if you want to figure it that way. She felt certain the boat would be torpedoed. The man kept trying to kid her out of it . . . laughing at her, making a joke of it. The night before the ship sank the woman came to my cabin. She'd had a horrible dream. A vision, she called it. She wanted me to promise that if anything happened to her and I lived through it, that I'd go to Russia, find the daughter, and work out some way of getting her out of the country."

Mason's eyes narrowed, but he said nothing.

"She gave me some jewels. She didn't have much money, but lots of jewelry. She said that if the boat reached port safely, I could give the jewelry back to her. Her husband wasn't to know anything about it."

"And she was drowned?" Mason asked.

"Yes. They were both in the first boat which went over. I saw it capsize with my own eyes. Then a big wave came up and smashed the second lifeboat against the side of the ship. However, Mr. Mason, all this is just preliminary. I'll only sketch what happened. I was saved. I went to Russia, located the child, and brought her out. It doesn't matter how. She was a wonderful girl with the blood of royalty in her veins. I wanted my own daughter to adopt her. My daughter was just getting married at the time. Her husband wouldn't listen to it. So I . . . I'm afraid I did something which was unpardonable, Mr. Mason."

"What?" he asked.

"I wasn't where I could keep her myself—that is, I thought I wasn't. I put her in a home."

"What home?" Mason asked.

"The Hidden Home Welfare Society."

"Where was that?" Mason inquired.

"In a little town in Louisiana. They made a specialty of caring for children whose parents couldn't keep them."

She paused for a moment as though trying to get the facts straight in her mind.

"Go ahead," Mason said.

She said, "I have to tell you a little something about that home, Mr. Mason, things I didn't know at the time but found out afterwards. It was a baby brokerage home."

"What do you mean by that?"

She said, "There's always been a great demand for children to adopt. Childless couples are always on the lookout. Well, this home didn't care how it got its children. I found out afterwards that most of the women who were employed on the premises were expectant mothers. They'd have children and leave. Some of them would arrange to pay for the child's care and maintenance, and some of them couldn't."

"You, of course, made arrangements for the care of this child?"

"Oh, yes. I sent them regular monthly remittances. I have my old cancelled checks to prove it. Thank God I kept them."

"And the child?" Mason asked.

"A year later," she said, "when my own affairs were in order, I went to the home to get her out. And what do you think I found?"

"That she wasn't there?" Mason asked.

"Exactly. They'd sold that baby for a thousand dollars. Think of it, Mr. Mason! Sold her just as you'd sell a horse or a dog or a used automobile."

"What was their explanation?"

"Oh, they were frightfully sorry. They claimed it had been a mistake. At first they said I hadn't paid them a cent. And then I confronted them with the cancelled checks—and they tried every means on earth to get those checks from me. I made a lot of trouble. The district attorney took it up, and The Hidden Home Welfare Society simply dissolved and vanished into nothing. I learned later what those places do. Whenever there's trouble, they simply move to some other state, give themselves another name, and begin all over again."

"But surely," Mason said, "their records would show what became of this child."

"They did, but the Home wouldn't admit it. They lied about those records. I should have hired a lawyer and gone right into court, but in place of that I started making complaints to the authorities, and I suppose they were dilatory. You know how public officials can be at times. The district attorney was taking his vacation, and he stalled me along. I went back to New York and waited to hear from him. He wrote me a letter and seemed very pleased with himself. He said that thanks to my efforts, The Hidden Home Welfare Society had been put out of existence, that there had been previous complaints, and that I was to be congratulated on having saved my checks and all that sort of stuff.

"I went right back down to Louisiana and told him that wasn't what I wanted, that I wanted the child. He said I'd have to engage private counsel, that his office was concerned with the broader aspects of the case. Think of it! The *broader aspects of the case.'* I could have choked him."

Rage glittered in her cold gray eyes.

"You employed private counsel?" Mason asked.

"I did. That's where I made my next mistake. It was too late for lawyers then. I should have employed good detectives. The lawyers took my money and puttered around. They said that the home had destroyed all of its records, fearing criminal prosecution, that it had scattered—as they said—to the four winds. . . . Four winds nothing! They'd simply moved to Colorado and started all over again under another name. That was something else I didn't know."

"How did you finally get the information?" Mason asked.

"By persistence and a little luck," she said. "One of the men, who had been in their bookkeeping department had, of course, remembered the entire transaction because of the commotion I'd raised, finally got in touch with lawyers who in turn got in touch with me. . . . They wanted to sell the information of course."

"What did you do?" Mason asked.

"I suppose I should have gone to the authorities, but I'd had a bitter dose of that medicine so I paid through the nose and got the information."

"Which shows?" Mason asked.

"The child was given the name of Byrl. She was adopted by a Mr. and Mrs. Gailord. They lived here in this city."

"How long ago was that?" Mason asked.

"Within two months of the time I'd left the girl at the orphanage, the Gailords came there looking for a child. They became completely infatuated with this girl. They insisted on having her. The Home told them that she wasn't as yet free for adoption, but they felt certain she would be within a few months, as their experience had convinced them that very few people kept up the payments, and the understanding was that whenever the payments ceased, the child was free for adoption.

"The Gailords couldn't wait. They offered to pay a fancy price—a thousand dollars. And I suppose there was a little bribe money passed at the same time. They said that if there was any trouble, they'd return the girl. . . . Perhaps they meant to at the time, but they'd become attached to her—and—well, you know how those things are."

Mason said, "But surely, Mrs. Tump, the girl has now arrived at the age of majority. She can do anything she pleases. She's free, white, and twenty-one. She . . ."

"That part of it's all right," Mrs. Tump said. "I've straightened all *that* out, but here's what happened. The Gailords were wealthy. Frank Gailord died. He left property, half to his widow, half to Byrl. Byrl's half was in a trust fund. She was to get it when she was twenty-seven. In the meantime, the trustee was to pay her such sums as he thought necessary for care, maintenance, and education.

"Mrs. Gailord married again—a man by the name of Tidings. They lived together five years, and then the woman died, leaving all of her property to Byrl under the same sort of trust and making Mr. Tidings the trustee without bonds. Tidings is no good. He married again, and there's been another separation. . . . You don't need to concern yourself with all these preliminaries, Mr. Mason. I'm giving them to you just so you'll have the background clear in your mind. The point is, that Albert Tidings is now trustee for Byrl's property, and it's a tidy little fortune. He has absolutely no right to be trustee. He's an improper person. He's a crook, if you want my opinion."

"You've seen him?" Mason asked.

"Naturally. I went to him and explained matters to him."

"What did he do?"

"He said, 'See my lawyer.'"

"And so you decided to come to me?"

"Yes."

"And you've explained matters to Byrl—about her parents?"

"I most certainly have. It came as something of a shock to her. She'd always considered the Gailords were her real parents."

"Where is she now?"

"Here in the city."

"What," Mason asked, "do you want *me* to do?"

"I want you to go after Tidings," she said. "I want you to prove that the original adoption was illegal, that it was a fraud, and was the result of bribery and corruption. I want Tidings out of there as trustee."

Mason's eyes narrowed slightly. "Meaning," he asked, "that you want to be appointed trustee in his stead?"

"Well, I certainly think Byrl is entitled to more of her money. She should travel, see something of the world, come into her own inheritance, and marry."

"She's free to marry whenever she wants to, isn't she?" Mason asked.

"Yes, but she can't meet the sort of people she should meet. . . . You can take one look at Byrl and realize that she has a most unusual heritage."

Mason said, "So far as the past history is concerned, Mrs. Tump, it has but little bearing on the legal situation. The trust doesn't depend on the adoption. Byrl is now of age. You have no legal standing in the case. You aren't related to her. The parents asked you to get the girl and protect her. You got her out of Russia. After that—I'll be frank with you, Mrs. Tump—a shrewd lawyer would make it appear that, having received the jewelry and smuggled her out of Russia, you suddenly lost interest in her. Beyond making your monthly payments, you were, to be frank, rather lax."

"I wasn't lax," she said. "I wrote the Home regularly asking how she was getting along, and they answered by telling me that she was a bright girl, and was doing well."

"You've kept those letters?"

"Yes."

"Of course," Mason pointed out, "Tidings wasn't a party to the original fraud, and as far as Byrl is concerned, she's in no position to complain. She has inherited property because of those adoption proceedings."

"But she never was formally adopted," Mrs. Tump said.

"No?"

"No."

"How did that happen?"

"Well, you see when they first took her, they knew that she wasn't eligible for adoption, and then, later on, when I made so much trouble, the attorneys for the Home wanted it kept entirely under cover. They were afraid that if adoption proceedings ever went through the courts, I'd find out about it and take Byrl away from them. As nearly as I can get it, their lawyer told them they could take care of Byrl's interests financially through a will, and simply let the child go on believing they were her parents. They'd gradually instilled that into her mind, making up a story to account for some of her childish memories."

"How," Mason asked with interest, "did you get her out of Russia?"

"That's a story I can't tell you right now. Some very influential people who were friends of mine were traveling on a passport with a child. The child died and—well, Byrl got into the United States all right. I suppose I could be prosecuted for my share in that, and the other people could, too. I've promised to protect them in every way. Byrl knows all about it now, and all about her real parents."

"Well," Mason said, "I can force an accounting in that trust matter. I can probably make Tidings give Byrl all of the income, and perhaps a part of the principal. Then, within a year or two, the young woman can take over the entire trust fund under the terms of the trust. If Tidings has been guilty of any misconduct, we can get him removed."

Mrs. Tump said, "That's all I want. I wanted you to get the picture. If you want to know anything about Albert Tidings, you can find out from a man who's very close to him. He's associated with him in some other trust matters—one of a board of three men who handle endowment funds for a university."

"That," Mason said, "will be valuable. Who is this man?"

"He's very influential and very wealthy," she said. "Incidentally, he's a great admirer of yours, Mr. Mason. He's the one who sent me to you."

"The name?" Mason asked.

"Robert Peltham," she said. "He's an architect. His address is 3212 Oceanic Avenue, but he has a downtown office, and you can reach him there."

Mason carefully refrained from even glancing in Della Street's direction. "That," he said, "is fine, Mrs. Tump. I'd like to get in touch with Mr. Peltham before I decide about taking your case."

"Why, I don't see what he has to do with it, except as he can give you some information. Why don't you take the case and *then* get in touch with Mr. Peltham? I'll pay you a retainer right now."

Mason thoughtfully flicked ashes from his cigarette. After a moment, he said, "Of course, Mrs. Tump, *you* have no legal standing in the matter. As I have pointed out, you aren't related to Miss Gailord. Any action would have to be instituted by Miss Gailord herself."

"I suppose that's right."

"And," Mason said, "before I started anything, I'd have to see Miss Gailord and have her give me a direct authorization to act."

Mrs. Tump, suddenly businesslike, glanced at a jeweled wrist watch. "At two o'clock tomorrow afternoon?" she asked. "Would that be convenient?"

Mason said, "I'd be very glad to give her an appointment for that time."

Mrs. Tump pulled herself out of the deep recesses of the leather chair. "I'll get busy right away," she said. "—Oh, by the way, Mr. Mason, I may have done something wrong. . . . Perhaps I got the cart before the horse."

"What?" Mason asked.

She said, "When Mr. Tidings told me to see his lawyer, I told him that *he* could see *my* lawyer, that Mr. Perry Mason would call on him at eleven o'clock this morning. I hope that was all right."

Mason did not answer her question directly. He said, "You're a resident of this city, Mrs. Tump?"

"No, I'm not," she said. "I came here recently because Byrl was here. I'm living at the St. Germaine Hotel."

Mason said, with elaborate unconcern, "Do you have her address, Mrs. Tump?"

"Why, of course—the Vista Angeles Apartments.... She's going to take a trip with me as soon as we can get matters straightened out. I'm financing her in the meantime. Understand, Mr. Mason, you'll make all arrangements through me. She'll be your client, of course, but I'll be the one who pays the fees, and therefore the one you'll look to for instructions."

"Is she," Mason asked, "listed in the telephone book?"

"Yes."

Mason said, "Thank you, Mrs. Tump. I'll see you at two o'clock tomorrow afternoon."

"And how about this appointment with Mr. Tidings?"

"I'll get in touch with him," Mason said, "and explain that I've been consulted, that the hour isn't convenient for me, and ask for a later appointment."

She gave him her hand. "You give me a real feeling of confidence, Mr. Mason. . . . You're so different from those other lawyers. I built up a phobia about the legal profession. But Mr. Peltham told me you'd be like this. He seemed to know a great deal about you. . . . You've met him personally, perhaps?"

Mason laughed. "I meet so many people—and so many people know me whom I don't know, that at times it's embarrassing."

"Yes, of course. That's what comes of being a famous lawyer. Well, I'll see you at two o'clock tomorrow afternoon."

Mason and Della Street remained motionless, watching Mrs. Tump walk across the office with firm, competent steps. She made no effort to leave by the door through which she had entered, but walked directly to the door which opened from Mason's private office into the outer corridor. She twisted the knurled knob which released the catch, and turned on the threshold to smile once more at them. "Don't forget about that eleven o'clock appointment with Tidings, Mr. Mason," she said, and pulled the door shut behind her.

When the latch had clicked into place, Mason trusted himself for the first time to look at Della Street.

"Ain't we got fun!" she said.

Mason grinned. "I knew there was going to be a joker in the thing somewhere."

Della, suddenly serious, tried to reassure him. "After all," she said, "the coincidence may be just that and nothing more."

"It *may* be," he admitted, in a voice that showed his skepticism. "One chance in ten million if you want to make it mathematical."

"Well," she said, "I suppose that Mrs. Tump would hardly be the woman who holds the other part of that ten-thousand-dollar bill."

"No," Mason said, "but what do you want to bet that Byrl Gailord isn't?"

"No takers," she told him. "This is your personally conducted excursion into the realm of mysterious women and masked mistresses. . . . Of course, if Byrl Gailord knew that Mrs. Tump was going to call on you and arrange for an appointment, she'd have been careful to keep you from hearing her voice. . . . But I don't see why all the secrecy."

Mason said, "Because she doesn't want Mrs. Tump to know that she's intimate with Peltham—if Byrl Gailord *is* the one who's intimate with him."

"And if she isn't?" Della Street asked.

Mason said, "Forget that. Ring up that *Contractor's Journal.* Tell them we have a personal ad which must go in their next issue. Look up the position of Byrl Gailord's name in the telephone directory, and compose a code ad asking if it's all right to represent her. . . . And some-how I feel as though I'm walking into a trap the minute I do *that.*"

"Couldn't you go ahead and represent her without it?"

"I could," Mason admitted, "but I don't want to. That ten thousand dollars looked as big as the national debt last night, Della, but it looks like trouble now. Go ahead and work out that ad. Tell Paul Drake to look up Tidings, and get Tidings on the telephone for me."

A few moments later, she popped her head in the door to say, "There's a one-thirty dead-line on that ad, Chief. I've got it ready and will rush it down. Albert Tidings is coming on the line in just a moment. His secretary's on now."

Mason picked up the telephone, and a man's rather high-pitched voice said, "Hello."

"Mr. Tidings?" Mason asked.

"No. This is his secretary. Just a moment, Mr. Mason. Mr. Tidings is coming right on. . . . Here he is."

A booming, resonant voice said, irritably, "Hello. Who the devil is *this?*"

"Perry Mason, the lawyer," Mason said. "I'm calling in regard to an appointment a Mrs. Tump made with you. She said I'd call on you at eleven. . . . Is this Albert Tidings?"

There was a moment of silence, then the voice said cautiously, "Yes, this is Tidings. I know all about what you want, and . . ."

"Mrs. Tump has just left my office," Mason interposed as the man at the other end of the line paused uncertainly. "She said she'd made an appointment for me to meet you at eleven o'clock this morning. That appointment was, of course, made without consulting my own convenience and . . ."

"I understand perfectly, Mr. Mason," the booming voice interrupted. "I was going to call you myself. . . . Hadn't got around to it yet. It's all damn poppycock. You don't want to waste *your* time on it, and I don't want to waste mine. She said eleven o'clock. . . . I knew you wouldn't drop your business and come running around to peddle a lot of old woman's gossip, but I didn't say anything to Mrs. Tump. I just figured I wouldn't hear any more about it, but I told my secretary to call you up just to make sure."

"It's quite possible," Mason said, "that I'll want to talk with your attorney—if you can tell me who he is."

"I have several attorneys," Tidings said, evasively.

"Can you tell me which lawyer will be handling this particular case?"

"None of them," Tidings said. "It's all bosh. I tell you there's nothing to it, but one thing I *will* tell you, Mason. If that woman doesn't quit her whispering campaign of poison propaganda, I'm going after her. Byrl's a swell girl. We get along fine, but that old buzzard is poison and she's laying up trouble for herself. She's a chiseler and is just trying to make Byrl dissatisfied so as to feather her own nest. I'm going after her if she doesn't quit. You can tell her that straight from me."

"Tell her straight from yourself," Mason said. "I only called up to cancel an appointment."

Tidings laughed. "All right. All right. I didn't mean it that way, Mason, but I'm getting irritated. . . . All right. Call up whenever you want to see me. Your secretary and mine can doubtless get together. Good-by."

Mason dropped the telephone receiver into place, pushed back his chair, got to his feet, and started slowly pacing the office.

3.

PERRY MASON was lying in bed reading when the telephone rang. He had been about to turn off the light, and there was a frown on his face as he picked up the receiver.

Della Street's voice greeted him. "Hello, Chief. How about the evening paper?"

"What about it?"

"Did you read it?"

"I glanced through it. Why?"

"I notice," she said, "that auditors have been called in to examine the books of the Elmer Hastings Memorial Hospital. Charges of mismanagement of funds have been made by a member of the Hastings family. A firm of certified public accountants were called on to make a preliminary audit of the books. The endowment funds are held in a trust administered by a board of three trustees. The members of that board of trustees are Albert Tidings, Robert Peltham, and a Parker C. Stell."

For several thoughtful seconds Mason was silent, then he said, "I guess that's what Peltham meant when he said I'd learn about him in the papers."

"Get this," Della Street went on, speaking hurriedly. "I didn't intend to disturb you over that newspaper business. I clipped the item out of the paper and figured it would keep until morning, but I was getting ready for bed and turned the radio on to get the evening broadcast. A news item came through that early this evening police investigated a parked automobile which had been found in a vacant lot, discovered that there were bloodstains on the seat cushion. A man's bloodstained topcoat was found pushed down on the floor boards near the gearshift lever. There was a bullet hole in the left side of the coat. The car was registered in the name of Albert Tidings, and a handkerchief in the right-hand pocket of the raincoat had Albert Tidings' laundry mark and some lipstick on it. A check-up shows that Tidings hasn't been seen since shortly before noon, when his secretary said he went out without saying where he was going."

Mason digested the information and said, "Now *that's* something. Any other clues?"

"Apparently that's all that found its way to the last minute news flashes. . . . Want me to call up Paul Drake and start him working on it?"

Mason said, "I'd better call him myself, Della."

"Look like the plot's thickening?" she asked.

"Positively curdled," he agreed, cheerfully. "It's like Thousand Island dressing. . . . Almost as bad as the cream gravy I tried to make on that hunting trip last fall."

"Can I do anything to help, Chief?"

"I don't think so, Della. I don't think *I'll* do very much. After all, we'll be hearing from Mrs. Tump on this, and in one way this will simplify matters."

"Sounds more complicated to me," she said.

"No. It'll work the other way. With the charges made in

connection with the trust fund of the Elmer Hastings Memorial Hospital, a court would want a pretty thorough accounting from Tidings on the Gailord trust. Tidings won't dare to let us drag him into court on that now. He'll make all sorts of concessions—that is, if he wasn't inside of that coat when the bullet went through. If he was, and should pass out of the picture, we'll then be in a position to have another trustee appointed and get an accounting from Tidings' administrator. . . . What worries me is the lipstick on the handkerchief in his coat pocket."

"Getting narrow-minded, Chief?" she asked banteringly.

"I was just wondering if the girl who owned that lipstick didn't perhaps have part of a ten-thousand-dollar bill in her purse. . . . I'm getting a complex about that bill, Della. I'm afraid to go to sleep for fear I'll dream of chasing a witch who turns herself into a beautiful young woman poking a part of a ten-thousand-dollar bill under my nose."

Della Street said, "More apt to be a beautiful young woman who turns into a witch. . . . Let me know if you want anything, Chief."

"I will. Thanks for calling, Della. 'Night."

"'Night, Chief."

Mason rang up the Drake Detective Agency. "Paul Drake—is he where you can reach him?" he asked of the night operator at Drake's switchboard.

"I think so, yes."

"This is Perry Mason calling. I'm at my apartment. Tell him to give me a ring soon as he can. It's important."

"Okay, Mr. Mason. I should have him within fifteen minutes."

Mason slipped out of bed, put on bathrobe and slippers, lit a cigarette, and stood in frowning concentration, his feet spread apart, his eyes staring intently down at the carpet. From time to time he raised the cigarette to his lips, inhaling slow deliberate drags.

The ringing of the telephone aroused him from his concentration. He picked up the instrument, and Paul Drake's drawling voice said, "Hello, Perry. I was wondering whether to call you tonight or wait until tomorrow morning. I've got some information on Tidings."

"What is it?" Mason asked.

"Oh, a bit of this and that," Drake said. "A bit of background, some gossip, and a little deduction."

"Let's have the high lights."

Drake said, "He's married. Been married twice. The first time to a Marjorie Gailord, a widow with a daughter. They lived together four or five years, then Marjorie died. A while later, Tidings married Nadine Holmes, an actress, twenty-eight, brunette, and class. They lived together about six months. She left him. He more or less publicly accused her of infidelity. She filed suit for divorce on grounds of cruelty, and then suddenly dismissed the action. Rumor is that after his lawyers told her lawyers what they had on her, she decided to be a good girl; but she won't go back and live with him, and he won't give her a divorce. He's either crazy about her or just plain mean.

"He's in the brokerage business, also director in a bank, reputed to be pretty well fixed. He's one of the trustees of the Elmer Hastings Memorial Hospital, and Adelle Hastings doesn't like him. They've had some differences, which culminated when Miss Hastings demanded an audit of the books of the trustees. She seems to have something rather definite to work on."

"Who is she?" Mason asked.

"Granddaughter of the original Hastings," Drake said. "The money in the family ran out along in the depression. She could sure use some of that money which the old grandfather scattered around to charity. She's poor but proud, thinks a lot of the family name, and points with pride to the hospital."

"Does she have anything at all?" Mason asked.

"Nothing except looks and social standing. She's working as a secretary somewhere, but the bluebloods all recognize her as being one of the social elite. She works during the week and goes out on millionaires' yachts and to swell country estates over week-ends. Some of her friends have tried to give her good-paying jobs, but she figures they're just making things easy for her. She prefers to stand on her own."

Mason said, "Okay, Paul. Now I've got something for you. Beat it down to police headquarters. They found Tidings' car parked in a vacant lot somewhere with blood on it and a topcoat with a bullet hole through it. Apparently, the coat belonged to Tidings, and he may have had it on when the bullet went through."

Drake said, "*That's* something! How did you get it, Perry?"

"Last minute flash on the news broadcast. Della phoned me a few minutes ago."

Drake said, "I'll get on the job. Want me to do any investigating on that car business?"

"Just tag along behind the police," Mason said. "Don't bother to do anything on your own hook as yet. Just gather facts and keep me posted."

"Call you later on?" Drake asked.

"No," Mason said. "I'm going to sleep. They dragged me up in the wee small hours this morning."

"I heard about that," Drake said. "By the way, Perry, that man the boys were covering for you was also on the board of trustees of the hospital with Tidings. . . . I presume you knew that."

"Uh huh."

"Mean anything?" Drake asked.

"I think so," Mason said, "but I don't know what—not yet."

"Want me to do any work on that angle?"

"I don't think so, Paul. I don't know just where I stand yet. Pick up what information you can without going to too much expense. Don't bother with it personally. Just put a good leg man on it, and we'll check over the dope in the morning."

"Okay," Drake said.

"Here's something I *am* interested in, Paul," Mason went on.

"Shoot."

"This has to be handled with kid gloves. I want the dope on it, and I want it just as fast as you can get it."

"What is it?"

"Robert Peltham," Mason said. "He must never know that I'm making the investigation, but I want to find out whom he's sweet on. I tried to telephone him this afternoon. He wasn't in, and his secretary said she didn't know when he'd be in. She was delightfully vague."

"Isn't he married?" Drake asked.

"I don't know," Mason said. "If he is, my best hunch is that his wife isn't the center of attraction."

"If he's married, he'll keep his love affairs pretty well covered up," Drake warned. "I may not be able to get you anything on it for a day or two."

"I'd like very much to have it before two o'clock tomorrow afternoon," Mason said. "See what you can do, Paul."

"Okay, I will."

Mason hung up the telephone, stretched out on the bed, picked up a book, and tried to resume his reading. He couldn't get interested in the book, nor on the other hand did he feel like sleeping. He tossed the book to the floor, sat up in a chair by the window, smoked three cigarettes, then turned off the lights, raised the windows, and got into bed. It was an hour before he dropped off to sleep.

By ten o'clock in the morning when he reached the office, events were gathering mass and momentum like a huge snowball rolling down a steep slope.

The preliminary investigations of the auditors had uncovered what amounted to a serious shortage in the trust funds of the Elmer Hastings Memorial Hospital. They were baffled, however, by the fact that all check stubs, all cancelled checks, and the check ledgers had disappeared. From the remaining books and available data, however, it was evident that some two hundred thousand dollars had been checked out of trust funds, and apparently this sum was not reflected in current assets or legitimate operating expenses. In view of the fact that the trustees had the discretionary right to sell stocks and bonds or other holdings and re-invest the proceeds, the auditors pointed out that it would be necessary to follow the trail of tangible assets through a complicated series of transactions in order to get an accurate picture.

Because withdrawals from the trust fund could be made only by checks signed by Albert Tidings and one other trustee, it appeared that there were what the newspaper cautiously referred to as "grave and far-reaching implications." The newspaper account mentioned that Robert Peltham was reported to be out of town on business. His office would give no information as to where the architect could be reached. Albert Tidings had mysteriously disappeared. Police, frantically working on clues in connection with the finding of Tidings' automobile with the telltale stains on the front seat and the bullet-pierced topcoat, were making a determined effort to learn more of where Tidings had gone after leaving his office. They had run up against a blank wall.

Parker C. Stell, the other member of the board of trustees, had consulted the firm of certified public accountants as soon as he knew that the investigation was under way. He had placed his own bookkeeping facilities at the disposal of the accountants. He announced he was deeply shocked and anxious to render every assistance possible. He said that he had been called on from time to time at the request of Tidings to sign some checks, that he thought Peltham had been the one who signed most of the checks with Tidings. He admitted that within what he termed "reasonable limitations" matters were left very much in Tidings' hands, and signing many of the smaller checks was considered a matter of routine formality once Tidings' name appeared on them. Larger checks, however, he said, were scrutinized carefully—at least those which he had signed with Tidings. These had represented monies paid out for securities in which the funds of the trust had been re-invested. The books of the trust fund had, he believed, been kept exclusively by Tidings who submitted detailed reports from time to time as to the state of the trust fund.

Adelle Hastings had not minced words in her characterization of the members of the board who administered the trust funds. Albert Tidings she accused of criminal mismanagement, Parker Stell of credulous inefficiency, and as for Robert Peltham, she insisted that he was honest, upright, and conscientious, and that Albert Tidings would never have dared submit any checks to him for signature which were not actual bona fide trust fund withdrawals.

Mason looked up from reading the newspaper to say to Della Street, "Well, I guess this is what he had reference to. . . . Strange, however, that it broke twenty-four hours later than he had anticipated."

She nodded, then after a moment said, "Chief, do you notice something peculiar about that?"

"What?"

"The way Adelle Hastings sticks up for Robert Peltham. After all, you know, Tidings has disappeared. That bloodstained coat could well be a blind to throw police off the track. Peltham has skipped out. Parker Stell is available and doing everything he can. Yet she accuses him of credulity and inefficiency."

"Keep it up," Mason encouraged. "You're doing fine, Della. If *you* can think this thing out, *I* won't have to work up a headache wrestling with a lot of confusing facts."

She said, "Miss Hastings apparently had some pretty definite information as to what was going on, something on which she could base definite accusations."

Mason nodded.

"She went to the bat and blew the lid off," Della Street said. "Now according to all outward indications, Peltham is just as deep in the mud as Tidings is in the mire, but Adelle Hastings sticks up for him. Parker Stell, judging from newspaper accounts, is the only one who is doing the logical, reasonable, manly thing. Yet Miss Hastings doesn't hesitate to accuse him of inefficiency."

"You mean," Mason asked, "that you think Adelle Hastings got her inside information as to what was going on from Robert Peltham?"

She said, "Goosy, wake up. I mean that Adelle Hastings holds the other half of the ten-thousand-dollar bill which we have in the safe."

Mason sat bolt upright in his chair. "Now," he said, "you *have* got something."

"Well," she went on, "it's just guesswork, but I can't figure Miss Hastings on any other basis. As one woman judging another woman, I'd say she was in love with Peltham. . . . At any rate, she has a faith in him which doesn't seem entirely justified by the circumstances, and she's taking pains to make that faith public.

"The rest of it all fits in. You can see what would happen if it should appear that Peltham, as one of the trustees, had been carrying on a surreptitious intimacy with Adelle Hastings."

"But why should it be surreptitious?" Mason asked. "Why couldn't he have courted the girl or gone out and married her? . . . assuming, of course, he wasn't already married."

Della Street said, "Probably because of things we'll find out later on. I'm just offering to bet that that Hastings girl holds the other half of your ten-thousand-dollar bill."

Mason was reaching for a cigarette when Paul Drake's knock sounded on the door which opened from Mason's private office to the corridor.

"That'll be Paul, Della," he said. "Let him in. . . . By George, the more I think of it, the more I believe you're right. That, of course, would mean that there'd be no objection on Peltham's part to our taking that Gailord case. . . . But I have ideas about Mrs. Tump."

"What sort of ideas?" she asked, opening the door to Paul Drake.

"I'll tell you later," Mason said. "Hello, Paul."

Paul Drake was tall and languid. He spoke with a drawl, walked with a long, slow-paced stride. He was thinner than Mason, seldom stood fully erect, but had a habit of slouching against a desk, a filing cabinet, or slumping to a languid seat on the arm of a chair. He gave the impression of having but little energy to waste and wishing to conserve that which he had.

"Hi, Perry. Hi, Della," Drake said, and walked over to the big leather chair. He dropped down with a contented sigh into the deep cushions, then after a moment raised his feet and twisted around so that his back was propped against one arm of the chair while his knees dangled over the other. "Well, Perry," he said, "I've got to hand it to you."

"What is it this time?" Mason asked.

"You sure can pick goofy cases. Did you know all this business about Tidings was going to break?"

Mason glanced at Della Street, then shook his head.

Drake said, "How'd you like to get some dope on Tidings' love-life, Perry?"

"On the trail of something?" Mason asked.

"Uh huh. May be on the trail of Tidings himself. If he's missing, I think I can put my finger on the person who saw him last."

Mason sat up in his chair to drum nervously with the tips of his fingers on the edge of his desk. "Darned if I know whether I want to try to capitalize on that or not, Paul," he said.

"How soon *would* you know?"

"After two o'clock this afternoon."

Drake said, "I don't think it'll keep that long, Perry. There's too much pressure being brought to bear. Some newspaper chap or some detective will stumble onto it."

"What have you got?" Mason asked.

Drake said, "Tidings told an intimate friend three days ago that he was going to spring a trap on his wife. He said he was going to move in on her and let her forcibly eject him. Seemed to think there was some legal point in that which would give him an advantage. He said his wife had been waiting to get a cause of action on desertion. He was going to move in on her just before the year was up.

"I looked her up through the records of the Bureau of Light and Power. It's a place up on one of those steep hillside subdivisions where there's a swell view and privacy. I have a hunch Tidings went there Tuesday after he left his office. Want to go find out?"

Mason said, "I guess so. . . . Della, get Byrl Gailord on the phone for me. If I'm going to mix into this now, I'd better know exactly where I stand."

"Where does she fit into the picture?" Drake asked, as Della Street noiselessly glided from the office.

"It's a long story," Mason said. "Apparently, she's the daughter of Tidings' first wife. In reality she isn't. There's a question of adoption mixed into it. . . . What else is new, Paul?"

"Oh, a lot of routine stuff," Drake said. "I can't find out anything about Peltham's girl friend."

"Is he married?"

"No. He's a bachelor, pretty much of a businessman, rather austere, something of an ascetic, and referred to by his friends as a cold, calm, reasoning machine. . . . Are you sure he has a heart-throb, Perry?"

Mason laughed. "*You,*" he said, "are giving *me* the information. I'm a lawyer protecting the confidence of a client. . . . You give, and I take."

Della Street opened the door of her secretarial office, holding a telephone in her hand. "She's on your line, Chief," she said.

Mason picked up the telephone on his desk. "Hello. Miss Gailord?"

A rich, well-modulated voice said, "Good morning, Mr. Mason. Thank you for calling. I believe I have an appointment with you for two o'clock this afternoon."

"You have," Mason said. "In the meantime, events are moving rather rapidly. I suppose you've seen the newspapers?"

"Yes. What does it mean?"

"I don't know," Mason said. "But I have a hot tip I'm going out to investigate now. The only information I have at present is that contained in the newspaper account. . . . I take it you're familiar with what Mrs. Tump has been doing in your behalf?"

"Yes."

"And that meets with your approval?"

"Yes, of course."

"You want me to represent you?"

"Certainly. Mrs. Tump is acting for me."

"Do *you* know Mr. Peltham?"

She hesitated for a moment, then said, "He's Mrs. Tump's friend. I believe he's the one who sent her to you."

"So I understand. Now you must be pretty well acquainted with Mr. Tidings?"

"Yes, of course."

"How do you get along?"

"We were always friendly. It never entered my head to doubt him until I started checking up recently. I tried to find out where I stood and Uncle Albert—I've always called him that—became furious. He said Mrs. Tump was poisoning my mind, that she was trying to get control of my property—but she isn't. I trust her absolutely. I know some things I can't tell even you, Mr. Mason, but she is empowered to act for me in every way."

"Thank you," Mason said. "That was what I wanted to find out. I'll see you at two o'clock, then."

He hung up and said to Della, "Get me that *Journal* on the phone, Della. Let's see if there's been an answer sent in to that ad of mine."

Della Street nodded, put through the call, and a few moments later signified to Mason that his party was on the line. Mason said, "Perry Mason talking. I put a personal ad in your paper to make the morning edition. I wonder if there's been any answer to it."

"Just a moment. I'll check it up with the classified ad department," the man said. Mason could hear steps retreating from the telephone, and a moment later returning; and the man's voice said, "Yes, Mr. Mason. A young woman left a reply at the counter not over an hour ago. It says simply, 'Okay. Go ahead. R.P.,' and it's headed, 'Answer to M.'—which, I take it, means your ad . . . . Anyway, we're going to publish the ad in tomorrow's edition so there's no reason to keep it confidential."

"Thank you very much," Mason said, hung up, and nodded to Paul Drake. "Okay, Paul," he said. "Let's go drop in on the thwarted wife."

4.

MASON SHIFTED into second at the foot of the grade. The road wound upward, twisting and turning around the steep sides of typical Southern California mountains. The subdivision was relatively new, and there were many vacant lots, some marked with a red placard bearing the word, SOLD. Here and there were scattered bungalows, obviously new. Up nearer the top of the grade, where a ridge offered more level building sites, half a dozen small homes were clustered.

"It'll be one of those," Drake said.

Mason looked at the house numbers and said, "Probably the last one in the row . . . Yes, here it is."

The bungalow faced to the south and east. Above it, on the west, towered the slopes of the hill, covered with a thick growth of chaparral. Below, to the east, the city stretched in glistening brilliance, the white buildings reflecting the brilliant sunlight, spotless gems of intense white below the red patches of tiled roofs.

Mason looked the place over before he went up to ring the bell. It was within two hundred feet of the end of the subdivision, and, just beyond the house, the road, taking advantage of the little bench on the hillside, terminated in a big circle where cars could be turned around. The sunlight was warm and the air balmy. The sky was a blue, cloudless vault. Off to the far north-east mountain crests sparkled, a white coating of snow suspended above the pastel blues of distant slopes.

Mason said, "Curtains drawn tight. Doesn't look as though anyone's home."

"If he's here," Drake said, "it's a hide-out."

Mason led the way up the short stretch of cement walk to the porch, and pressed his thumb against the bell button. They could hear the ringing of a bell on the inside of the house, but there was no answering sound of motion. There was about the place that dead silence indicative of an untenanted house.

"Might try the back door," Drake suggested.

Mason shook his head, pressed his thumb against the button once more, and said, "Well, I guess . . . Wait a minute, Paul. What's this?"

Drake followed the direction of his eyes. Just below the threshold was a jagged, irregular splotch of rusty, reddish brown.

Mason moved his feet and said, "There's another one, Paul."

"And another one back of that," Drake said.

"All within eighteen inches of the doorstep," Mason pointed out. "Looks as though someone had been wounded and gone in, or had been wounded and gone out. He must have been losing quite a bit of blood at that."

"So what?" Drake asked.

Mason pulled back the screen door, examined the front door, and said, "It isn't tightly closed, Paul."

"Let's keep our noses clean," Drake warned.

Mason bent down to examine the bloodstains. "They've been

here for a while," he announced. "Wonder if the sun would shine in here later on in the afternoon. . . . They look baked."

He raised his eyes to determine the course of the shadows. The porch consisted of a slab of cement with a gable roof extending not over three feet from the side of the house, furnishing a somewhat scanty protection for the door, a roof which was more ornamental than useful.

"How about it, Perry?" the detective asked.

By way of answer, Mason knocked on the door, at the same time pushing against the panels with his knee.

The door swung slowly open.

"There you are, Paul," Mason said. "You're a witness to what happened. We knocked on the door, and the force of the knocking pushed the door open."

"Okay," Drake said, "but I don't like it. Now what?"

Mason stepped inside. "Anyone home?" he called.

It was a typical bungalow with wide windows, gas radiators, an ornamental half-partition opening to a dining room, and a swinging door evidently leading to a kitchen. On the side of the living room were two doors which evidently opened into bedrooms.

The house had the atmosphere of a place that had been lived in. There were magazines on a wicker table in the center of the living room, with a comfortable chair drawn up near the table, a floor lamp behind it. A magazine lay face down and open on the wicker table.

Mason lowered his eyes to the floor on which were several Navajo rugs.

He pointed to a red splotch on one of the Navajo rugs. A few inches farther on was another. Then there was a spattering drop with irregular edges on the floor, another on the rug nearest the bedroom door on the left.

Mason followed the trail directly to the closed door of the bedroom.

Drake hung back. "Going in?" he asked.

By way of answer, Mason turned the knob and opened the door.

A blast of hot, fetid air rushed out of the bedroom to assail their nostrils. It was the oxygen-exhausted air of a room tightly closed in which gas heat has been generated, and it was an atmosphere which held the suggestion of death.

It needed only a glance at the fully clothed figure lying on the bed to confirm the message of that superheated, lifeless air.

Mason turned back to Paul Drake. "Call Homicide, Paul," he said. "There's a phone."

The detective whirled to the telephone.

Mason stepped into the room and gave a quick look around.

Apparently it was a woman's bedroom. There were jars of cream and bottles of lotion on the dresser. There were blood-stains on the floor. There was no counterpane on the bed. The top blanket had been soaked with blood which had dried into a stiff circular stain beneath the still body.

The corpse was clothed in a double-breasted gray suit, with the coat unbuttoned. Red had trickled down the trousers to dry in sinister incrustations. There were no shoes on the body. Gray, silk, embroidered socks which harmonized with the gray trousers covered the feet. The man lay on his back. His lids were half closed over glassy eyes. The jaw was sunken, and the interior of the partially opened mouth showed a grayish purple. About the lips was a crimson smear, which might have been the faint traces of lipstick, a stain which would hardly have been noticeable in life but which was now strikingly evident against the pallid skin of the dead man.

The gas radiator was hissing at full blast. The windows were tightly closed, the shades drawn.

Somewhere in the room a fly was buzzing importantly.

Mason dropped to one knee, looked under the bed, and saw nothing. He opened a closet door. It was filled with articles of feminine wearing apparel. He looked in the bathroom. It was immaculate save for rusty red splotches on the side of the wash bowl. A towel on the floor was stiff with dried blood. Mason opened the door into the adjoining bedroom. It was evidently used as a spare room for guests. There was no sign that it had been occupied recently.

Mason retraced his steps to find Paul Drake just hanging up the telephone.

"Tidings?" Drake asked.

"I wouldn't know," Mason said. "Probably."

"Look in his clothes?"

"No."

Drake heaved a sigh of relief. "I'm glad you're showing *some* sense. For God's sake, Perry, close that door. . . . Let's open a few windows, first."

Mason said, "No, let's go outside. We'll leave things here just as they were when we came in."

Drake said, "We've got our fingerprints on things. The boys from Homicide aren't going to . . ." He broke off to listen. "Car coming," he said.

A car purred past the house, swung in a turn at the end of the roadway, came back, and stopped.

Drake, who was nearest the front window, slid one of the drapes a few inches to one side, and said, "Coupe. Class at the wheel . . . She's getting out . . . Swell legs . . . Overnight bag, brown coat, fox fur collar . . . Here she comes. What do we do, Perry? Answer the bell?"

Mason said, "Push that door shut with your foot, Paul. I think there's a spring lock. Try and get the license number on the car."

Drake said, "I can't see it right now. She's parked right in front of the house. If she drives away, I'll get it."

"Sit still and shut up," Mason said.

They could hear the click-clack of heels on the cement, the sound of the screen door opening. They waited for the doorbell to ring, but heard instead the scrape of a key against the metal lock plate on the door. Then the latch shot back, and a woman entered the room.

For a moment her eyes, adjusting themselves to the subdued light of the interior, failed to take note of the two men. She started directly for the bedroom, then suddenly stopped. Her eyes became wide and round as she saw Mason. She dropped her bag and the coat from nerveless fingers, turned, and started toward the door. A key container dropped with a muffled clang to the wooden floor.

Drake stepped from the window to stand between her and the door.

She screamed.

Mason said, "Hold it."

She whirled, at the sound of his voice, back to face him. She stared steadily for a moment, then said simply, "Oh."

Mason said, "I'm an attorney. This man is a detective. In other words, we're not thieves. Who are you?"

"How . . . how did you get in?"

"Walked in," Mason said. "The door was unlocked and slightly ajar."

"It was locked just now when I . . . when I . . ." She gulped as her voice caught in her throat, laughed nervously, and said, "This has knocked me for a loop. What's it all about?"

She was in the late twenties or early thirties, a striking brunette with jaunty clothes which set off her figure to advantage, and she wore those clothes with an air of chic individuality. Her face had been drained of color, and the pattern of the orange rouge showed clearly against the pasty white of her skin.

"Do you," Mason asked, "happen to live here?"

"Yes."

"Then you're . . ."

"Mrs. Tidings," she said.

"Does your husband live here?"

"I don't know why you're asking me these questions. What do you want here anyway? What right did you have breaking in?"

"We didn't break in," Drake said. "We . . ."

"We just walked in," Mason assured her, keeping Drake out of the conversation by interruption. "I think it will be to your advantage to answer that question, Mrs. Tidings. Does your husband live here?"

"No. We've separated."

"Didn't you patch up your differences recently?"

"No."

"Weren't there negotiations looking toward that?"

"No," she said, and then added with defiance in her voice, "—if it's any of your business, which it isn't."

Color was returning to her cheeks now, and her eyes flashed with resentment.

Mason said, "I think you'd better just sit down and take it easy for a few minutes, Mrs. Tidings. Officers are on their way out here."

"Why should officers be on their way *here?*"

"Because of something we found in the bedroom." And Mason pointed to the stains on the floor.

"What's that," she asked, "ink? What *is* that on my floor? Good God! I ..."

She took a step forward, stared down at the stains, and then a gloved knuckle crept toward her mouth. She bit hard on the black leather stretched taut over her knuckles.

"Take it easy," Mason said.

"Who ... who ... what ..."

Mason said, "We don't know yet. I think you'd better prepare yourself for a shock. I think it's someone you know."

"Not ... not ... Oh, my God, it can't be ..."

"Your husband," Mason said.

"My husband!" she exclaimed. There were both incredulity in her voice and a something which might have been relief. Then there was sudden panic again. "You mean that he ... he might have done it, might have ..."

"I think that the *body* is that of your husband," Mason explained.

She gave a half-stifled exclamation and moved swiftly toward the bedroom door. Mason caught her arm.

"Don't do it," he said.

"Why not? I must find out ..."

"You will, later. Right now, don't spoil any of the fingerprints on that doorknob."

"But I have a right to know. Can't you see how I . . ."

"Quit looking at it from your viewpoint," the lawyer interrupted. "Figure it from the police viewpoint. Do a little thinking."

She stared at him silently for several seconds, then crossed over to sit down on the davenport. "What happened?" she asked.

"Apparently he was shot."

"When?"

"I don't know. He was in his office yesterday morning. I talked with him on the telephone. He must have come out here shortly afterwards. . . . Would you know anything about that?"

"No," she said. "I've been away ever since Monday afternoon."

"May I ask what time Monday?" Mason asked.

"Why?"

Mason smiled and said, "The officers will ask these questions. After all, it's your house, you know. I thought perhaps it might help you a little if I gave you a chance to collect your thoughts before the officers get here."

"That's thoughtful of you," she said. "Was it suicide?"

"I don't know," Mason said. "I haven't made any investigation."

"How about this detective?"

"He's a private detective employed by me."

"Why did you come here?"

"We thought Mr. Tidings might have come out here after he left his office Tuesday. Had you seen him lately?"

"No. We—didn't get along at all."

"Now then," Mason asked, "would you mind telling me where you went on Monday afternoon?"

"I drove nearly all night," she said. "I was upset."

"And where did you drive?"

"To a friend's house. I spent a couple of days with her."

"You didn't take much baggage," Mason pointed out.

"No. I decided to go on the spur of the moment. I've had—well, troubles of my own."

"Where does this friend live?"

"In Reno."

"And you drove to Reno Monday?"

"Yes. I got in about daylight Tuesday morning. I felt a lot better after the drive."

"And you've been there ever since?"

"Until late last night. I left about ten o'clock."

"Where did you stay last night?"

She laughed nervously, and shook her head. "I don't drive that way. When I want to go some place, I start driving. When I get sleepy, I pull off to the side of the road and get a few minutes' sleep, then I start driving again. I much prefer to drive at night. I don't like the glare of the sun on paved roads."

"You slept some last night?"

"Yes, a few cat-naps here and there along the side of the road."

Mason said, "The officers will probably want to check your time pretty carefully. If you can give them all the data they need it will make it a lot easier for you. I'm just telling you as a friend. Here they come now."

A siren screamed up the hill. A police radio car finished the ascent, raced along the level stretch of roadway, and swerved sharply to park up against the curb. An officer jumped out of the car and came striding toward the house.

Drake opened the door.

The radio officer looked at Drake, pushed a foot through the door. "Which one of you telephoned Homicide?" he asked.

"I did," Drake said. "I'm a private detective."

"Your name Drake?"

"Yes."

"Got a card on you?"

Drake handed him a card.

"How about the woman and this other guy?" the officer asked.

"This is Mrs. Tidings. She came in right after I telephoned headquarters."

The officer stared at her suspiciously.

"I just this minute returned from Reno," she explained. "I drove."

"When did you leave there?"

"Last night."

"She lives *here*," Mason explained. "This is her house. She's been visiting a friend in Reno for a couple of days."

"I see. And who are you? Oh, I place you now. You're Perry Mason, the lawyer. What are *you* doing here?"

"We came out to see Mr. Tidings."

"Find him?"

"I think he's the dead man in the next room."

"I thought you said this woman came here *after* you did."

"She did."

"Then how'd you get in?"

"The door was unlocked and slightly ajar," Mason said.

"Well, Homicide will be here in a minute or two. The radio dispatcher rushed us out to hold things until Homicide could get here. You haven't touched anything, have you?"

"No, nothing important."

"Doorknobs and things like that?"

"Perhaps."

The officer frowned. "Okay," he said. "Get out. It's a pleasant day. You can wait outside as well as in. Let's not get any more fingerprints around. . . . You didn't touch the body, did you?"

"No."

"Go through the clothes?"

"No."

"Where is it?"

"In that bedroom."

"Okay," the officer said. "Go on out. . . . What's this—blood on the floor?"

"That's what led us to the corpse," Mason said. "We noticed the bloodstains on the floor. You notice they go from the outer threshold into the door of the bedroom."

"Okay," the officer said. "Go on out. I'll take a peek in that bedroom." He opened the door, looked in, then stepped back and pulled the door shut.

Mason said, "There's some reason to believe the body is that of Albert Tidings, this woman's husband. Wouldn't it be well to have her make an identification?"

"She can do that when Homicide gets here," the radio officer said. "I'm just keeping the evidence lined up. Go on. Out with you. I'll call you if I want anything."

Mason led the way out into the fresh air and warm sunlight. The radio officer followed them to the door and called to his partner, who sat behind the wheel of the radio car. "Keep an eye on this outfit, Jack. There's a stiff in here. It's a job for Homicide right enough."

He stepped back inside the house and slammed the door.

Mason offered Mrs. Tidings a cigarette, which she accepted gratefully. Drake shook his head in refusal. Mason placed one between his own lips, and snapped a match into flame. As he held the light to Mrs. Tidings' cigarette, the grind of a motor running fast in second gear could be heard from the grade.

"That'll be Homicide," Mason said.

The Homicide car flashed swiftly around the turn, hit the more level stretch of roadway along the ridge, and swept down upon them. Men jumped out. The radio officer got out from his car and reported in a low voice. The other radio officer appeared at the door of the house. "In here, boys," he said.

Sergeant Holcomb strode across to Mason. "Hello, Mason."

"Good morning, Sergeant."

"How's it happen you're here?"

"I had some business with Albert Tidings," Mason said. "I had a tip I could find him here."

"Did you?"

"I think it's his body," Mason said. "On a guess, I'd say it had been here at least since yesterday afternoon. The gas heat's turned on, and the windows and doors are tightly closed. That's a condition you'll have to take into consideration in determining the time of death."

"When did you get here?"

"About half an hour ago."

"You didn't have any reason to think you'd find a body?"

"No."

"You've seen him before?"

"No."

"Talked with him over the telephone?"

"I called his office yesterday, yes."

"What time?"

"I don't know. I would say it was shortly before eleven o'clock."

"What did he say?"

"I had a tentative appointment with him," Mason said. "I wanted to cancel it, and make one at a later date."

"Have any argument?"

"Not exactly."

"What was your business with him?"

Mason smiled and shook his head.

"Come on," Sergeant Holcomb said. "Kick through. If we're going to solve a murder, we've got to have motives. If we knew something about that business you wanted to discuss with him, we might have a swell motive."

"And again," Mason said, "you might not."

Sergeant Holcomb clamped his lips shut. "Okay," he said. "Don't leave here until I tell you you can. . . . That your car?"

"Yes."

"Who's the other one belong to?"

"Mrs. Tidings . . . Mrs. Tidings, may I present Sergeant Holcomb?"

Sergeant Holcomb didn't remove his hat. "What are you to him?" he asked.

"His wife."

"Living with him?"

"No. We've separated."

"Divorced?"

"No, not yet. . . . That is, no. I haven't divorced him."

"Why not?"

She flushed. "I prefer not to discuss that."

"You'll have to, sooner or later," Sergeant Holcomb said. "I don't want to pry into your private affairs, just to be doing it, but you can't hold out on the police. You stick right around here. I'm going in."

The others had already gone on into the house, and Sergeant Holcomb joined them. Mason dropped his cigarette to the cement, ground it out with the sole of his shoe.

"Just as a matter of curiosity, Mrs. Tidings," he said, "had your husband been here before?"

"Once."

"On a friendly visit?"

"A business visit."

"Was there some question of alimony between you?"

"No. Well, it wasn't serious. Alimony was a detail. I didn't care about that."

"You wanted your freedom?"

"Why do you ask these questions?"

"Because it might help my client if I knew some of the answers, and the police are going to make you answer them anyway."

"Who," she asked, "is your client?"

Mason said, "I'm not ready to make any statements yet."

"Is it that Gailord girl?"

"Why?" Mason asked. "What makes you think it's she?"

She watched him with narrowed eyes. "That," she said, "isn't answering *my* question."

Mason said, "And you aren't answering mine."

He strode out to the curb to stand gazing thoughtfully. The radio officer watched him narrowly. Paul Drake stood close by, his manner seemingly detached.

Suddenly Mason turned to Mrs. Tidings. He said, "You look like a nice girl."

"Thank you."

"You wouldn't by any chance be trying to kid anyone, would you?" Mason asked.

"Why, what do you mean, Mr. Mason?"

Sergeant Holcomb opened the door of the house, motioned to Mrs. Tidings. "Come in here," he said.

Mason took his cigarette case from his pocket and carefully selected another cigarette. "Watch your step," he said in a low voice, his eyes turned toward the distant horizon with its gleam of snow-capped mountains. "And if you have anything to say to *me*, you'd better say it *now*."

Mrs. Tidings shook her head in a swiftly decisive gesture of negation and walked firmly toward the house.

5.

DELLA STREET was waiting in the doorway of Mason's private office as he came down the corridor. She beckoned to him to come in without going through the reception room of his office.

"Someone laying for me, Della?" he asked.

"Mrs. Tump and Byrl Gailord."

Mason said, "Her appointment wasn't until two o'clock."

"I know it, but they're all worked up about something. They say that they have to see you right away."

Mason said, "I thought I'd pick you up for a bite of lunch."

"I've tried to stall them off," she said. "They won't stall. . . . They're biting fingernails and whispering."

"What's the girl look like?"

"Not what you'd call beautiful, but she has a swell figure, and she can turn on plenty of personality. Her features aren't much, but she could get by in a bathing-girl parade anywhere. Her hair is darkish, her eyes black. She goes in for vivid coloring in clothes, throws lots of hand motions in with her talk, and seems full of life."

Mason said, "I'll see them now and get it over with. . . . We ran into something out there, Della."

"What was it?"

"Albert Tidings," he said, "nicely drilled with a revolver shot, probably a thirty-eight caliber, not suicide because there were no powder burns on the clothes or skin; and the officers can't find the fatal gun. There was a thirty-two caliber revolver in the right hip pocket. It hadn't been fired, and it wasn't the murder gun. What's more, the officers can't find Tidings' shoes. There's lipstick on his mouth."

"When was the body discovered?"

"When we got there."

"You mean—you were the one who discovered it?"

"That's right."

"Think Paul Drake had a hunch what you'd find?" she asked.

"No, not Paul. He'd have had a fit. The police think we find too many corpses. Paul's jittery about it."

"Well, you *do* get around, Chief," she said.

"I have to," he told her, grinning. "I met Mrs. Tidings out there. She'd been visiting friends in Reno and walked in on us."

"What sort?" Della Street asked.

"Class," Mason said. "Took it like a little soldier. Stood up and told the officers frankly that she didn't love him, that he'd been doing everything he could to make things difficult for her, that she wanted a divorce and he wouldn't give her one. She was a little indefinite about his methods, but he evidently had something on her."

"Doesn't that make her look like a logical suspect, Chief?" Della Street asked.

"That's what the officers seem to think. They're going to check her alibi. Holcomb put through a long distance call to Reno while I was there. Apparently, there's no question but what she was with friends just as she said. . . . However, I got my usual complex."

"What do you mean?"

Mason grinned. "Made a stab in the dark," he said, "figuring that she might hold the other part of that ten-thousand-dollar bill."

"Any results?"

"No. She couldn't have been the one, anyway. She left town Monday afternoon. Her friends say she arrived in Reno before daylight. The Reno police are checking up, but it sounded pretty good over the telephone. Even Holcomb accepted it. . . . Well, let's get Mrs. Tump and the Gailord girl in here and see how they react to the news."

"There won't be any need for you to represent them if Tidings is dead, will there, Chief?"

"Probably not," he said. "I can keep an eye on things; but there's nothing much to be done. The court will appoint another trustee."

"Mrs. Tump?" Della Street asked.

Mason said, "Probably not. It's more apt to be some trust company. The accounts will take a lot of going over."

"Want them in now?" Della Street asked.

"Uh huh," Mason said, and crossed over to the washstand. He ran water into the bowl and was drying his hands on the towel when Della Street ushered in Mrs. Tump and an attractive, willowy girl whose eyes flashed about the room in a swift glance, and then registered approval as they appraised Perry Mason.

"This is Mr. Mason, Byrl," Mrs. Tump said, and to Mason, "Byrl Gailord."

Mason caught a glimpse of red lips parted to disclose flashing teeth, of intense black eyes, and then Byrl Gailord's hand was in his as she smiled up in his face. "I'm afraid I'm a nuisance, Mr. Mason," she said, "but when I told Mrs. Tump about what you'd said over the telephone—you know, about investigating a hot tip—well, we just couldn't wait."

"That's quite all right," Mason said. "The tip panned out. Won't you sit down?"

"What was it?" Mrs. Tump asked. "What have you found out?"

Mason waited until they were seated. "Albert Tidings is dead," he said. "We found his body stretched out on a bed in a bungalow owned by his wife. We notified the police. He'd been shot in the left side. Police can't find the gun. There was one in his pocket, but it hadn't been fired, and it's the wrong caliber anyway. There was a faint smudge of lipstick on his lips."

Byrl Gailord stifled a faint exclamation. Mrs. Tump stared at Mason with startled eyes. "You're sure it was he?" she asked.

"Yes," Mason said. "Mrs. Tidings identified him."

"The body was found in her house?"

"Yes."

"Where was she?"

"She'd been in Reno," Mason said. "She happened to return at about the time we discovered the body."

Byrl Gailord said, simply, "I'm glad it wasn't suicide. I'd always have felt that we—well, hounded him into it."

"Nonsense," Mrs. Tump said.

"I couldn't have helped feeling that way," Byrl Gailord insisted. "I liked him a lot, although I distrusted him in some ways. I think he was the kind who would have taken a lot of financial liberties, figuring that things were going to turn out all right."

"He was a crook," Mrs. Tump said. "His whole record shows it."

"He was very kind to me personally," Byrl observed, biting her lip and fighting back tears.

"Of course he was kind to you," Mrs. Tump said. "He was embezzling your money. Why shouldn't he have kidded you along? You were Santa Claus."

Byrl said, "The accounts may be out of balance, but his intentions were the best. If he'd made some poor investments, he'd have tried to plunge in order to get them back. I don't think he'd deliberately embezzle any of my money, but I did resent his attitude towards *you*."

Mrs. Tump said nothing.

"When . . . when did it happen?" Byrl Gailord asked, at length.

"Sometime after noon on Tuesday," Mason said. "The coroner rushed the body to an autopsy to have an examination made that would give him an exact time."

"And where does that leave Byrl?" Mrs. Tump asked.

"The court will appoint another trustee," Mason said. "There'll be a complete check-up on the accounts."

Mrs. Tump met his eyes steadily. "Very well, Mr. Mason. Let's be businesslike. . . . Does this mean that we don't need *your* services?"

Mason said, "Yes."

"I don't see why," Byrl Gailord said.

"Because there's nothing he can do now," Mrs. Tump said. "There's no need to pay Mr. Mason a fee if there's nothing he can do."

"That's right," Mason agreed.

"Isn't there *any*thing you can do?" Byrl Gailord asked. "No way in which you can—well, sort of look after my interests?"

"I can keep an eye open," Mason said. "If I find something that will justify my employment, I'll take it up with you. The court will probably appoint some trust company as a trustee. The trust accounts will have to be carefully examined."

"Can I be appointed?" Mrs. Tump asked.

"Perhaps," Mason said, "but a court would be more inclined to appoint a company which had auditing facilities at its command."

"I'd serve without compensation just to get things straightened up."

"We'll have to wait a few days until we can find out more about it," Mason said. "A court might permit Miss Gailord to nominate the trustee."

"I'd want Mrs. Tump, of course," Byrl Gailord said.

The telephone on Mason's desk rang sharply. Mason said, "Excuse me," picked up the receiver, and heard the voice of his receptionist saying, "Sergeant Holcomb is here. He says he must see you immediately. There's a man with him."

Mason thought for a moment. "Did you tell him I was busy, Gertie?"

"Yes."

"Didn't give him the names of my clients, did you?"

"No. Certainly not."

"Tell him I'll be right out," Mason said.

He hung up the telephone and excused himself to his clients. "Sergeant Holcomb of the Homicide Squad is outside," he said. "He wants to see me at once. I won't be long. Excuse me, please," and went out to the reception office, carefully closing the door of his private office behind him.

Sergeant Holcomb said, "Let's go some place where we can talk."

"The law library is available," Mason said, opening the door to the long room with its shelves lined with books.

The officer nodded to the young man who was with him, and said, "All right, Mattern. Come along."

Mason shifted his eyes to make a quick appraisal of the young man. He was somewhere in the late twenties with a head which seemed too large for his body. The bulging, prominent forehead and slightly protruding eyes gave him an appearance of owlish intellectuality which was emphasized by large, dark-rimmed spectacles.

Mason led the way into the law library and closed the door. "What is it, Sergeant?" he asked.

Sergeant Holcomb jerked his head toward the narrow-shouldered young man. "Carl Mattern," he said, "Tidings' secretary."

Mason nodded in acknowledgment of the introduction. Mattern didn't say anything. He seemed intensely nervous.

Sergeant Holcomb said, "You're representing Byrl Gailord?"

Mason hesitated a moment, then said, "On certain matters, yes."

"What's that other name?" Holcomb asked Mattern.

"Tump. Mrs. A. E. Tump."

"Know her?" Holcomb asked Mason.

"Yes."

"She your client?"

"Not exactly. What are you getting at?"

Sergeant Holcomb said, "Mattern says you called up and talked with Tidings yesterday about an appointment."

"Yes. I told you I'd talked with him on the phone."

"That appointment was to discuss Byrl Gailord's affairs?"

"In a way, yes."

Sergeant Holcomb said, "Where can I find Byrl Gailord now?"

Mason said, "That's something I don't feel called upon to answer—not as matters stand now."

"Not being much help, are you?" Sergeant Holcomb asked.

Mason said, "If you'll come down to earth and tell me what you're driving at, I might be able to help you."

Sergeant Holcomb said, "I'm checking up on motives, that's all. Mrs. Tump and Byrl Gailord were making things pretty hot for Tidings. They tried to see him Monday afternoon, and Tidings refused to talk with them. They were hanging around outside his office, waiting for him to come out. Tidings said he'd see Miss Gailord, but he'd be damned if he'd talk to Mrs. Tump; said she was a hellcat."

"So she killed him?" Mason asked with a smile.

"Nuts," Holcomb said. "You know what I'm after, Mason. I want the low-down. I want to know what they knew about him, and whether they accused him of embezzling funds. After all, when a man's killed, we check up on his enemies. You know that as well as I do. . . . As far as that's concerned, a woman could have killed him as well as a man. . . . That lipstick makes it look like a woman."

"I don't think Mrs. Tump uses any," Mason said with a smile.

Sergeant Holcomb frowned and started to say something, but paused as the door leading to the reception office opened, and Gertie said, "I'm sorry to interrupt. There's someone on the line who says he must speak with Sergeant Holcomb right away."

Sergeant Holcomb looked around the room. "Can I take the call on this phone?" he asked, indicating an extension phone on a small table near the window.

Gertie said, "I'll connect you," and stepped back into the reception room, closing the door to the law library.

Sergeant Holcomb picked up the telephone, said, "Hello," then after several seconds said again, "All right . . . hello. Who is it? . . . All right. Go ahead."

Carl Mattern said in a low voice to Mason, "This has upset me frightfully. I'm so nervous I can hardly think straight."

Mason looked down at the wide, greenish-blue eyes which stared steadily up from behind the horn-rimmed glasses. "I presume it was quite a shock," he said. "It must . . ."

He broke off as Sergeant Holcomb, muttering an oath, slammed the receiver back into place, and, with no word of explanation, took two quick strides toward the door which led to Mason's private office.

"Don't go in there," Mason said.

Sergeant Holcomb ignored Mason. He jerked open the door, strode into the private office.

The two women, sitting huddled in a whispered conference, looked up in surprise.

Holcomb swung back to face Mason. "Holding out on me, eh? If I hadn't been tipped off that she was on her way to your office, I'd have fallen for it. . . . That sort of stuff isn't going to get you any place, Mason."

Mason said, "I don't have to report to you when a client calls on me. I'm having a conference with these women."

"Well, ain't that too bad?" Sergeant Holcomb said. "That conference is going to wait until *I* ask a few questions. . . . You two women were having some trouble with Albert Tidings, weren't you?"

Abigail Tump took the conversational lead. "Certainly," she said. "And the Hastings Hospital was having trouble with him. Mr. Tidings was a crook."

"You know he's dead?" Sergeant Holcomb asked.

"Yes. Mr. Mason told me."

"All right," Sergeant Holcomb said. "Now you went to Tidings' office Monday afternoon to try and see him. He told his secretary to tell you that he'd talk with Byrl Gailord, but he'd be damned if he'd talk with you. Isn't that right?"

"Yes," Mrs. Tump said.

"But you did talk with him?"

"Yes."

"Where?"

She said, "We waited outside in the parking lot where he keeps his automobile. Byrl knew where it was. We parked our car right next to his."

"What time did you talk with him?"

"Right after he left the office Monday, about four-thirty or quarter to five."

"Did you make any threats?"

Mrs. Tump took a deep breath and seemed to swell up with indignation. "Did *I* make any threats?" she asked. "Well, I like *that!* Threats indeed! That man threatened to have *me* arrested for defamation of character. He said I'd poisoned Byrl's mind against him. He said that under the trust he had absolute discretion as to what he'd give her and when he'd give it to her, and if I didn't quit interfering, he wouldn't give Byrl one damn cent. Those were his exact words, young man. One damn cent. Does that sound as though I was threatening *him?*"

"And what did you tell him?" Sergeant Holcomb asked.

She said, "I told him that he was going to be forced to make a complete accounting on that trust fund, and tell Byrl exactly how her affairs stood, that I wasn't anybody's fool, and that I was going to consult a lawyer."

"Then what?" Holcomb asked.

"Then," she said, "I told him that Mr. Perry Mason was going to be my lawyer, and that Mr. Mason would call on him at eleven o'clock the next morning. And that seemed to knock him for a loop. He mumbled something we couldn't hear, and started his car and drove away."

Sergeant Holcomb glanced inquiringly at Byrl Gailord. "You were there?" he asked.

She nodded.

"How does that check with your recollection of what happened?"

Byrl Gailord lowered her eyes thoughtfully for a moment, then said almost inaudibly, "It isn't the way I remember it."

Sergeant Holcomb pounced on her statement. "What's wrong with it?" he asked.

She said, "Uncle Albert—that's Mr. Tidings—wasn't quite as short and irritable as it would seem from the way Mrs. Tump tells it."

"He was, too," Mrs. Tump said indignantly. "He was very abusive. He . . ."

"I don't think you understand Uncle Albert as well as I do," Byrl Gailord interrupted. "He's exceedingly nervous when he's in a hurry, and he was in a hurry then."

"Yes," Mrs. Tump admitted, "he did say something about an appointment."

"An appointment?" Sergeant Holcomb asked eagerly. "Who with?"

"He didn't say," Mrs. Tump said.

"A lady," Byrl Gailord corrected.

"Yes, that's right. He did say something about he couldn't keep a lady waiting," Mrs. Tump agreed, "but he didn't say definitely that it was an appointment."

"Well, not in so many words," Byrl supplemented, "but I gathered that he had an appointment with a young woman."

"A social engagement?" Sergeant Holcomb asked.

Byrl twisted her gloves. "Personally," she said, "I think it was a business appointment, and I think it was something which worried him very much, something which made him preoccupied and irritable."

"You're giving him altogether too much credit," Mrs. Tump said. "The man was rude, impertinent, and—and ugly. He was trying to be abusive."

Byrl Gailord shook her head decisively, and met Sergeant Holcomb's eyes. "That isn't true, Sergeant," she said. "Mrs. Tump didn't know him well, that's all. If you investigate, you'll find Mr. Tidings had a very important appointment, and he was in a hurry to keep it. It was an appointment which meant a great deal to him, either personally or in a business way."

Carl Mattern said, "That agrees with what I told you, Sergeant."

Sergeant Holcomb frowned to him. "You said that Tidings knew these women were hanging around the parking place."

"I think he did," Mattern said. "He saw them drive in there, but I told you that I thought Mr. Tidings had an important appointment. That appointment was with a woman, I'm quite certain.... And I think it was on business matters."

"You don't know what business?"

Mattern chose his words carefully. "It was with a woman who had been making some trouble for Mr. Tidings, or was in a position to make some trouble for him. I know that."

"You can't give me her name?"

"No."

"When did Tidings come to his office Tuesday morning?"

"Around nine-thirty. Between nine-thirty and ten."

"And he didn't say anything about having kept an appointment Monday night?"

"No."

"Didn't say anything about where he'd been or whom he'd seen?"

"Not a word."

"Could you tell anything from his manner?"

"Well, he seemed more at ease, I thought.... A little less nervous, but that may have been merely my impression."

Sergeant Holcomb turned back to Mrs. Tump. "Now then, Mrs. Tump," he said. "You went back to Tidings' office on Tuesday morning, didn't you?"

Mrs. Tump fidgeted uneasily in her chair.

"Go ahead," Sergeant Holcomb said. "Answer the question."

"Yes, I did."

"Why?"

"Well," she said, "I figured . . . I don't know. I just wanted to give him one more chance."

Sergeant Holcomb said, "You figured that you'd arranged with

Mason to ring him up and frighten him, that the thought that Perry Mason was going to represent Byrl Gailord would scare Tidings into making some sort of a settlement, and you intended to see him and make a settlement direct and chisel Mason out of a lawyer's fee, didn't you?"

Mrs. Tump said indignantly, "I did nothing of the sort," but her eyes avoided those of Mason and of Sergeant Holcomb.

Sergeant Holcomb smiled frostily at Mason. "Why *did* you want to see him?" he asked Mrs. Tump.

"I . . . Well, I wanted to explain to him that—well, I wanted to tell him that Mr. Mason was going to act for Byrl."

"That was the only information you wanted to give him?"

"Yes."

Sergeant Holcomb grinned triumphantly. "We'll let it go at that. What time did you get there?"

Mrs. Tump nodded to Mattern. "His secretary knows. It was shortly before noon."

"And Tidings wasn't in his office?"

"The secretary *said* he wasn't in his office."

"But you didn't believe that?"

"Well, not exactly."

"You went over to the parking lot again?"

"I looked around there, yes."

"And then you went to Mr. Tidings' club?"

There was a distinct pause before Mrs. Tump said, "Yes."

"And somewhere along the line," Sergeant Holcomb said triumphantly, "you found out where Tidings was. You followed him out to the home of his wife, where the body was found, and you had your last conversation with him there, didn't you, Mrs. Tump?"

She met his eyes then with indignant denial. "I did nothing of the sort," she said. "You have absolutely no right to make such a statement. I can make trouble for you on that."

"Where were you at one o'clock Tuesday afternoon?"

"Why, I . . . I'd have to think. . . . Wait a minute. I was at my hairdresser's. I had a twelve-thirty appointment."

Sergeant Holcomb frowned thoughtfully. "Where were *you*, Miss Gailord?"

She said, "Why, I don't know . . . Tuesday . . . Oh, I know. I was having lunch with Coleman Reeger. . . . I guess you know him. He's the polo player. His family is very prominent socially."

Sergeant Holcomb walked over to the telephone on Mason's desk, picked it up, and said, "Put me through to police headquarters. I want to get the autopsy surgeon who's working on the body of Albert Tidings. I'll hold the phone."

He stood with the receiver held to his ear.

Mattern said to Mason, "I can tell you some things now, Mr. Mason, which I wasn't at liberty to say before. As far as Miss Gailord's affairs are concerned, I know something about them. The very last thing Mr. Tidings did was to make a most advantageous deal for Miss Gailord."

"What was it?" Mason asked.

"He sold out ten thousand shares of stock in the Seaboard Consolidated Freighters, and invested the proceeds in Western Prospecting. Just before he left the office, he told me to be sure to take the check down to Loftus & Cale, to see that the deal was put through."

"How much was the check?" Mason asked.

"Fifty thousand dollars."

"What's Western Prospecting? Is that a listed stock?" Mrs. Tump asked.

"No, Mrs. Tump. It's not listed."

"I never heard of it," Mason said.

"Well," Mattern said, "confidentially, they've struck. . . . I'm sorry, Mr. Mason, but I can't divulge details, but Mr. Tidings made a complete investigation. Out of that one deal, Miss Gailord will net—well, let's call it a handsome profit."

"Why so cagey?" Mason asked.

"Because," Mattern said, "the information is highly confidential, and you know there's nothing on earth so dangerous as having information leak out on a stock deal. I didn't intend to say anything about the stock as an investment. I merely mentioned it to show that Mr. Tidings was working in Miss Gailord's interests. He devoted weeks of study to the situation. He'd had a mining expert making confidential reports on the holdings of Western Prospecting, and had been to considerable pains to get detailed, accurate information on *one* of their holdings—a mining property."

Mason said, "There's no reason why you can't give Miss Gailord any information you have about that stock."

Mattern said, "You're a lawyer, Mr. Mason. I'm not. I'm not going to match wits with you, and I'm not going to argue law; but I presume Mr. Tidings' estate will have to be administered. The administrator will have a lawyer. I'll turn my information over to the administrator, and you can talk with the administrator's lawyer. . . . I think you can appreciate my position."

"What time did you take this check over to the broker's?"

"Shortly before eleven."

"Tuesday morning?" Mason asked.

"Yes, sir. I left with the check a short time after you called."

"And that was a personal check issued by Mr. Tidings?"

"No, sir. It was a cashier's check. . . . The amount was rather large, and for certain reasons Mr. Tidings was very anxious to have the matter concluded without waiting for a personal check to clear. He'd got the cashier's check Monday."

"*He* didn't take it over personally?" Mason said.

"No, sir. He sent me. That's one of the things I'm for, to relieve him of detail work of that sort."

"And when did Tidings leave his office?"

"At the same time I did. He went down in the elevator with me."

"And didn't tell you where you could reach him to report on the completion of the transaction?"

"No, sir. He called me."

"When was that?" Sergeant Holcomb asked, putting his hand over the mouthpiece of the telephone.

"I would say it was shortly before noon."

"Tuesday morning?"

"Yes."

"Did he say where he was calling from?" Mason asked.

"No, sir. He didn't."

Mason said, "Then the last we know of . . ."

"Hold it," Sergeant Holcomb said to Mason, and then into the telephone transmitter, "Yes. Hello. This is Sergeant Holcomb, Doctor. I want the dope on Albert Tidings. I want to know exactly when he died. . . . Yes, of course, I understand you haven't completed your examination, but you've certainly gone far enough to give me a pretty good guess . . . Well, what's the temperature of the room got to do with it? . . . I see . . . What? . . . What's that?

. . . Now, wait a minute. That doesn't check with the evidence. . . . No, it couldn't have been that early . . . Ten o'clock at the latest? . . . You'll have to up that by three hours . . . Well, get busy on it . . . Of course, I want the exact facts, but I don't want you to make a monkey out of yourself and the department, too. . . . You get the chief autopsy surgeon on that."

Sergeant Holcomb banged up the receiver.

Mason grinned at Byrl Gailord, then turned to Sergeant Holcomb and inquired courteously, "What did he say, Sergeant?"

Sergeant Holcomb said, "He doesn't know. He hasn't completed his examination. . . . Those doctors are a pain in the neck. I left word they were to go to work on that the minute the body was received at the coroner's office."

Mason smiled at Mrs. Tump. "Well, Mrs. Tump," he said. "I guess you won't have to produce any alibi to show that you didn't drag Tidings out of his club, shoot him, and drive him up to Mrs. Tidings' house. The autopsy surgeon has just advised Sergeant Holcomb that the man has been dead since ten o'clock Tuesday morning."

Sergeant Holcomb frowned at Mason. "You're using a lot of imagination," he said.

Mason picked up the telephone, and when he heard Gertie's voice on the line, asked, "Did you listen in on that telephone conversation, Gertie?"

"Uh huh," she said.

Mason said, "Thanks. That's all."

He dropped the receiver back into its cradle, and smiled at Sergeant Holcomb's discomfiture.

"Those doctors," Sergeant Holcomb said, "are a bunch of

boobs. How the devil can a man work up a case with a lot of nitwits tying his hands?"

Mattern said, "Why, I know he was alive shortly before noon. I talked with him over the telephone."

Mason said, "You talked with someone who *said* he was Tidings."

"I talked with Tidings."

"You recognized his voice?"

"Well . . . well, I thought so at the time."

Mason said, "Voices can be imitated, you know."

"Exactly *when* did he leave the office?" Sergeant Holcomb asked.

Mattern said, "Well, to tell you the truth, Sergeant, I don't know the exact time. It was right after his conversation with Mr. Mason—just a few minutes after that."

"Can you," Sergeant Holcomb asked Mason, "fix the exact time of that conversation?"

Mason said cautiously, "I might reconstruct it from data which I could assemble, Sergeant, but I can't give you the *exact* time right now."

Sergeant Holcomb said irritably, "What are you so damned cagey about, Mason? Your clients are in the clear—if their alibis hold up. Why not tell me *exactly* when that conversation was?"

Mason glanced significantly at Byrl Gailord. "I think," he said, "that there's one matter I'll have to investigate first."

"What's that?"

"The stock of the Western Prospecting Company."

Carl Mattern said, "I can tell you all about that, Mr. Mason."

"You haven't done so, so far," Mason said.

"It's a good investment."

"I prefer to make my own investigations and draw my own conclusions."

"Well, you'll find it's a good investment."

Sergeant Holcomb nodded to Mattern. "All right," he said, "that's all. Let's go." He turned to Mason and said, "The next time I'm investigating a murder and want to talk with clients of yours, and they're in your office, don't try to hold out on me."

"I didn't," Mason said. "I simply wanted my clients to make their own appointments."

Sergeant Holcomb stared at Mason, "You," he said, "don't co-operate very much with the authorities. Some day, it's going to get you into trouble. . . . Come on, Mattern."

They left the office.

Mason turned to the two women. He said, "I told you that I couldn't be of any particular assistance. . . . I think now that I can."

"What do you mean, Mr. Mason?" Mrs. Tump asked.

Mason said, "I want to know more about that deal covering the Western Prospecting Company stock. We may be able to set that sale aside—if we want to."

"But I don't see how," Mrs. Tump said.

Mason said, "Neither do I as yet, but Sergeant Holcomb is in a fix. The autopsy surgeon is going to say Tidings was killed within ten or fifteen minutes of the time he left his office Tuesday morning."

"Well?" Mrs. Tump asked.

Mason said, "A dead man can't buy stock."

Mrs. Tump and Byrl Gailord exchanged glances. Then Mrs.

Tump said, "But suppose it should turn out the stock really *is* a good buy?"

"Then," Mason said, "we'll simply sit tight. . . . Now then, you run along and let me get busy."

The women arose. Byrl Gailord gave him her hand, and said, "I have implicit confidence in you, Mr. Mason. Thanks very much."

Mrs. Tump said nervously, "Mr. Mason, I didn't want you to think that I was trying to double-cross you. I . . . Well, I wanted to see Mr. Tidings and let him know that I wasn't bluffing; that I said I'd go to you and that I'd gone to you."

Mason said, "Forget it. Even if you *had* been trying to effect a last minute settlement with him, it would have been all right with me."

"Thank you, Mr. Mason. You're so kind. You make me feel like a . . . like a . . ."

"Like a heel," Byrl Gailord interrupted, laughing. "But really, Mr. Mason, Mrs. Tump was working for my best interests, and she wants to save every dime of my money she can. Come on now, Abigail. 'Fess up."

Mrs. Tump laughed. "I don't need to 'fess up, Byrl. I've been caught with the goods. . . . Good-by, Mr. Mason."

Mason and Della Street watched them out of the office.

"The chiseler," Della Street said.

Mason nodded. "They'll all do that," he said, "if they're smart enough. . . . Get my broker on the line, Della. Tell him to find out everything about Western Prospecting, what the stock can be sold for, and who unloaded a block of fifty thousand dollars' worth on Tuesday morning."

"Do you want to talk with Loftus & Cale?" he asked.

"Not yet," Mason said. "I want to be loaded for bear when I talk with them."

"Why?"

"I don't know," Mason said. "Call it a hunch if you want. I think there's something fishy about that stock deal. Tidings was being crowded. He must have known that Adelle Hastings was going to put the screws on him. . . ."

"His Monday night appointment was with her?" Della Street asked.

"Looks like it," Mason said. "Sergeant Holcomb didn't mention any names, so I didn't. . . . Ring Paul Drake. Tell him to find Robert Peltham, and ring up the *Contractor's Journal* and put in a classified ad. Simply say, 'P: Must talk with you, personally if possible. Otherwise over the telephone. Will mention no names over the telephone but must have additional accurate information at once. M.'"

Della Street's pencil flew over the lines of her shorthand notebook. "Okay, Chief," she said. "Anything else?"

"No," Mason said, "but get busy on that stock deal, and tell Drake to keep his ear to the ground on that murder case."

Della Street said, "If your clients are in the clear, Chief, why worry about the murder?"

Mason said, "Because, Della, I'm caught in a trap. I'm afraid some woman is going to come into this office at such time as suits her convenience, and hand me the other part of that ten-thousand-dollar bill, and say, 'Go ahead and represent me, Mr. Mason.' And it's an even money bet that the hand holding that part of the ten-thousand-dollar bill will be the one that held the gun when Tidings was killed."

"Within fifteen minutes after he left his office Tuesday morning?" Della Street asked skeptically.

"*Somebody* killed him," Mason said.

"Then you don't believe that it was Tidings who called the secretary at noon Tuesday to find out whether the deal had been completed?"

"The autopsy surgeon doesn't," Mason said significantly.

6.

MASON ENTERED his office on Thursday morning to find Paul Drake waiting for him. He nodded to Gertie, took Drake's arm, and escorted him into the private office where Della Street was busy sorting the morning mail.

"'Lo, Della. Anything new?" Mason asked.

"Nothing particularly important," she said. "Hello, Paul."

"Hello, Della. How's tricks?"

"Swell."

Drake jackknifed himself into his favorite pose across the arms of the big, black, leather chair.

"Got something?" Mason asked.

"Odds and ends," Drake said. "Peltham's skipped out. The officers want him damn badly. They can't find him, and I can't find him."

"Any charge against him?" Mason asked.

"They figure he's the one who signed the checks with Tidings. . . . The checks that left the hospital holding the sack."

"You can't find out anything about a girl friend?"

"Not a thing. He lived in an apartment, and as far as is known, no woman ever visited him in that apartment. He's a cold-blooded, mathematical individual with no more emotions than a banker turning down a loan application. Anything that he did would have been done skillfully, thoroughly, and with ample attention to details. If he had a love affair with a married woman, for instance, the thing would be all blueprinted, nothing would be left to chance."

Mason said, "Okay. Here's an important job for you, Paul. I put an ad in the *Contractor's Journal*. That's confidential. I don't want even your operatives to know about it. The point is, sometime during the day a person will send in an ad in answer to mine. Plant a man there at the office, Paul, and when an answer to my ad shows up, arrange for a tip-off from behind the counter, and tail that person."

"Okay," Drake said. "Anything else?"

"Yes. Mrs. Tump had a run-in with an orphan asylum, The Hidden Home Welfare Society. It made quite a stink. . . . She's in touch with a former bookkeeper of that society. I have a hunch this bookkeeper is here in the city. I'm going to make her want to get in touch with him sometime after . . . Oh, say ten-thirty this morning. You watch her hotel, check on the people who inquire for her at the desk, and watch her outgoing telephone calls. . . . Do you think you can fix that up?"

"The telephone calls aren't easy," Drake said, "but it can be managed."

"All right," Mason said, and then to Della Street, "Promptly at ten-thirty, Della, ring up Mrs. Tump and tell her that Mr. Mason says there's some question as to the endorsements on the back of the cancelled checks from The Hidden Home Welfare Society. Tell her the claim has been made that they're forgeries, that The Hidden Home Welfare Society never received any of that money in the first place, and that the person endorsing the checks was never connected with the society. Ask her if she knows anything about it. . . . Get her worried, but be a little vague. You know. You're only my secretary calling during my absence from the office and repeating my instructions. . . . You can act just a little dumb if you want to. It won't hurt anything."

"Be your own sweet self," Drake supplemented.

Della ran out her tongue at him and made a note. "Ten-thirty," she said.

"That's right."

"You have a man planted on the job by that time, Paul," Mason said to Drake.

"Okay."

Mason said, "I want to find out something about Byrl Gailord, Paul. The story Mrs. Tump tells doesn't hold water."

Della Street looked up in surprise. "How so, Chief?" she asked. "I thought it was very dramatic."

"You bet it was dramatic," Mason said. "Too dramatic. The hands clutching at the steel sides of the vessel, people being swept away on waves and all that. . . . But what she overlooked was certain routine matters of procedure. In the first place, the Russian nobleman *and* his wife wouldn't have gone over in the first lifeboat—not with Mrs. Tump standing on the rail looking down into the dark waters. It's a rule of the sea that women and children go first.

"Mrs. Tump gives a swell picture, but it's only the way she's imagined it. She pictures herself standing on the rail, looking down with a detached, impersonal interest. If she'd actually *been* on that ship, she'd have spoken about how hard it was for her to stand up on the slanting deck, how she struggled to get on her life preserver, and how officers kept blowing whistles and herding passengers around from one boat to another. . . . That shipwreck sounds phony to me. Notice she didn't give any data about the name of the ship. Whenever she'd come to statistics, she'd wave her hand and say, 'All this is preliminary, Mr. Mason.'"

Della Street said, "When you come to think of it, it does sound fishy. . . . But *why?*"

Mason said, "On a guess, she's lying about some things, telling the truth about others. If it weren't for that correspondence she has, I'd have figured that she was just trying to tell Byrl a fairy story and horn in on the trust fund."

Drake said, "Well, I'll get busy," and started to straighten up from the chair.

Mason said, "Wait a minute, Paul. I've got one more thing for you. Carl Mattern, the secretary to Albert Tidings. Get all the dope you can on him. Find out who his sweetheart is, whether he intends to get married, whether he plays the horses, hits the hooch, or what he does for relaxation."

"Okay. Anything else?"

"That's all, right now."

As Drake moved out through the exit door, the telephone rang, and Della Street said, "Here's your broker on the line with that information about Western Prospecting."

Mason picked up the telephone, said, "Okay. This is Mason talking. Let me have it."

His broker gave him the information in concise, dry-as-dust statistics. "Western Prospecting," he said, "capital stock, three million dollars. Two million five hundred thousand shares issued. Each share has a par value of one dollar. Much of it given in exchange for mining properties. Some sold to the public at a dollar a share, then it went up, and there were several sales at a dollar and a quarter, a dollar and a half, and at two dollars. Then the pressure was removed, and the stock drifted back. Right now, there's no open market for it at any price. The corporation isn't making any sales at less than a dollar, but reports are that private stockholders will sell out for anything they can get from two cents up. No one wants it.

"Tuesday, shortly before noon, the sale of a big block of stock went through. The stock was transferred on the books of the corporation to Albert Tidings, trustee. Doesn't say trustee for whom or for what. . . . I don't know what broker handled the deal, and I don't know what the consideration was. It shouldn't have been over three or four thousand dollars. The company has a bunch of prospects all of which look good, but there's a big difference between a prospect and a mine. Anything else you want?"

"Yes," Mason said. "Where did the stock come from that was sold to Tidings?"

"They're trying to be secretive about that," the broker told him, "but my best guess is the president of the company unloaded his personal holdings."

"Who's the president?"

"Man by the name of Bolus—Emery B. Bolus."

"Western Prospecting Company have offices here?"

"Uh huh. . . . Think they keep them simply to sell stock. Pretty good suite of offices under a lease which hasn't expired yet. No business activity. One stenographer, a vice-president, a superintendent of operations, a president, and a bookkeeper. . . . You know the type. . . . If you get rough, don't let anyone know where you got the information."

"Thanks," Mason said. "I'm going to get rough—and I won't let anyone know where I got the info."

He said to Della Street, "Get me Loftus or Cale on the line. . . . Brokerage firm of Loftus & Cale. I want either one."

She nodded and put through the call. While Mason was waiting for the connection, he pushed his hands down deep in his pockets and paced the floor of the office thoughtfully.

"On the line," Della Street called. "Mr. Loftus, senior partner."

Mason took the line, said, "Hello, Mr. Loftus. This is Perry Mason, the lawyer. I find that I'm interested through one of my clients in a transaction which was concluded through your office on Tuesday morning."

"Yes?" Loftus asked, his tone reserved and cautious.

"A sale of Western Prospecting Company stock to Tidings as trustee."

"Oh, yes."

"What can you tell me about it?" Mason asked.

The answer was prompt. "Nothing."

"I'm representing Byrl Gailord, the beneficiary of the trust which Tidings was administering," Mason explained.

"Are you, indeed?" Loftus inquired.

Mason's face darkened. "Can you come over to my office?" he asked.

"No."

"Do you," Mason asked, "have an attorney who handles your business?"

"Yes."

"Would you mind telling me who he is?"

"I see no occasion for doing so."

"All right," Mason said, raising his voice, "if you won't come to my office, I'll come to yours. You can have your attorney there if you want. If you take my advice, you'll have him there. You'll also have Emery B. Bolus, the president of the Western Prospecting Company there. . . . I *was* willing to give you guys a break. *Now,* I'm going to stick you for exactly fifty thousand bucks. And so you'll have something to worry about, I'm going to tell you in advance exactly how I'm going to do it. . . . I'll be there in fifteen minutes, and I won't wait."

He slammed the telephone receiver back on its hook, then suddenly started to laugh. "Dammit," he said to Della Street. "One of those frosty, reserved, human adding-machines gets under my skin worse than a dozen shysters who try browbeating tactics."

He walked over to the closet and put on his hat.

"Going over to beard the lion in his den?" she asked.

"I'm going over to throw a scare into that old buzzard he'll never forget," Mason said, "and I'm going to skate on damn thin ice doing it. I hope he has his lawyer there, and I hope his lawyer tries to argue with me. . . . Wish me luck, sweetheart, because I'll need it."

It was exactly fifteen minutes later that Perry Mason entered the imposing offices of Loftus & Cale. An attractive young woman looked up from a desk on which a brass plaque stamped "Information" had been fastened to a prismatic-shaped bit of wood.

"Mr. Loftus," Mason said.

"Your name?"

"Mason."

"Oh, yes," she said. "Mr. Loftus is expecting you."

"That's nice," Mason said.

"Will you wait a few minutes?"

Mason said, "No."

She appeared ill at ease. "Just a moment," she said, and, turning in the swivel chair, plugged in a telephone line. "Mr. Mason is here, Mr. Loftus. He says he won't wait."

There was evidently an argument at the other end of the line. The young woman listened attentively, then said simply, "But he won't wait, Mr. Loftus."

There followed another moment of silence, then she turned to smile at Perry Mason. "You may go right on in," she said, indicating a gate which led to a hallway. "It's the second door on the left."

Mason pushed through the gate, marched down the corridor, and opened a door marked "Mr. Loftus, Private."

The man who sat behind the massive mahogany desk was somewhere in the sixties, with florid complexion, a face which was inclined to jowls, a cold lackluster eye, and thin white hair.

Mason smiled coldly. "I told you over the phone I wouldn't wait," he said.

Loftus said, in a rasping, authoritative voice, which was evidently more accustomed to giving orders than asking favors, "Sit down. My attorney is on his way over here."

"If you'd told me that earlier," Mason said, "I'd have made an appointment which would have suited his convenience."

Loftus clenched his right fist, extended it in front of him, and gently lowered it to the desk. There was something more impressive in the gesture than would have been the case had he banged the top of the desk with explosive violence. "I don't like criminal lawyers," he said.

"Neither do I," Mason admitted, seating himself in what appeared to be the most comfortable chair in the office.

"But *you're* a criminal lawyer."

"It depends upon what you mean," Mason observed. "I'm a lawyer. I'm not a criminal."

"You defend criminals."

"What is your definition of a criminal?" Mason asked.

"A man who has committed a crime."

"And who decides that he has committed a crime?"

"Why, a jury, I suppose."

"Exactly," Mason said, with a smile. "So far, I have been very fortunate in having juries agree with me that the persons I represented were not criminals."

Loftus said, "That isn't conclusive."

"Judges think it is," Mason said, still smiling.

"What interest can a man of your ilk possibly have in our business?"

"I don't like that word *ilk,*" Mason observed. "It may be I won't like your business. In any event, I told you why I was calling on you. If you'd given me the information I asked over the telephone, you might have spared yourself a disagreeable interview."

"It'll be disagreeable to you," Loftus said, "not to me. I hate to go to the expense of consulting my legal department every time some pettifogging attorney wants to pry into my business. . . . But now I've started, I'm going to see it through."

"Very commendable," Mason observed, carefully selecting a cigarette from his cigarette case, and lighting it.

"Well, aren't you going to tell me what you want?"

"Not until your lawyer gets here," Mason said.

"But you said you wouldn't wait."

"I don't like to wait in outer offices," Mason observed, "unless it's necessary, and I don't like to discuss legal points of business with a man I'm going to trim unless his attorney is present. . . . Suppose we talk about baseball or politics."

Loftus half rose from his chair. His face assumed a slightly purplish tinge. "I'm going to warn you, young man," he said, "that you're due for the surprise of your life. Your rather spectacular courtroom victories have been made possible because you were pitted against underpaid public servants and political appointees. You're going up against the best and highest-priced brains in the legal business now."

"That's nice," Mason said. "I always like to . . ."

The door was pushed open. A tall, broad-shouldered man with high cheekbones came bursting into the office. He was carrying a brief case in his hand. "I told you not to see him until I got here," he said to Loftus.

Mason smiled affably. "I wouldn't wait," he said. "I take it you're the legal department."

The man eyed him without cordiality. "I'm Ganten," he said, "senior partner of Ganten, Kline & Shaw. You're Mason. I've seen you in court. What do you want?"

"I asked Mr. Loftus over the telephone," Mason said, "to tell me what he knew of a transaction involving the sale of fifty thousand shares of stock in the Western Prospecting Company to Albert Tidings as trustee. He refused."

"He did quite right to refuse," Ganten said coldly, seating himself and carefully placing his brief case on the floor by the side of his chair.

Mason smiled. "Personally, I think it was poor judgment."

"I don't care to have you question my judgment," Loftus said angrily.

Mason said, "Perhaps I'd better explain my position, and call your attention to certain facts. I'm representing Byrl Gailord, the beneficiary under the trust. . . . That is, I've been consulted in her behalf."

"Go ahead and represent her," Loftus said. "We have nothing to do with what happens between her and the trustee."

"For your information," Mason said, "Albert Tidings was killed."

Loftus and Ganten exchanged glances. Ganten said, "If you don't mind, Mr. Loftus, I'll handle the interview."

"I'm not going to be browbeaten," Loftus said. "I read about Tidings' death in the paper. It doesn't mean a damn thing—not so far as . . ."

"Please, Mr. Loftus," Ganten interrupted. "Let me do the talking. This lawyer is trying to trap you into making some admission."

Mason laughed. "*I* was the one who suggested to Mr. Loftus that he have his attorney present at this interview."

Ganten said coldly, "Well, I'm here. Go ahead with the interview."

Mason seemed to be enjoying himself. He inhaled deeply, and then watched the cigarette smoke as he exhaled it through half-parted lips. "Unfortunately," he said, "there seems to be some difference of opinion as to when Tidings met his death."

"What has that to do with the stock sale?" Loftus asked. "We had no infor—"

"*Please,* Mr. Loftus," Ganten interposed hastily.

Mason said, "It may have a good deal to do with that stock sale. The transaction, as I understand it, was concluded by Mr. Tidings' secretary. Tidings had left his office before the matter was concluded. Tidings was acting in the capacity of trustee."

"What does all that have to do with us?" Ganten asked.

Mason said, "Simply this. The medical examiner claims that Tidings couldn't possibly have been alive after ten o'clock Tuesday morning."

"That's poppycock," Loftus said. "His secretary saw him after that. His secretary talked with him over the telephone after the deal had been concluded."

"His secretary might have been mistaken," Mason said.

"Bosh," Loftus remarked explosively.

Ganten said, "Apparently it hasn't occurred to you, Mr. Mason, that the medical examiner might be mistaken."

"It has," Mason admitted. "I'm willing to grant you the possibility that the medical examiner was mistaken. You're not willing to grant me the possibility that it was Tidings' secretary who made the mistake."

Ganten half turned in his chair so that he was facing Mason. "Is it your position," he inquired coldly, "that if it should appear that Mr. Tidings was dead at the time the secretary concluded the transaction, there is any liability on the part of my clients?"

"Fifty thousand dollars' worth of it," Mason announced cheerfully.

Ganten assumed the manner of one talking to a child. "I am afraid, Mr. Mason, that your legal experience has been confined too much to courtroom technicalities, under the distorted rules of criminal procedure."

"Suppose you leave *my* legal experience out of it," Mason suggested, "and get down to brass tacks."

"Very well," Ganten announced, and then turned to Loftus. "There's absolutely nothing to this, Mr. Loftus," he said. "He hasn't a leg to stand on. Even conceding for the sake of the argument that Tidings was dead at the time of the transaction, there can be no liability on your part. He can't even question the authority of the trustee.

"Under the law, the death of a trustee creates a vacancy which is filled by the appointment of another trustee in a court of competent jurisdiction. Until that appointment is made, the administrator of the decedent trustee assumes charge of the property. . . . There is no question but what Mr. Mattern was acting in accordance with specific instructions given by Mr. Tidings. There's absolutely nothing to this claim."

Loftus said, with a smile which was almost a sneer, "You see, Mr. Mason, Mr. Ganten is an expert in matters of this sort. He's a specialist on contracts."

"And contractual relationships," Ganten supplemented.

"That's nice," Mason said. "How is he on the law of agency?"

"I have also specialized on that," Ganten said.

"Then," Mason observed, "perhaps you have given some thought to the law of agency as it applies to *this* case."

"It doesn't apply to this case at all," Ganten observed patronizingly. "My clients are acting as brokers. That's a definite subdivision of the agency relationship. They act as intermediaries . . ."

"Forget it," Mason said. "I'm talking about Mattern."

"About Mattern!" Ganten said in surprise. "What in the world does *he* have to do with it?"

Mason said with a smile, "You closed the deal with Mattern. You treated Mattern as the agent of Tidings. He was the agent of Tidings. But the very minute Tidings died, that relationship was automatically terminated by law. The authority of an agent—unless it is coupled with an interest—expires immediately upon the death of the principal."

Loftus said, "Bosh," again, but a quick glance at Ganten's face caused him to show sudden signs of concern. "What is it, Ganten?" he asked.

Ganten said, "That's not going to get you anywhere, Mr. Mason. A complete agreement had been reached between the parties. Mattern was merely the instrumentality by which that agreement was consummated, and Tidings had given Mattern specific, definite instructions prior to his appearance at our office. ... As you study the law of agency, Mr. Mason, you will find that there are various fine distinctions limiting the application of the general code sections on which you seem to be relying."

"Well," Mason said, "you might examine *Restatement of the Law*. Take for instance pages 309-310 of the volume on Agency and notice the illustrations therein cited as representing judicial applications of the doctrine that death of the principal terminates the authority of the agent. I call your attention particularly to the following:

"'P purchases an option on Blackaire and authorizes A to sell it. Two hours before the expiration of the option and while A is in the process of executing a sale of it to T, P dies. A's authority is terminated.

"'P employs H, a stockbroker, to purchase at the market 10,000 shares of stock in A's name but for P's account. P dies, this being unknown to anyone. A few moments thereafter, A purchases the shares. A had no authority to purchase.'"

Ganten blinked his eyes rapidly, his only outward symptom of nervousness, but he avoided glancing in the direction of his client.

Once more the door was pushed open, and a short, thickset, genial individual in the early fifties pushed his way into the room. "Good morning, Mr. Loftus," he said. "Good morning," and walked across the office to grasp Loftus' hand and pump it up and down. Then he turned to include the other two occupants of the room with his genial smile.

"Mr. Ganten of my legal department," Loftus introduced, "and Mr. Perry Mason who is trying to upset that fifty-thousand-dollar sale of Western Prospecting stock. . . . Gentlemen, this is Mr. Emery B. Bolus, the president of the Western Prospecting Company."

Bolus remained genial. He shook hands with Ganten, and then grasped Mason's hand cordially. "Glad to meet you gentlemen," he said. "What's this about upsetting that sale? The sale has already been completed. The transaction, so far as our company is concerned, is closed."

"Stock transfer been duly entered on the books?" Mason asked.

Bolus hesitated a minute, then said, "Yes."

"Don't answer his questions," Ganten said after a moment. "I'll do the talking. Your interests and those of my client are identical, Mr. Bolus."

Mason said, "Rather a damaging admission coming from an attorney who has specialized in the law of agency and of contracts, Mr. Ganten. . . . I don't want to suggest how you should conduct your office, but if your investigation *should* disclose that the facts are as I contend, then it would be very much to the interest of your clients to help me impound that fifty thousand dollars until the validity of the transaction can be determined. Otherwise, any judgment which we might recover would leave your clients holding the bag. If we're going to get judgment, it's to your interest to see that it's paid with that fifty thousand dollars Bolus is holding, instead of fifty thousand your clients will have to dig up out of their own pockets."

Mason got to his feet.

Bolus said genially, "Come, come, boys. What's all this?"

Loftus said, "Mason contends that Tidings was dead when we closed the deal on that stock. It's in the morning papers."

For a moment there was silence in the room, then Bolus turned to Ganten. "Well, Mr. Ganten," he said, "as attorney for Loftus & Cale, you can take care of our interests in the matter. Personally, I'm not going to concern myself with legal technicalities."

Loftus said raspingly, "Just a minute, Ganten. Are we apt to tie our hands doing that? You heard what Mason said."

Ganten said cautiously, "Well, perhaps it would be better, under the circumstances, for Mr. Bolus to consult his own counsel."

Bolus said, "Come, come, Loftus. You're not going to let Mason's goofy ideas interfere with *our* cordial relationship, are you?"

"Where's that fifty thousand dollars?" Loftus asked.

Bolus tugged at his ear. "Well now," he said, "let's find out just where *we* stand before I start making statements to you. Do you consider there's any possibility you folks might try to go after that fifty thousand dollars?"

Mason said, "Of course, they're going after it."

Ganten glared at Mason. "The whole situation is absurd," he said. "Tidings was alive and well when that agreement was concluded. There's positive, irrefutable evidence to that effect."

Mason yawned.

Bolus said, "That's not answering my question. *Is* there any possibility that you people are going to try and impound that fifty thousand dollars?"

Ganten said, "It might not be a bad idea to simply hold matters in abeyance until we've investigated the case in all its ramifications."

"What do you mean by holding them in abeyance?"

"Oh, just take steps to preserve the *status quo*."

Bolus lost his smile. "I don't know what you mean by the *status quo*," he said.

"Just see that everyone is protected," Loftus explained hurriedly.

Bolus said, "The way I'm going to protect myself is by putting that fifty thousand dollars into circulation."

"I don't think that would be wise," Loftus said.

"Why wouldn't it?" Bolus asked, his eyes glinting. "Your own attorney has said that the claim is absurd."

"Nevertheless, it's a claim."

"And what do you propose to do about it?"

"We'll investigate it," Ganten said.

"Go ahead and investigate," Bolus said. "Investigate all you damn please, but don't pull any of this *status quo* business on me. It's *my* money isn't it?"

"The corporation's money," Ganten corrected.

Bolus said, "You folks have the stock. I have the money. I don't give a damn what you do with the stock, and you aren't going to tell me what to do with the money."

"Now wait a minute," Ganten said. "You'll admit that you don't want to become involved in litigation. I think the whole thing is absurd. I think a few days' investigation will clear up the entire matter. We will use all of our facilities to see that that investigation is made promptly and thoroughly."

"And in the meantime?" Bolus asked.

"Well, in the meantime," Ganten said, "it's to the interest of all of us to see that the situation doesn't become any more complicated."

"What are you driving at?"

"Well, you should co-operate with us."

"In what way?"

"In making the investigation."

"Anything else?"

"Well, of course if the transaction *should* be declared invalid, we'd all of us want to be in such a position that we could protect ourselves."

Bolus said, "As far as I'm concerned, I made a deal. I'm going to stand back of it. . . . That stock's a good investment, a mighty good investment. There are things the general public doesn't know anything about. I'm not at liberty to say what they are, but within sixty days that stock is going to be worth— Well, it will be worth plenty."

Loftus nodded.

Mason said casually, "Then why did you unload all of *your* holdings, Bolus?"

Bolus whirled on him angrily. "I didn't unload all of my holdings."

"How much stock do you have at the present time in your own name in the company of which you're president?"

"That's none of your damn business."

"Did any substantial part of that fifty thousand dollars go into the corporation's treasury?"

"That also is none of your business. I don't have to answer your questions."

"That's right," Mason agreed affably, "you don't," and once

more devoted his attention to the cigarette smoke which eddied upward from the tip of his cigarette. "As I understand what happened, you'd be foolish if you did."

Ganten and Loftus exchanged glances.

"Well," Bolus asked, "are you standing with me in this thing, or are you against me?"

"We're not against you," Loftus said hastily.

"What my client means," Ganten corrected, "is that in many respects our interests are in common. That is, it's to the interest of both of us to show that Tidings was alive when the deal was completed."

"Do you mean to say that if he was dead when the stock was actually turned over and the cash was passed, you can come back on *me?*"

"Of course," Ganten said, "if the transaction was void for any reason, then we'd want to see that you had the stock back and that the money was returned to the proper person."

"Why?"

"Well, because we acted as brokers, and in the highest good faith. . . . I think you should answer Mr. Mason's question about what happened to that money and assure him that the sale was of treasury stock."

"I don't have to assure anyone of anything," Bolus said. "You wanted fifty thousand dollars' worth of stock. You got it. I got the money."

"You individually?" Mason asked. "Or as president of the corporation?"

"I don't like your damned insinuations," Bolus said.

"There's one way of preventing a repetition of them," Mason pointed out. "Simply answer the question."

"I think it would be perfectly in order for you to answer Mr. Mason's question," Ganten said.

"Well, I don't," Bolus snapped.

Loftus stroked the angle of his chin. His eyes shifted from his attorney to the president of the Western Prospecting Company, then over to Mason, and were hastily averted.

Mason said, "Well, I'll be going. I simply wanted you gentlemen to know where I stood."

"I don't think your client is adopting a fair attitude," Loftus said.

Mason said, "Don't let my departure interfere with your discussion, gentlemen."

Loftus arose from his chair, started around his desk, and stopped. "Just *what* are you trying to do, Mr. Mason?" he asked.

"Protect the interests of my client," Mason said, "and educate your legal department." With an inclusive bow, he left the office.

Mason returned to his office in rare good humor.

"Do any good?" Della Street asked.

"I think so," Mason said. "I've got those brokers plenty worried, and their legal department's running around in circles. By the time they get done stirring things up, we'll know when Tidings died. The way things are shaping up now, Sergeant Holcomb won't be able to dig up additional clues and keep them from me."

"You mean they'll do the investigating for you?"

"That's right. They can bring pressure to bear on Holcomb, and make him talk. I can't."

She said, "Paul Drake wants you to call. Shall I get him?"

"Uh huh."

She got Drake on the line. As Mason picked up the receiver, he heard Drake's voice over the wire, saying hurriedly, "Listen,

Perry. A girl went into the *Contractor's Journal* with an answer to that ad you placed. From there she went to a beauty parlor and is getting herself all slicked up: shampoo, wave, manicure, massage. I've got a man staked out in front of the beauty parlor. . . . Now, if you'd like to get a look at this baby first hand, we've got time to run down there and give her the once-over when she comes out."

"Got your car downstairs, Paul?"

"Sure."

"Okay," Mason said. "I'll meet you down in the parking lot. You do the driving. I'll do the looking."

He hung up the telephone, said to Della Street, "We've got a customer on that *Contractor's Journal* ad. . . . Probably the same girl who turned in the last ad. I'm going to go take a look at *her*."

"Think she's got the other half of that ten-thousand-dollar bill?" Della Street asked.

Mason grinned. "I'm getting so I think everyone has it. I'm on my way. If this girl turns out to be Byrl Gailord, we'll know a lot more in an hour."

Mason walked rapidly down the corridor, took the elevator, and found Paul Drake seated in his automobile, waiting in front of the entrance. Mason climbed in.

"Think you'll know this girl when you see her, Perry?" Drake asked.

"Uh huh," Mason said. "—I hope so, and I'm afraid so."

"Who is she, Perry?"

"My client," Mason said.

Drake looked at him in surprise. "Don't you know your own clients?"

Mason grinned. "I have a wide practice."

Drake said, "Perry, this case keeps getting goofier and goofier. Why should you want to shadow your own client?"

"Just to give you boys a job, Paul. You've had a lot of hard cases, so I thought I'd give you an easy one."

Mason remained thoughtfully silent while Drake piloted the car through traffic. A signal turned against them, and Drake, stopping the car, said, "It's a couple of blocks farther on. We may not be able to find a parking space."

"We can roost in front of a fire plug," Mason said. "I want to get a good look at this girl, but I don't want her to see *me*. . . . Got a pair of dark glasses, Paul?"

"Yeah. In the glove compartment. . . . Dark glasses are as near as we come to using disguises—and usually they're all that's necessary."

The signal changed, and Drake eased the car into gear. "Got a description of her?" Mason asked.

"Not too much to go on," Drake said, "just what I picked up over the telephone. The operative was calling from a cigar stand across the street from the beauty parlor. She has a swell figure, is around twenty-eight, a brunette with large, dark eyes."

Mason frowned thoughtfully.

"Doesn't it fit?" Drake asked.

"It depends on the eyes," Mason said. "The girl I have in mind has dark eyes, but I wouldn't pick them as being a particularly noticeable feature."

"This operative is young and impressionable," Drake said. "He made her sound like a follies' beauty on the loose."

He turned the car to the left, and said, "There's the stakeout—this car right ahead. Have to hand it to that boy. He's managed to take up two parking spaces so we can squeeze in behind."

"That's swell," Mason said.

Drake pressed lightly on the horn button, and the operative looked behind, nodded, started his motor, and pulled his car forward until its bumper was touching that of the car ahead. Drake managed to work his own car into the space behind. "Want to talk with him?" he asked.

Mason nodded.

They got out and walked across to the agency car.

"Think she'll be out pretty quick now," the operative said.

"You tailed her here from the *Contractor's Journal* office?" Mason asked.

"Yeah. It's only three or four blocks. She evidently had an appointment at the beauty parlor. I think the girl in the beauty parlor knows her. But I haven't tried as yet to get the address or any information in there."

"You can do that after she leaves," Mason said. "—No, wait a minute. I don't want her to think anyone's trailing her. We'll wait and keep that beauty parlor as an ace up our sleeve."

"Okay. You want me to stay here?"

"Yes. You can follow along in the car. I'll get out and try to follow her on foot. If she gives me the slip, you carry on from there, and find out where she goes."

"That'll be swell. She may duck into a department store or something. A man's lost trying to follow a pedestrian in an automobile when they pull a stunt like that."

Mason said, "Okay. Stay on the job. How's she dressed?"

"Dark woolen dress with a red fox jacket and one of those good-looking little hats."

"Easy on the eyes?" Mason asked.

"Gosh, I'll say. She's a beauty. I could go for that number in a big way."

Drake winked at Mason.

"Okay. We'll go back and wait in our car," Mason said. "You tag along and see what you can do."

Mason and Drake walked back to sit in Drake's car while they waited.

"You got some ideas on the time of Tidings' death, Perry?" Drake asked.

"I think I have."

"What are they?"

Mason said, "I don't know. The thing doesn't make sense. . . . Not the way Homicide has it figured out."

"How do they have it figured out?"

"Holcomb figured it two ways. Once he figured that Tidings was shot in the bungalow, and once he figured he was shot in the automobile and the body dragged into the bungalow."

"How do *you* figure it?"

"I figure he was shot in the automobile and came into the apartment under his own power—probably with quite a bit of assistance. He died practically as soon as he was stretched out on the bed. . . . Funny thing, Paul, about his shoes."

"What's funny about them?"

"They weren't on."

"Well, a man wouldn't get into bed with his shoes on."

"A dying man wouldn't stop to take his shoes off. If someone was helping him in, that someone would hardly think to take the shoes off—unless it happened to be a woman."

"Something to that," Drake agreed.

"The boys from the Homicide Squad couldn't find those shoes," Mason said. "I looked around for 'em myself when I was in there. I didn't see them in the closet, and didn't see them under the bed."

"Why would anyone take his shoes?"

"I don't know, but I have an idea."

"What's the idea?"

Mason said, "Let's look at it this way, Paul. The autopsy surgeon says he's been dead some time. He figures ten o'clock Tuesday morning as the very latest. I have an idea he'd like to put it quite a bit before that, but in view of the other evidence, he's stretching things to the limit."

"That gas being on and the room being closed up didn't help things any," Drake pointed out.

"I know, but that's a significant thing in itself."

"How do you mean, Perry?"

Mason said, "Let's look at it this way, Paul. Tidings might have gone into the house under his own power. It *might* have been during the daytime. . . . But there are quite a few things which make me think otherwise. One of them is the gas.

"*I* don't think that the gas was turned on simply to create conditions which would cause a more rapid decomposition of the body and make it more difficult to fix the time of death with any degree of accuracy."

"Why was it turned on then?" Drake asked.

Mason said, "It was turned on because it was cold in the room. Whoever turned it on wanted to heat the room. That means it was turned on at night."

"Tuesday night?" Drake asked.

Mason said, "No, Paul. *Monday* night."

Drake stared at him. "Monday night! But that's impossible!"

Mason said, "Let's look at it this way, Paul. It was either Monday night or Tuesday night. The man wasn't dead when he was brought into the house. The bloodstains on the floor indicate that. The nature of the bloodstains on the bed show that there was considerable hemorrhage after he was put to bed."

"That's right," Drake admitted.

"According to the testimony of the autopsy surgeon, it *had* to be Monday night and not Tuesday night. Remember, he says the man had been dead since at least ten o'clock Tuesday morning."

"But, Good Lord, Perry, you talked with him over the telephone. His secretary says he was . . ."

"How do I know I talked with him over the telephone?" Mason said. "I talked with someone who *said* he was Tidings. I talked with the secretary first."

"But how do you account for the fact that the secretary says he was in the office, and that the secretary said . . . Gosh, Perry, do you mean that the secretary's lying?"

"Exactly," Mason said. "I don't see any other way out of it. The secretary *has* to be lying."

"Why?"

Mason said, "Your guess is as good as mine, but let's look at the thing from a viewpoint of sound common sense. To begin with, we're pretty safe in assuming that Tidings wasn't dead when he was taken into the house. He was mortally wounded. Apparently he died very shortly after he was stretched out on the bed. Whoever helped Tidings into the house, and stretched him out on the bed, turned on the gas heat to warm up the room, probably went into the bathroom to get some towels to stop the flow of blood, or perhaps ran to the telephone to get a doctor—and Tidings died.

"Then they got in a panic, surveyed the situation, and decided to skip out; and having made that decision, whoever it was had every reason to believe that it would be a considerable period of time before the body was found—that it would be difficult if not impossible to fix the exact time of death. So off came Tidings' shoes."

"Why?"

"Don't you see?" Mason said. "The shoes furnish a valuable clue."

"To what?"

"To the time of death."

"No," Drake said, "I don't see."

Mason said, "I think the shoes were taken off after Tidings died, and that the person who took them off was a woman."

"Just what do the shoes have to do with it, Perry?"

"There was mud on the shoes," Mason said. "Not a great deal of mud, but just enough to show that it had been raining outside, a hard, driving rain which had made not for a thick, sticky mud, but for a thin coating which would have adhered to the soles of the shoes.

"There's no counterpane on the bed. That means the counterpane was pulled out from under the body after death because it contained some telltale clue—probably the marks left by muddy shoes and wet smears made by a wet topcoat."

"You figure Tidings was wearing a topcoat at the time?"

"That's right. I figure that Tidings either drove or was driven up to the bungalow. Someone helped him up the walk to the house, across the living room, and into the bedroom. Tidings stretched out on the bed and was dead within a very few minutes. There were bloodstains on the counterpane, mud on his shoes, and wet smears made by the topcoat.

"Someone took off his shoes, managed to get off the topcoat, and then pulled the counterpane out from under the body. . . . That made rather a bulky bundle. The topcoat was disposed of by putting it back in the bottom of Tidings' car. Then Tidings' car was planted where the police would find it sometime the next day, but not where they'd find it *before* the next day.

"That brings us to the most significant clue of all, Paul, the fact that those bloodstains stop an inch or two beyond the threshold of the house. Remember, it was raining cats and dogs Monday night. That's a cement porch, and a cement walk. Now I'll tell you why the bloodstains stop near the door. It's because the driving rain washed them away, except for those two or three drops which were protected from the rain by that little roof over the front door. That again fixes the time of the murder—Monday night."

Drake said, "Okay, Perry. You win. That last clue clinches things. Standing by itself, it's almost enough. . . . All right, he was killed Monday night. Where does that leave us?"

Mason said, "I don't know."

"How about going to work on that secretary of Tidings' and seeing if we can get a confession out of him?"

Mason said, "That's the logical thing to do—if I knew where I stood."

"What do you mean, Perry?"

Mason said, "Frankly, Paul, I don't know who my client is."

"Come on," Drake said. "Talk sense."

Mason said, "I've been retained by someone to protect a woman. I *think* I was hired to defend this woman from the charge of murdering Albert Tidings."

"That wasn't specifically mentioned?" Drake asked.

"No, Paul. It wasn't. A man come to my office after midnight Monday. It was raining then—raining hard. There was a woman with him. The woman wouldn't let me hear her voice, wouldn't let me see her face. The man made arrangements by which she could be identified. When that identification was complete, I was to receive a very substantial fee.

"Now, I can't figure anything which would have justified all of that frenzied effort—that business of getting me out of bed to protect someone, unless it had been an emergency and a serious one. I figure a murder would be most apt to fill the bill.

"Of course, when I learned of Tidings' murder, I thought at once that that must be it. But I was employed on *Monday* night. The murder apparently hadn't been committed until *Tuesday*. Then I started checking up on clues, and everything that I found indicated Tidings died on Monday night. . . . And my best guess is that it was before midnight on Monday."

"I still don't see why your move isn't to try to force a confession out of the secretary," Drake said, "—if you're certain your client was a woman."

Mason said, "Because I'm not certain the secretary murdered him."

"Good Lord, Perry! If he's lying about Tidings' having been in the office, and if he impersonated Tidings over the telephone in talking with you . . ."

"It doesn't prove a damn thing," Mason interposed, "except that the secretary had some very definite reason for not wanting anyone to know that Tidings wasn't there in the office. Suppose, for some reason, it was vital to have it appear Tidings was sitting in his office on Tuesday morning. The secretary did the best he could to create the impression Tidings was there. Then Tidings' body was found, and the indications pointed to the time of death as Monday night—little things which wouldn't be significant to a stranger, but which caused the secretary to realize what he was up against.

"You can see what a fix the secretary was in. He didn't dare to back up and reverse his previous statements, because that would put *him* in an awful jam. He simply *had* to go ahead and bluff the thing through.

"Now then, Paul, suppose the secretary isn't guilty of murder, but merely used a subterfuge to make it appear Tidings was in the office on Tuesday morning. Then suppose I rush in, browbeat Tidings' secretary with a lot of facts, force him to confess. He confesses that he was lying about Tidings, but advances some logical reason for the lie. Thereupon, the police come down on my client and charge her with murder. My officious interference has wiped out the only defense she could possibly make in front of a jury."

"What do you mean?"

"An alibi for Tuesday morning and for Tuesday afternoon and evening."

"What makes you think she has such an alibi?"

"Because," Mason said, "the shoes and the counterpane were missing."

"Talk sense, Perry."

"I am talking sense. Don't you see, Paul? The only reason for taking the man's shoes from his feet and the counterpane from the bed was to conceal the fact that it was raining when Tidings entered that house. That means that this person knew that that particular location would be the last place on earth where anyone would think to look for Tidings. It means that the person who did it knew that Mrs. Tidings wasn't in the city and didn't expect to return for several days. The only logical solution is that this person must have left my office Monday night, and then started building an alibi . . . This looks like the party we want, Paul."

Drake glanced swiftly at the young woman who was standing in the door of the beauty shop drawing on dark gloves.

"Looks like it," he said. "The operative didn't miss it far. She could get my vote for Miss America any time."

Drake shifted his eyes to Mason's face as the lawyer remained watchfully silent. "What's the matter, Perry?" he asked.

Mason said, "I would have bet ten to one that she would be a woman I'd seen before. I didn't expect to find a stranger."

"She's the one we want all right," Drake told him. "The operative in the car ahead is giving us the high sign."

Mason lowered his head so that his hat brim shielded a portion of his face. "Keep your eye on her, Paul," he said. "She may know me when she sees me. Tell me what she's doing."

"Finishing drawing on her gloves," Drake said. "There she is out on the sidewalk. . . . Just a curious and flickering glance at the operative in the car ahead. . . . Seems to have passed *us* up entirely. . . . Okay, Perry. She's on her way. Want to tag along?"

"Yes," Mason said. "And get this, Paul. . . . Look up that secretary, Mattern. Find out all you can about him. Investigate particularly whether there's any connection between Mattern and a guy named Bolus who's the president of the Western Prospecting Company. I'm on my way."

Mason stepped to the sidewalk, sauntered casually over to the inner lane of traffic, and moved quietly along behind the young woman.

She was walking with a brisk step, but her gait was not sufficiently hurried to destroy the easy swing of perfectly co-ordinating muscles. Her hips moved in graceful rhythm as she strode easily but rapidly, very apparently headed toward some definite objective.

Mason followed her to a drgustore where she went into a telephone booth and remained long enough to dial a number and engage in swiftly rapid conversation with some unknown party. She hung up, swept past the counter where Mason was buying a toothbrush, and again reached the sidewalk. Once more, she flashed a quick glance at the car which the operative was driving, but it was no more than a mere flicker of the eyes.

Out in the street, she seemed to lose much of her former haste. Her step became more leisurely. Twice she paused to look in at store windows. The second time she seemed to tear herself reluctantly away from the inspection of a black velvet dinner dress, which was draped on a model in the window. She walked half a dozen steps, then abruptly turned to come back and once more study the dress, giving Mason an opportunity, after an uncomfortable second or two, to wander past, noticing as he did so, that her eyes were only interested in the department store window.

Mason stepped into the doorway of the department store and waited for her to walk past.

Instead she marched swiftly through the doorway, and mingled with the crowd which was moving slowly through the aisles. She branched off toward the elevators, then abruptly turned, walked around a staircase, back to the ready-to-wear department, and out of the door to another street.

Mason, following behind, was entirely unprepared when she suddenly stopped. He was faced with the necessity of making himself conspicuous by also stopping or else trying to saunter casually past. He decided to keep moving.

A well-modulated voice said, "Good morning, Mr. Mason. Was there something you wished to say to me?"

Mason raised his hat, and looked into intense black eyes in which there was just a twinkle of mocking humor.

"I don't think I know you," he said.

She laughed up into his face. "That's the line a woman falls back on when she's trying to make up her mind whether to fall for a pick-up," she said. "Surely the great Perry Mason should be expected to do better than that! Why are you following me?"

"Just my appreciation of the beautiful."

"Don't be silly. . . . Come along. If you want to tag me around, there's no reason why you should walk along behind me."

She tucked her arm through his, smiled up at him, and said, "There. That's better. I was going to turn to the left. I presume that means you were also going to turn to the left."

He nodded.

"Did you," she asked, "notice the two cars that were also following me?"

"Two?" Mason asked.

"Well," she admitted, "one of them I'm certain of. The other, I'm not positive about."

"You seem to be rather popular," Mason said.

"Apparently, I am."

"Really, I don't recall having met you."

She laughed. "Oh, I've seen your picture dozens of times, and had you pointed out to me in nightclubs. You probably don't realize it, Mr. Mason, but you're something of a popular idol here in the city—definitely more than a celebrity."

"I'm flattered," Mason murmured.

She looked up at his profile, and said, "My, I'd certainly hate to have you cross-examine me."

"And I," Mason said, "would hate to have to crossexamine you. Anyone who can avoid questions as well as you would make a deadly witness."

"Why? What question was I avoiding?"

"You haven't told me your name—as yet."

She laughed and said, "That's right. I haven't. I'm not even certain that I will, Mr. Mason. . . . Rather clever, those detectives, aren't they?"

"What do you mean?" he asked.

"One of them evidently stayed at the entrance where I went in. The other's circling the block. Here he comes now. Shall we try to ditch him, or string him along?"

Mason said, "Oh, let's string him along. They're getting paid by the day, and we may as well give him a break. I hope my entering into the picture doesn't cause complications."

"Why? Why should it?"

"Oh," he said, "you don't know to whom they're reporting, and, of course, they don't know why I was following you. As a result, their reports will read, 'Shortly after subject left beauty parlor, Perry Mason started to follow. After observing that coast was apparently clear, Mason contacted subject, and they departed arm in arm, talking earnestly.'"

She frowned and said, "That *would* complicate things. I wouldn't want—well, you know. It looks rather peculiar when you mention it that way."

"That's undoubtedly the way a detective would write it up in his report," Mason said.

"Were you following me all the way from the beauty parlor?"

"Yes."

"I didn't spot you until the drugstore," she said. "What do you want with me?"

"I'd like to know who you are," Mason said.

"Suppose I don't tell you?"

"Then it will probably take me all of half an hour to find out."

She said, "Don't be silly, Mr. Mason. There are a dozen ways I could ditch you."

Mason said, "You wouldn't stoop so low as to try the rest-room trick on me, would you? That's hardly sporting."

"Good heavens, no!" she said. "It's so obvious. . . . And then I'm not entirely certain about you. I'm not even certain you'd stop at the rest-room door. You look as though you'd call any ordinary bet—perhaps raise it. You're capable of it."

"Well then, why not be a good scout and tell me."

"Because that's the one thing I don't want you to know. I'm not quite ready for you to know."

"When will you be ready?"

"When I know why you were following and what led you to me in the first place. I also want to know whether you know anything about those detectives who were trailing me in the automobiles. In other words, Mr. Mason, I seem to have achieved a very sudden and flattering popularity. To be shadowed by one detective is bad enough. To have two detectives on the job is disconcerting, and then to look back and see the city's most famous attorney taking an unusual interest in my activities is enough to run my pulse up in the hundreds."

"Are you," Mason asked, "going to tell me who you are?"

She turned then to face him. "No," she said, "and I'm not going to let you follow me. I'm warning you, Mr. Mason, that I want very much to be left alone. . . . Now then, suppose we shake hands and part friends. I'll stand here and watch you walk down that street. When you're a block away, I'll resume my afternoon shopping."

Mason shook his head. "Having gone to all this trouble to find you," he said, "I don't intend to let you escape so easily."

"Then they're *your* detectives!"

Mason said nothing.

She tilted her head defiantly. "Very well," she said. "You brought this on yourself."

"Do we have to declare war?" Mason asked.

"Yes," she said, "unless you retreat."

"Answer four or five questions," Mason said, "and I'll sue for an armistice."

"No."

"All right," he said, "it's war then."

They had been swinging along the sidewalk as they talked, apparently a couple gaily chatting with each other. Only a close observer would have noticed the dogged determination on the lawyer's face and the nervous uneasiness in the girl's manner.

A signal changed. The crossing officer turned with the approaching stream of pedestrians, walking quietly to stand at watchful attention near the edge of the crossing, his eye shrewdly appraising the automobile traffic, alert to detect the first symptoms of a prohibited left-hand turn.

Abruptly the young woman at Mason's side pushed him

away violently and called out, "Officer! This man is annoying me! He . . ."

Moving with lightning swiftness and before the officer could turn to get them in his field of vision, Mason snatched the purse from under her arm.

Speechless with surprise and indignation, she whirled to stare at him with startled eyes. Mason raised his hat and said, "I'm only trying to return the purse, Madam."

The officer pushed toward them. "What's all this? What's all this?" he asked.

"He's annoying me," the young woman said. "He grabbed . . ."

Mason smiled. "A young woman left her purse on the counter in the drugstore," he explained to the officer. "I believe the purse belongs to this young woman, but I won't give it up until she can identify it. That's only reasonable, isn't it? Here, *you* can take it if you want."

Mason calmly opened the purse and said, "You can see for yourself, officer. There's . . ."

She jumped toward Mason, grabbing frantically at the purse. "Don't you dare . . ."

Mason turned so as to present one of his broad shoulders to her rushing attack. He pulled a leather folder from her purse, opened it to glance quickly at her driving license, and said, "You can see for yourself, officer. The name and address of the owner of the purse are here on this driving license. All she has to do is give me her name, and I'll surrender the purse."

There were quick tears of humiliation and indignation in her eyes.

The officer said, "Say, buddy. You're acting kinda funny about this."

"I fail to see anything strange about it," Mason said with dignity. "Permit me to introduce myself, officer. I'm Perry Mason, the attorney. I . . ."

"Say," the officer exclaimed, "you are for a fact! Pardon me, Mr. Mason. I didn't recognize you. I've seen you in court some, and seen your picture in the papers a lot."

Mason bowed and smiled acknowledgment, then said to the young woman, in his most conciliatory manner, "You can appreciate my position. I *think* this is your purse. I certainly can't turn it over to you unless you can at least identify it."

"Oh, very well," she said. "The name on the driving license is Adelle Hastings. The address is 906 Cleveland Square. There's even a fingerprint of my thumb on the driving license in case you want any further identification."

Mason said, "It's quite all right, Miss Hastings. I'm satisfied it's your purse. That's the name and address on the driving license."

The officer looked past them to the curious onlookers who had stopped to listen. "On your way," he growled. "This is an intersection, not a club-room. Keep moving. Don't be blocking the traffic."

Mason raised his hat, bowed to the officer, and said to Adelle Hastings, "Are you going my way, Miss Hastings?"

She blinked back the tears. "Yes," she said, and then added after a moment, "I am now," and fell into step at his side.

Mason said, "I was sorry I didn't have an opportunity to make a more detailed investigation of your coin purse."

"Why?" she asked.

"I thought I might find a torn bill in there."

"A torn bill?" she asked, looking at him with raised eyebrows.

"Well, at least one that had been cut along the edges."

She said, with quick vehemence, "I haven't the faintest idea of what you're talking about, Mr. Mason."

"Well," he said, "we can discuss that later. Why didn't you want me to know who you were?"

"For various reasons."

"Can you tell me what they are?"

"I can, but I won't."

"Don't you think it might be well for you to be frank with me?"

"No."

"You're the one who insisted on the investigation which disclosed the shortage in the hospital trust fund?"

"Yes."

"How did you know Tidings had been embezzling funds?"

"I simply asked for an investigation," she said. "I made no charges."

"The question still stands," Mason said.

"So does the answer," she retorted.

Mason said, "Well, we'll try it from another angle. I'm very anxious to talk with a certain architect. Of course, I can wait until tomorrow and read the answer to my ad in the *Contractor's Journal*, but I thought it would simplify matters if you told me what Mr. Peltham had said."

She stood stock-still, and Mason, looking at her, saw that her face was drained of color. The eyes were dark with panic. Her lips quivered. She tried twice to speak before she managed to say, "Oh," in a choking voice that was half a sob. Then after a moment, she said again, "Oh, my God!"

Mason said, "No need to be so upset, Miss Hastings. Just tell me what he said."

She clutched his arm then, and he could feel the tips of her fingers digging into his flesh. "No, no," she cried. "No, no! You mustn't ever, ever let anyone know about that. . . . Oh, I should have known you'd trap me!"

Mason patted her shoulder. Noticing the curious glances of several pedestrians, he piloted her toward a doorway. "Take it easy," he said. "Perhaps there's some place we can talk. . . . Here's a cocktail lounge. Let's go in."

She permitted him to pilot her into the cocktail lounge, and seated herself as though glad to relieve the strain of her weight on wobbling knees.

"How did you know that?" she asked, as Mason seated himself on the other side of the little table.

A white-coated waiter appeared, and Mason raised his eyebrows at Adelle Hastings.

"A double brandy," she said.

"Make it two," Mason ordered, and, when the waiter had withdrawn, Mason said in a kindly voice, "You should have known you couldn't get away with it."

"But I could have," she said, "if I'd . . . if I'd only used ordinary prudence. I can see it all now. I can see the trap you set for me."

Mason brushed her remark aside. "Let's quit this business of beating around the bush," he said. "Haven't you something to say to me?"

"About what?"

"About your first visit to my office."

Her eyes narrowed. "What about it?" she asked.

Mason said, "If you need me, you know, arrangements have already been made."

"I don't know what you're talking about."

Mason said, "That isn't going to get you anywhere."

"But I don't. I really don't."

"All right," Mason said. "You've had your chance. Remember that I protect my clients to the best of my ability. People who are not my clients have to be on their guard."

She laughed nervously. "If you think I'm not going to be on my guard with you from now on, Mr. Mason, you have another think coming."

"All right. We'll handle it that way then," Mason said with calm, patient persistence. "Now let's get back to Robert Peltham. First, what did he say in answer to my ad?"

As she hesitated, Mason added, "I can find out by the simple expedient of ringing up the *Contractor's Journal.* After all, they're going to publish it, you know."

She bit her lip. For a moment her dark eyes were veiled from his by lowered lashes, then she suddenly looked up at him, and he had a glimpse of flashing teeth as she smiled. "Mr. Peltham," she said, "says he can't meet you—for you to carry on."

"But," Mason observed, "I'm groping in the dark."

"You seem to be doing very well at it, Mr. Mason," she said, and Mason realized that something had given her a sudden return of self-confidence. Her manner was archly gay, a jaunty assumption of carefree banter.

Mason studied her, trying to find some reason for the transformation, to learn whether it was due to something he had said, or simply because she had suddenly conceived some new plan which offered such possibilities of ultimate success as to restore her confidence.

Mason said, "I'm in too deep to back out right now. I'm going ahead."

"Do," she said. "Mr. Peltham seems to think you're doing splendidly."

"Have you talked with him?"

"Well, let's put it this way: I've been in communication with him."

"Over the telephone?"

"I'm afraid I'm going to have to start avoiding questions again, Mr. Mason."

Mason scowled. "All right," he said, lashing out at her with sudden belligerency. "Let's quit playing ring-around-the-rosy. What's your alibi for Monday night?"

She smiled at him sweetly. "Tuesday from noon on, Mr. Mason," she said.

"You heard my question. Monday night."

"You heard my answer," she replied smilingly. "From noon Tuesday, Mr. Mason."

"I hope it's a good one."

"It is."

"Just by way of satisfying my curiosity," he asked her, "what *were* you doing Monday night?"

"What I was doing Monday night doesn't have anything to do with the case. You know it doesn't. The newspaper says you, yourself, talked with Tidings Tuesday morning around eleven o'clock. . . . And I see you're representing that Gailord girl . . . I wish you luck with her."

"Are you," Mason asked, "trying to change the subject?"

"No, of course not."

"What do you know about Miss Gailord?"

"Nothing."

"You know her?"

"I've met her, yes."

"Where?"

"Oh, several times—at social functions."

"She moves in your circle?"

"Not exactly. She tries to . . . wait a minute, I don't mean it that way."

"Yes, you do," Mason said. "That's exactly what you meant. The remark may have slipped out, but you meant it."

"All right, then, I did. It's just what she's doing."

"She's a social climber?"

"If you want to put it that way. Good Lord, what if her father was a grand duke? Who cares?"

Mason, watching her narrowly, said, "At a guess, she has specific ambitions toward marriage?"

"I guess all women do, don't they?"

"I wouldn't know. What's the catch she's after?"

"I'm sorry, Mr. Mason. I don't care to discuss it."

"Simply because she's a rival?"

"What do you mean? What are you insinuating?"

Mason said, "I may know more than you give me credit for."

She said hotly, "You look here, Mr. Mason. Coleman Reeger and I are good friends, and that's all. I don't care whom he marries—only I'd hate to see him walk into a trap."

"You think that's what he's doing?"

She said firmly, "That's enough, Mr. Mason. We aren't going to discuss that matter, and we'll leave Coleman Reeger out of it."

"All right, we will if you'll tell me where you were Monday night."

She laughed and said, "You're laying another trap for me, aren't you, Mr. Mason?"

The waiter brought their drinks.

Mason said, "Look here. You weren't just playing a hunch on that trust fund business. You've been sticking up for Peltham. You're in communication with him. You have the most implicit faith in him. That means that—well, you know what it means."

"What does it mean?" she asked.

Mason said, "You may mask your face, but you can't mask your feelings."

She twisted the stem of her glass, rotating it by a slow motion of the thumb and forefinger while she kept her eyes from his. "I don't think I'm going to make any answer to that," she said.

"You mean you don't understand me?"

"N-n-no. Not exactly that, but I'd want you to be very definite before I—before I said anything at all."

Mason tossed off his drink, pulled a bill from his pocket, and dropped it on the table. "Now listen," he said, "we've played ring-around-the-rosy and button-button-who's-got-the-button until I'm sick of it. You can either talk to me now and talk to me frankly and fairly, or I'll walk out, and *you* can chase *me* around."

"But why should I want to chase you around, Mr. Mason? It's the other way around. *You* were following *me.*"

"Forget it," Mason said. "I'm tired of playing horse. Do you want me to walk out, or don't you?"

Her eyes showed a quick flash of some baffling expression. "Mr. Mason," she said, with feeling, "if you'd get up from this table, walk out of that door, and not ask me any more questions, I'd think—I'd think it was one of the biggest breaks I'd ever had in my whole life."

Without a word, Mason pushed back his chair, picked up his hat, and started for the door. He turned midway to glance back at her surprised features and said, "You know where my office is,"—then walked out and left her.

7.

DELLA STREET looked up as Mason unlocked the door of his private office and came striding into the room.

"Oh—oh," she said. "Was it as bad as all that?"

"Worse," Mason told her, taking off his hat and throwing it on a chair. "I'm getting fed up with things. I've bought a pig in a poke, and it's the last time."

"But Paul Drake telephoned that you'd picked her up, and that everything seemed all right."

"Drake," Mason said, "is a damn poor judge of feminine character. I don't know but what I'm not as bad. . . . When did Drake telephone?"

"A few minutes ago. He said he guessed there was no need for him to keep a shadow on the woman, but he'd done it just on general principles, that she was Adelle Hastings, that you'd left her in a cocktail lounge, that she'd gone out right after you had left—within a matter of minutes—and had gone straight to her apartment. If you'll give me the other half of that ten thousand dollars, Chief, I'll take it down to the bank and make a deposit."

Mason laughed mirthlessly.

"What's the matter? Haven't you got it?"

"No."

"Didn't she have it?"

"She must have it," Mason said, "and she's taking me for a ride to the tune of ten grand."

"How do you figure?"

Mason spread out his hands in a gesture of resignation. "A sucker," he said. "Just a plain pushover. I was so damn conscientious that I stuck my finger in the porridge and started stirring. Now I've stirred out all the lumps, and haven't anything to show for it except a burned finger."

"You mean she isn't going to give you the other half of that bill?"

"Why should she? Peltham is satisfied, and she's satisfied. Things are moving fine. She has an iron-clad alibi for Tuesday morning. At least, she says she has, and I give her credit for being smart enough to be telling the truth. If she fixed up an alibi, she fixed up a good one.

"I've prodded Holcomb into the position of bringing pressure to bear all along the line, to fix the time of that murder as immediately after noon on Tuesday. I have the smaller piece of that ten-thousand-dollar bill. I can't do anything with it until I get the other half. . . . If I'm a big enough sap to work for nothing, why should anyone pay me for it?"

She said thoughtfully, "It *does* look that way, doesn't it?"

He nodded moodily. "Anything else?" he asked.

"Drake says his men shadowed Abigail Tump, that she led them to the man he thinks is the secretary for the orphan asylum you want. He also picked up a copy of the ad which was left in the *Contractor's Journal* by Miss Hastings."

"What does the ad say?" Mason asked, dropping into his big

swivel chair, elevating his feet to the desk, and taking a cigarette from the office humidor.

Della Street consulted her shorthand notebook and read, "'Have nothing to add to situation. Granting interview this time would be unwise. You're doing fine. P.'"

Mason said, "That's rubbing it in. . . . I'm doing fine, am I? Yes, Della. Take this down. Type it out and rush it over to the *Contractor's Journal.* Have them carry it in their earliest possible issue: 'P. I don't like to contract for work without blueprints. Arrange to deliver detailed plans and specifications or anticipate serious defects in finished structure.' Now read that back to me, Della."

She read it back to him.

Mason nodded grimly. "Okay," he said.

She looked at him with eyes that showed a trace of concern. "Wouldn't it be better, Chief, to sit tight now and let things develop?"

"I'm not built that way," he said. "It would probably be the prudent thing to do. In any event, it would be the conventional thing to do, but you never get far being prudent and conventional. Right now, this case is wide open. If I sit back and wait, it'll crystallize against the client I'll eventually have to represent."

"But if you keep doing things which are advantageous to that client, you'll never be paid," she pointed out.

Mason said, "From now on the things I'm going to do will make their hair stand up. . . . Take that ad down to the *Contractor's Journal* and leave word in Drake's office that he's to come in here as soon as he gets back to the office. . . . That little devil, Adelle Hastings, figures she can trump my aces and make me like it."

"How can you stop her playing it that way, Chief, as long as you keep working on the case?"

Mason grinned, but without humor. "I'm going to make it no-trumps," he said.

Della Street adjusted her hat in front of the office mirror. "Well," she observed, "there's no use telling you to be careful."

"Whoever got anything in life by being careful?" Mason retorted. "Every time you stop to figure what the other fellow's going to do, you unconsciously figure what *you'd* do in his place. The result is that you're not fighting him, but yourself. You always come to a stalemate. Every time you think of a move, you think of a perfect defense.

"The best fighters don't worry about what the other man may do. And if they keep things moving fast enough, the other man is too busy to do much thinking."

"Something tells me," Della Street grinned, as she made for the door, "that things are going to move fast."

Paul Drake's voice from the corridor said, cheerfully, "Against the light, your legs are swell, Della. They'd get by in front of any window."

"Sometime when you're not too busy, tell Perry all about them, will you, Paul?"

Drake, in a rare good humor, circled Della Street and edged in at the open door. "Gosh, Perry," he said, "that was a slick stunt you pulled with that purse. I thought I'd die laughing. When she called the officer and said you were annoying her, I thought I'd have to appear in the police court to give you a good character reference."

"What's all this about?" Della Street asked.

"Your boss," Drake said, "has become a pursesnatcher."

Mason said, "Come in here and close that damn door. I don't want all the tenants in the office listening in on my conferences."

"If Paul's through admiring my figure, I'll be going," Della observed.

Drake clicked the door shut behind him.

"What the devil was that last crack about?" Mason asked.

Drake grinned. "Don't you *ever* notice your secretary's legs?"

Mason said, "For God's sake, snap out of it! There's work to be done."

"What sort of work?"

By way of answer, Mason picked up his desk telephone, plugged it in on the office line, and said, "Gertie, I want you to get Dr. Finley C. Willmont on the line. You'll find him at his office. His nurse will tell you he's seeing patients and can't come to the telephone. Tell her it's Perry Mason calling, and it's important. I want to talk with Dr. Willmont personally."

"Right away," Gertie promised. "Do you want to wait?"

"No, ring me when you have him on the line."

Mason hung up and said to Paul Drake, "That little devil's holding out on me."

"Della?" Drake asked in surprise.

"Come down to earth," Mason said. "Adelle Hastings."

"I thought you had her eating out of your hand."

"No," Mason said. "I bought her a drink. She drank it out of a glass."

"You act as though someone had put a burr under your saddle blanket," Drake said.

"Someone has."

"Who?"

"I don't know."

"Well, can't you take the burr out?"

Mason said, "I don't want to. I prefer to start bucking."

"What do you want me to do?"

"You have the name and address of that bookkeeper for The Hidden Home Society?"

"Yes."

"Who is he, where does he live, and what does he look like?"

"Arthmont A. Freel, Montway Rooms, around sixty, and mousy, a little wisp of a fellow with stooped shoulders, faded eyes, faded hair, faded clothes, and a faded personality, shabby in a genteel sort of way. Put him in a group of three, and you'd lose him in the crowd. He doesn't stand out any more than cigar ashes on a gray rug on a misty morning."

Mason said, "Feeling pretty good, aren't you, Paul?"

"Uh huh."

"Why?"

"I don't know. Just the way I feel. I got an awful bang out of seeing you turn the tables on that girl when she tried to call the cop. You sure put that one over, Perry. The cop was nodding to himself when you walked away, as though he'd discharged his duties to the taxpayers in noble shape and was entitled to a merit badge."

The phone on Mason's desk rang. He picked it up and heard Gertie say, "Dr. Willmont's coming on," and then a moment later, Dr. Willmont's crisply professional voice saying, "Yes, Perry. What is it?"

Mason said, "I want a blood donor, Doctor—about a pint."

"What type?" Dr. Willmont asked.

"The type that will keep its mouth shut," Mason said.

"I know, but what type blood?"

"Human blood," Mason said. "That's all I require."

Dr. Willmont hesitated. "This is rather unusual. You can't have a transfer, Perry, without getting types of both the donor and the patient. You . . ."

"There isn't any patient," Mason said. "There isn't going to be any transfusion. I simply want a donor."

"But what do you want done with the blood?"

"Put it in a bottle," Mason said, "and forget about it."

"How would you want it handled?"

"That's up to you. I'll pick up the blood while it's still fresh. I'll keep in touch with your office and let them know just when and where I'll want it. You get the donor lined up."

Dr. Willmont hesitated. "I suppose I *could* explain it was for laboratory purposes," he said. "Could you keep me out of it, Perry?"

"Uh huh."

"What do you want it for?"

"Purposes of a laboratory experiment in criminology," Mason said glibly.

"Okay, that's fine. I'll try and arrange it."

"I'll call you later," Mason said. "You make the arrangements and have the donor on hand."

He hung up, and turned to Paul Drake. "Okay, Paul, let's go."

"Where?" Drake asked.

"The Montway Rooms," Mason said.

"Your car or mine?"

"Yours."

"Now?"

"Right now. Let's get going."

Drake's loquacious good humor evaporated under the influence of the lawyer's savage grimness. He essayed a quip or two, then lapsed into a silence which persisted until he parked the car in front of the rooming house. "This is the joint," he said. "Are you going to get rough with him, Perry?"

"I'm going to get rough with everyone," the lawyer said, "until I smoke someone into the open. Come on, let's go."

In silence they opened the car doors, slammed them shut, and entered the rooming house. There was no one at the desk, and Drake said, "It's on the second floor near the back. I have the number of the room."

They climbed creaking stairs, pounded their way down a thin ribbon of worn, faded carpet which stretched between the rows of doors down the length of the upper corridor. Drake silently motioned to a door.

Mason knocked.

A man's reedy voice on the other side of the door said, "Who is it?"

"The name's Mason," the lawyer said.

The voice sounded now closer to the door. "What is it?"

"News."

A key clicked in the lock. The door opened, and a man, whose face hardly came to Mason's shoulders, looked up over the top of steel-rimmed reading spectacles. "What sort of news?" he asked.

"Bad," Mason said, and walked in.

Drake followed the lawyer into the room. Mason flashed him a swift glance of inquiry, and the detective nodded almost imperceptibly. Drake moved over to a chair by the window and sat down. The chair was still warm from human occupancy. Freel, still holding a newspaper he'd been reading between thumb and forefinger, glanced from one to the other. "I don't think I know you," he said.

"You will," Mason said. "Sit down."

Freel sat on the bed. Mason possessed the only other chair in the room, a rickety, cane-bottomed affair which creaked as he sat down.

It was a small, cheerless bedroom with an iron bedstead, a thin mattress, and a mirror which gave back distorted reflections. Dripping water had left a pathway of reddish incrustations spreading fan-shaped from beneath each faucet in the washstand. There were only the two chairs, a rug worn thin from much use, a wardrobe closet, the bed, and some faded lithographs as furnishings of the room.

Beneath the bed appeared the ends of a suitcase and a hand-bag. A worn, tweed overcoat was folded across the white enameled foot of the iron bed. The grayish white counterpane had been patched in two places and was worn almost through in another place.

Freel nervously pushed his newspaper to one side. In the silence of the room, the rattle of the paper sounded unusually loud. "What is it?" he asked.

"You know what it is," Mason said, watching him narrowly.

"I'm sure I haven't the faintest idea what brought you here, or what you're talking about."

"Your name's Freel?"

"Yes."

"You were a bookkeeper and accountant for The Hidden Home Welfare Society years ago?"

The man's nervousness increased perceptibly. "Yes," he said.

"What," Mason asked, "are you doing here?"

"Looking for work."

Mason's snort was contemptuous. "Try again," he said. "This time try telling the truth for a change."

"I don't know who you are. I don't know what right you have to make these insinuations."

"I *could* make accusations," Mason said.

The stooped shoulders straightened. There was a sudden glitter of hard defiance in the faded gray eyes. "Not against me, you can't," the man said.

"No?" Mason asked sarcastically.

"No."

Mason suddenly pointed a forefinger squarely at the man's chest. "I could," he said, "for instance, accuse you of the murder of Albert Tidings."

The little man on the bed jumped as though an electrical discharge had sparked from Mason's forefinger to his chest. His mouth sagged in astonishment and consternation. *"Me!"* he shrilled in a voice high-pitched with fear and indignation.

"You," Mason said, and lit a cigarette.

The silence of the room was broken only by the creak of the bedsprings as Freel shifted his position uncomfortably.

"Are you," he asked, "the police?"

"This man," Mason said, indicating Paul Drake with a gesture of his thumb, "is a detective," and then added after a moment, in a lower voice, "private. He's working on that Tidings case."

"What's he got to do with me?"

"You mean what's he going to do *to* you? When did you last see Tidings alive?"

"I don't know what you're talking about."

"You mean you don't know Tidings?"

"No," Freel said defiantly. "I don't know who he is."

"You've been reading about it in the paper," Mason said.

"Oh, that! You mean the man who was found dead?"

"That's the way murdered people are generally found."

"I just happened to be reading about him. I didn't even connect the name."

"Well," Mason said, "the name connected you."

Freel straightened and inched forward to sit on the extreme edge of the thin mattress. "Now you look here," he said. "You can't come in here and pull this kind of stuff on me. You can't . . ."

"Forget it," Mason interrupted. "Quit trying to dodge the question. When did you last see Tidings alive?"

"I never saw him. I never knew him."

"You're certain of that?"

"Yes."

Mason just laughed.

There was another interval of strained, uncomfortable silence broken by Mason's sudden question. "When did you last see Mrs. Tump?"

"Who?"

"Tump."

"You look here," Freel protested, in his thin, high-pitched voice, "I didn't murder anyone. I . . . I had some business dealings with Mrs. Tump, that's all."

"And how about Tidings?"

Freel averted his eyes, "I didn't know him."

"Guess again," Mason said, "and you'd better guess right this time."

"Well, I'd only met him casually. He . . . he hunted me up."

"Oh, he did, did he?"

"Well, in a way, yes."

"When was that?"

"Oh, I don't know. A week or ten days ago."

"You didn't hunt him up?"

"No."

"Did you hunt up Mrs. Tump?"

"Well . . . What did you say your name was?"

"Mason."

"You're Perry Mason, the lawyer?"

"Yes."

"Why, you're representing Byrl Gailord."

"Mrs. Tump told you that?"

"Yes."

"What else did she tell you?"

"She said you were going to get Byrl's money for her."

"What do you know about Byrl?"

Freel settled back on the bed. He said unctuously, "Understand, Mr. Mason, I wasn't a party to any of that original fraud. The Hidden Home Welfare Society was guilty of numerous irregularities. You know how it is in that baby business. A couple wants to adopt a baby. It takes quite a while to get one that's been properly vouched for and whose parents are known. There's quite a demand for such children and always has been. Sometimes couples have to wait a year or even longer after their application is put in. . . . A baby's something people don't like to wait for. That is, lots of them don't.

"A society like The Hidden Home can play the game coming and going. People go there and pay to have babies that will be released to the Home for adoption. A good many times the mother tries to arrange with the Home to support the child. She thinks she's going to work and keep on making payments. In ninety-nine cases out of a hundred she can't do it."

The little old man stopped and cleared his throat nervously. His eyes peered furtively over the tops of the reading glasses which had slid down on his nose, studying the faces of his listeners in the hopes that he could read their reactions in their facial expressions.

"Go on," Mason said.

"That's all there is. If the homes are on the square, they wait until the mother quits payments before they do anything about it, but sometimes they take a gamble."

"What do you mean by taking a gamble?" Mason asked.

"They just go ahead and release the child for adoption. . . . You see, a very young baby gets a better price than an older child."

"Why?" Mason asked.

"After a child is four or five years old—old enough to remember about life in the Home—it realizes that it's been adopted. Most people never tell children they've been adopted. They want the child to look on them as its real father and mother."

"All right," Mason said. "How about Byrl Gailord?"

"They took a gamble with her—and they lost."

"Where did they get her in the first place?"

Freel said glibly, "She was Russian. Her parents were killed in a shipwreck. Mrs. Tump left her with them. At that time, she was older than the Home liked to have children, but with the heritage she had, it was a cinch for them to get a high price."

Freel moistened his lip with his tongue and started nodding his head up and down, giving silent emphasis to his words.

Mason studied the man narrowly for several seconds. Abruptly, he said, "Mrs. Tump has a daughter, hasn't she?"

Freel's head jerked in a quick half-turn as his eyes searched Mason's. "A daughter?" he asked.

"Yes."

"Why . . . what sort of a daughter?"

"A daughter," Mason said. "You know what the word means, don't you?"

"Oh, yes. Yes, of course. . . . I'm sure I can't remember. A lot of those things have escaped my recollection—little details. I presume they got Mrs. Tump's history when the child was given to them."

"Why would they do that?" Mason asked.

"Oh, they want to know all about the child, everything they can find out. They usually make the girls give them the names of the fathers. The girls hate to do that. . . . It's strange the way they try to protect the men who have betrayed them. It's the natural loyalty women have for men. Women are a lot more loyal to men than men are to women, Mr. Mason."

Mason took a last drag at his cigarette and ground it out in the ash tray.

"All right," he said. "Let's get back to Tidings."

Freel said, "Tidings tried to pump me. He wanted to find out everything I knew. I think he was looking for some flaw somewhere, something that would show that Byrl Gailord wasn't . . ."

"Wasn't what?" Mason prompted.

"Wasn't entitled to the money."

Mason stared thoughtfully for several seconds at the faded carpet. Freel studied him with the anxious scrutiny of a marksman who is anxious to see just where his bullets have struck in the target.

"Did the Home investigate that story about the torpedoed ship?" he asked.

"Oh, yes. Yes, indeed, Mr. Mason. They made a very complete investigation. They always want information about the parentage, you know. That information means dollars and cents to any home."

Mason got up from his chair, walked over to the narrow window with its dingy lace curtain over the lower portion of it. He raised a tattered, green shade, and stood with his elbows resting on the molding which divided the upper from the lower part of the window, and stared meditatively down into a dingy alley and at the blank wall of a brick building opposite.

Freel turned to Drake. "You believe me, don't you?" he asked.

"Sure," Drake said carelessly.

"Know Coleman Reeger?" Mason asked, still staring out of the window.

"No," Freel said. "Who's he?"

"You don't know anything about him?"

"No."

"Ever heard the name?"

"No, I'm quite certain I haven't. I have a good memory for names."

"You take a lot of prompting," Mason said. "It took quite a while to get you to remember Tidings."

"I was lying about Tidings," Freel confessed. "I thought it would be better not to let anyone know. . . . Well, you know how it is."

"He came to you?"

"Yes. He wanted to bribe me."

"What did Mrs. Tump say when you told her that?"

There was sudden panic in Freel's voice. "I didn't tell her," he said. "You mustn't tell her. She must never know about that."

Mason continued standing at the window. The tips of his fingers drummed thoughtfully on the narrow projection against which his elbows were propped. Suddenly, he whirled to face Freel. "You're lying," he charged.

"I am not, Mr. Mason. I swear to you that I'm telling the God's truth."

Mason said, "I see the whole business now. How much are you getting out of it?"

"Nothing, I'm simply giving my testimony in an attempt to right a wrong in which I feel I have unwittingly participated. . . . Of course, I knew what was going on there at the Home, but then, I was just an accountant. I had charge of the books, and that was all."

"Where are those books?"

"I don't know. I was discharged."

"But you remember a lot of details?"

"Yes."

Mason, watching him with level-lidded intensity, said, "Your testimony wouldn't be worth a damn, Freel. It's too long ago. No jury would trust your memory."

"I made notes," Freel said. "I made a complete set of notes of certain cases that impressed me as being . . . well, being apt to come up again."

"Why?"

"Because if I were ever called on to testify, I wanted to be certain that I could give the true facts."

Mason said, "You mean you wanted something for blackmail."

Freel's shoulders seemed to slump. "I don't know what you're talking about," he said, his eyes avoiding those of Mason.

Mason said, "Look up at me, Freel."

For a moment Freel continued to avoid his eyes, then, with an obvious effort, looked up at the lawyer.

"What's back of all this business about Byrl Gailord?" Mason asked.

"Just what I told you," Freel said, and his eyes slithered away from those of the lawyer.

"Look up at me, Freel."

Mason waited until the man had slowly raised his eyes.

"Now," Mason said, "I'll tell you the whole business. Byrl Gailord is no more the daughter of a grand duke than I am. Byrl Gailord is the illegitimate daughter of Mrs. Tump's daughter. That grand duke business was invented within the last few months by Mrs. Tump to give the child a background of respectability. Gailord's will referred to her as an adopted child. She inherited a lot of money under that will, but that will also disclosed the fact that she had been taken from a welfare home somewhere, and had never been formally adopted, that she was the illegitimate offspring of an illicit affair. . . . No, don't shift your eyes, Freel. Look up at me. Keep looking at me. . . . Mrs. Tump wanted to get the girl into society. Byrl Gailord attracted the interest and attention of Coleman Reeger. Reeger's family are high society with a capital H.S. They'd never have consented to a marriage with a young woman of Byrl Gailord's real antecedents, so Mrs. Tump took it on herself to furnish a fictitious background. She knew she couldn't do it by herself, so she hunted you up and planted you as a witness."

Freel fidgeted. The bedsprings squeaked uneasy accompaniment.

"How much?" Mason asked.

"Fifteen thousand dollars," Freel said in a thin, reedy voice.

"How much of it have you actually received?"

"One thousand. The other comes when . . . when . . ."

"When she marries Reeger?" Mason asked.

"Yes," Freel said, his eyes still avoiding those of the lawyer.

"Go ahead and tell me about it."

"That's all there was to it. I was out of work, and desperate. Mrs. Tump had detectives hunt me up. She made me this proposition. That thousand dollars looked big to me. I'd have agreed to anything."

"And that's all bunk about this Russian blood in the girl's veins?"

"Not entirely. The father is a Russian, the son of a headwaiter who was a refugee from Russia."

Mason abruptly turned away from the little man and started pacing the floor. His hands were thrust deeply down in his trousers pockets. His eyes from time to time swung to study Freel's face.

Drake, manifestly uncomfortable in the conventional, straight-backed, rickety chair, watched Mason in silent interest.

After several minutes of thoughtful floor-pacing, Mason said, with slow deliberation, "I can't understand what interest Tidings had in bribing you to change your testimony. . . . Exactly what *did* he want?"

"I don't know, Mr. Mason," Freel said hastily. "It never got that far. He tried to bribe me, and I let it be known right at the start that I wasn't interested—that I wasn't that sort of a man."

Mason said, "But you *were* that sort of a man. You'd let Mrs. Tump bribe you to testify to a lot of lies."

"But that was different, Mr. Mason. This man wanted me to sell Mrs. Tump out."

"Why?"

"I tell you, I don't know. He didn't say."

"Exactly what did he want?"

"He wanted me to change my testimony."

"In what way? Did he want you to tell the truth?"

"No. He didn't know the truth."

"Well, what *did* he want?"

"I tell you, I don't know."

"How did he get in touch with you?"

"I don't know that. He found me the same way you did. I was here in my room when he came to me."

"More than once?"

"No, just once."

"When was that?"

"I don't know. Around a week ago."

"And what did he say?"

"He said he could make it worth my while if I'd cooperate with him."

"Co-operate how?"

"Well, something about changing my story."

"But what earthly advantage would that give him?" Mason asked.

"I don't know. I tell you, I don't know anything at all about it."

"How much money did Mrs. Tump give you?"

"A thousand dollars."

"When?"

"That was two months ago."

"And you took a little while fixing up your story—perhaps forging a few records?"

"Well, naturally, I wanted to make my story stand up."

Mason said suddenly, "Freel, *you* went to Tidings. He didn't come to you. Your first contact was with Tidings. You wanted to sell him information about Byrl Gailord. Because he was the trustee of her funds, you thought there'd be a chance for a shakedown. And then you found out about Mrs. Tump, or she found out about you, and you cashed in on that. But you were still doing business with Tidings. There was something he wanted. . . . *Now what did Tidings want?*"

Freel put his hands on his knees. His head was lowered until his voice sounded muffled as he said, "You've got me wrong, Mr. Mason. It wasn't anything like that at all."

Mason strode over to him, placed his hand on the collar of the little man's coat, and said, "Get up off that bed," and, as he spoke, jerked Freel to his feet.

Mason whipped the pillows from the bed and felt underneath them. He turned to Paul Drake. "Give me a hand with this mattress, Paul," he said. "We might as well try here first."

Mason took the head of the mattress, Drake the foot.

"Flip it over."

They turned the mattress over.

Freel came running forward to grab at Mason's arm. "No, no," he cried, tugging futilely at the lawyer's right arm.

Mason shook him off.

"You can't do that," Freel screamed indignantly.

Near the center of the mattress on the under side, inch-wide strips of adhesive tape had been interlaced into a network. Mason took out his penknife and cut through the strips of tape.

Once more Freel lunged at him, and Mason said, without looking up, "Take care of that guy, Paul. He might get hurt on the knife."

Drake slipped an arm around the man's shoulders. "Come on, Freel," he said. "Take it easy. No one's going to hurt you."

Freel struggled with frantic effort against Drake's restraining arm. Mason, cutting through the strips of adhesive tape, disclosed a little recess which had been hollowed out in the padded cotton stuffing of the mattress. A roll of bills, fastened with two elastics, became visible in the opening. Mason pulled out the roll and unsnapped the elastic.

There were ten one-thousand-dollar bills in the roll.

Mason turned to Freel. "All right, Freel," he said. "Who gave you the money?"

"Mrs. Tump," Freel said.

"Tidings," Mason corrected.

Freel's eyes shifted. He shook his head nervously. Mason put the bills back into a roll, snapped the elastics around them. "All right, Freel," he said, "if you're going to act that way, this money goes out of the room with me. I'll turn it over to the police."

Freel moistened his lips. "What do you want?" he asked.

"The truth," Mason said.

"Then will you give me my money?"

"Yes."

Freel said, "Tidings gave it to me."

"Tell me about it," Mason said.

"I double-crossed Mrs. Tump," Freel admitted miserably. "You're right. Maybe I have done a little blackmailing. I've had to live since the Home let me go. If I've collected from a few people, it was because I had to. And I've never been able to get very much—just a little here and a little there—and I had to be careful because I only dared to work in the cases where they couldn't complain to the police—cases where the publicity would have ruined someone. Sometimes I'd collect a little money from the father, sometimes from people who had adopted children and didn't want the children to know about the adoption."

Freel was whining badly now. "I didn't ask for much money, Mr. Mason, only enough to get by on. I figured that the world owed me a living."

"Go ahead," Mason said. "Tell me about Tidings."

"I went to Tidings. I told him what I knew about Byrl Gailord."

"What did Tidings do?"

"He laughed at me and kicked me out."

"Then what?"

"Then out of a clear sky, Mrs. Tump hunted me up. She offered me a thousand dollars in cash and fifteen thousand dollars later on if I'd bolster up her story about the adoption proceedings and about the Russian parentage of the girl. . . . The entire thing was made up out of whole cloth. The girl was the illegitimate child of her daughter. The daughter's married to a Des Moines banker. He'd have a fit if he ever found out. ... But that wasn't the game that Mrs. Tump was gunning for. Byrl was getting along in society. Mrs. Tump had a marriage staked out with this man Reeger."

"And then Tidings came back into the picture?"

"Yes."

"What did he want?"

"He wanted me to promise that when the time came, I'd tell the absolute truth. That was all he asked."

"What did you do?"

"I tried to protect Mrs. Tump. I told him that I couldn't. He laughed at me, and said he had enough on me to convict me of perjury if I didn't; and then he offered me ten thousand dollars and . . . well, there was nothing I could do. I had to take the money. Otherwise, I'd have had to do just as he wanted, and wouldn't have had a cent for it. You see, he had me. . . . Anyone could have had me who was willing to go to court. My record for the last few years wouldn't stand investigation. I knew it as well as anyone."

"Did you," Mason asked, "kill Tidings?"

"No, of course not."

"Tidings had plenty on you," Mason said. "Tidings was a hard man. He might have crowded you too far."

"No," Freel said tonelessly. "I didn't kill him. I never killed anyone."

Mason tossed him the ten thousand dollars. "All right, Freel," he said, "here's your money. Come on, Paul."

Freel watched the two men out into the corridor. Then he darted over to close and lock the door.

"Put an operative on him," Mason said to Drake.

"He'll skip out," Drake said.

"I want him to skip out," Mason said, "and I want to know where he goes."

Drake stopped at the corner drugstore to call his office. When he emerged, he nodded to Mason. "An operative will be on the job in ten minutes, Perry."

"Now," Mason said, climbing into Drake's car, "tell me something about Peltham."

"What about him?"

"He lived in an apartment?"

"Yes."

"I believe you said he was rather circumspect."

"Very."

"Secretive?"

"Very."

"Does the apartment house have a garage?"

"Yes. In the basement. There's an attendant who has charge of the cars."

"Did Peltham leave in his automobile?"

"No. His car's still there."

"Got the license number and a description?"

"Yes. It's on the report that we sent into your office."

"The number of his apartment and all that?"

"Yes."

"I suppose police have searched the place?"

"Yes. They've gone through it with a fine-toothed comb."

"Do you know if they are still watching it?"

"No, but they probably are."

Mason said, "That's going to complicate the situation a little."

Drake said suddenly, "Perry, I'll appreciate it a hell of a lot if you don't tell me anything more about what you're going to do. I don't like the sound of it."

Mason settled back against the cushion of Drake's car. "Neither do I," he said.

8.

MASON, WEARING a low, black felt hat, a topcoat, and gloves, stepped casually from the taxicab in front of the Giltmont Arms Apartment Hotel. A liveried doorman reached for the two travel-stained suitcases which the cab driver handed out, suitcases which bore the labels of half a dozen foreign countries.

Mason paid off the cab driver, gave him a generous tip, and followed the doorman into the apartment hotel.

A heavy-set man, wearing square-toed, rubber-heeled shoes with heavy soles, looked up from a newspaper as Mason entered. He gave the lawyer a quick, flashing scrutiny, and then returned to his paper.

Mason said to the clerk, "I may be here for as much as two months. My niece is driving up her automobile for me to use. I'll want garage space for it. I don't care to be too high above the street, nor too near it. Something on about the tenth floor would be satisfactory. I am willing to go as high as two hundred and fifty dollars a month."

The clerk nodded. "I think I have just the thing," he said. "Mr. . . . er . . ."

"Perry," the lawyer said.

"Yes, Mr. Perry. I'll have a boy take you up for an inspection." He nodded to a bellboy. "Show Mr. Perry to 1042," he said.

Mason followed the bellboy to the elevator.

1042 was a well-furnished, three-room apartment with two exposures. Mason announced that it was quite satisfactory and had the bellboy bring up his suitcases. When he had been settled, he picked up the telephone and said to the clerk, "I told you my niece is bringing an automobile for my use. Kindly notify me when she arrives, and I'll go down and make arrangements for proper storage."

"That won't be at all necessary, Mr. Perry," the clerk said. "I'll instruct the garage man and . . ."

"No, thank you," Mason interposed firmly. "I want to make certain that the car is parked where it will be available at rather unusual hours. I'll talk with the garage man myself. A bit of a tip sometimes is most efficacious I've found."

"Yes, Mr. Perry," the clerk said suavely. "I'll let you know as soon as your niece arrives."

Mason hung up the receiver, opened one of his suitcases, took out a bundle of keys, and compared them with his door key. He selected three passkeys of similar design and started experimenting on his own door.

The second key worked the lock easily and smoothly. Mason detached it from the bundle and slipped it into his pocket. He closed the door of his apartment quietly behind him, and walked down the corridor until he came to the door bearing the number 1029. This was Peltham's apartment, and Mason, moving with calm assurance and a complete lack of nervousness, fitted his passkey to the door. The lock clicked back, and Mason entered the apartment.

He didn't switch on the lights, but took from his pocket a miniature flashlight about half the size of his little finger. Using that to guide him, he moved directly toward the clothes closet.

He selected a dark topcoat and made certain that the name of the tailor and the initials "R.P." appeared in the label on the inside of the inner pocket.

He folded the overcoat, put it over his arm, closed the closet door behind him, his gloved hands leaving no fingerprints, and quietly left the apartment.

Two minutes later, safely ensconced in his own apartment, Mason telephoned Della Street at the drugstore where she was waiting.

"Okay, Della," he said.

"Everything under control?" she asked.

"Clicking like clockwork."

"I'm on my way."

Mason hung up the receiver and sat waiting. Within a few minutes the telephone rang, and the clerk said, "Your niece is here, Mr. Perry."

The detective in the lobby was still reading his newspaper when Mason stepped from the elevator into the lobby. He gave the lawyer only a cursory glance.

The clerk said, "The garage is around the corner to the right and down the incline, Mr. Perry."

"Thank you," Mason said. "I'll find it."

Della Street tucked her arm through Mason's. She was jaunty and chic in a sports outfit with her hat tilted at a saucy angle. "Hello, Uncle," she said.

"Hello, darling."

Della's car was parked at the curb. "Take off that wire?" Mason asked.

"Uh huh."

"All right," Mason said. "Wait here."

He walked rapidly to the corner, turned to the right, and walked down the incline which led down to the basement garage.

The garage attendant was seated in a sedan by the door, engrossed in a radio program. When he saw Mason, he hurriedly shut off the radio, and made a great show of being busy parking the car.

Mason waited until he had finished, then significantly took his wallet from his pocket.

"My name," he said, "is Perry."

The garage man nodded.

"I have just moved into 1042," Mason said. "My niece has kindly placed her car at my disposal for the duration of my stay. For some reason, her car won't start. She drove it up to the entrance all right and shut off the motor. Now, it won't start. Do you suppose you can get it going and bring it down for her?"

"Sure," the garage man said. "She's flooded the carburetor, that's all. Janes do that all the time. I'll go out and bring it in."

Mason had to move two cars before he could drive Peltham's car out to the street.

The garage man was still struggling with Della Street's refractory automobile as Mason glided smoothly by on the cross street. Looking back, he had a glimpse of Della Street's arm and hand extended through the window of the car, waving him on his way.

Mason drove some ten blocks, stopped at a drugstore, and telephoned Dr. Willmont at his club.

"Okay, Doctor," Mason said. "I'm ready for that experiment."

"How soon do you want it?"

"As soon as I can get it."

"Half an hour at the Hastings Memorial Hospital," Dr. Willmont said.

"All right. Put it in a can and leave it at the desk for me."

"I have a thermal unit which I use occasionally for transportation," Dr. Willmont said. "It'll be in that unit at the desk. See that I get the unit back when you've finished with the experiment."

"Okay," Mason told him. "That'll be tomorrow. You're sure it'll be ready in half an hour?"

"Yes. Everything's all ready. The donor's waiting, and my assistant is on the job awaiting instructions."

"Okay," Mason said, and hung up.

Mason piloted Peltham's automobile out to a place which was sufficiently isolated to serve his purpose. Stopping the car, he shut off the motor and spread Peltham's overcoat over a clump of brush, took a thirty-eight caliber revolver from his pocket, held the weapon close enough to leave powder burns in the cloth of the coat, and fired a shot into the left breast.

Tossing the coat into the car, Mason thrust the revolver back into his pocket and drove to the hospital. He picked up the thermal container with its content of human blood, and then drove Peltham's automobile to the exact place where Tidings' car had been found by the police.

Mason poured blood onto the overcoat around the hole which had been made by the bullet, both on the inside and outside. He saw that there were stains smeared liberally over the seat of the car and on the floorboards. He left spots on the steering wheel and trickled a rivulet down the inside of the overcoat to form in a puddle on the seat and floor.

When he exhausted his supply of blood, he surveyed the effect with critical appraisal and nodded with satisfaction.

Carrying the thermal container, he swung out in a long, brisk stride, heading northward. Headlights loomed ahead before he had gone two blocks, and Della Street slid her car into the curb.

"Okay, Chief?" she asked.

"Not a hitch anywhere," he said.

"Just what," she asked, "will this do?"

"It's going to smoke someone out into the open," Mason said, lighting a cigarette and settling back against the cushions of the car.

Fifteen minutes later Mason sent a telegram addressed to Miss Adelle Hastings at 906 Cleveland Square, which read:

HIGHLY IMPORTANT TO ASCERTAIN FROM P IF THERE IS ANY OBJECTION TO SETTING ASIDE SALE OF WESTERN PROSPECTING STOCK TO GAILORD TRUSTEE. PLEASE ASCERTAIN AT ONCE AND NOTIFY ME BY WIRE SENT TO MY OFFICE. M.

9.

TIDINGS' SECRETARY, Carl Mattern, opening the door of his apartment in response to Mason's knock, regarded the lawyer with his characteristic owlish scrutiny.

"Why, good evening, Mr. Mason."

"There's a minor matter I wanted to clear up, Mattern," Mason said. "I thought you could help me."

"Certainly. Won't you come in?"

"Thank you."

Mason entered the modest apartment. Mattern indicated a comfortable chair, and Mason dropped into it.

"What," Mattern asked, "can I do for you?"

"Not much for me," Mason said. "It's really for you."

"What do you mean?"

Mason said, "I'm not going to mention names, Mattern, but the claim has been made that you left the broker's office right after the completion of that stock deal and went out to report to Tidings, and while you were talking with him, there was a quarrel, that Tidings accused you of having a personal interest in the transaction and confronted you with proof, and that you shot him."

"That's absurd," Mattern said.

Mason nodded affably. "Thought I'd mention it to you," he said, "so you'd have a chance to clear it up."

"In the first place," Mattern said, "I can account for every minute of my time from the time I left that brokerage office."

"That's fine," Mason said. "Would you mind running over the schedule with me?"

Mattern took a notebook from his pocket. "Not at all," he said. "When I realized that it was going to be necessary for me to remember what had happened that day, I thought I'd better jot it down on paper."

"Good idea," Mason said.

"To begin with," Mattern said, "I left the brokerage office at eleven-eight. I made a point to notice the time when the deal was closed. I returned to my office, and Mr. Tidings called me just about noon. I told him that the deal had been concluded satisfactorily. Mrs. Tump had been trying to see him, and I told him about that. Then I rang up a friend of mine in one of the other offices and asked her to have lunch with me. We went down in the elevator at five minutes past twelve, and I returned with her at five minutes before one o'clock."

"I presume she can verify not only the occasion but the time," Mason said.

"Certainly. She works in an office where they go by the clock. Her lunch hour is from twelve to one. She has to be back at her desk promptly at one o'clock."

"I see," Mason said, "and after that?"

"After that," Mattern said, "I went back to Mr. Tidings' office. There were some matters to take up with the manager of the building, and I rang up the manager's secretary and asked for an appointment as near one-thirty as was convenient."

"You got one?"

"Yes, at one-twenty-five. I talked with the manager of the building for fifteen minutes. I had told his secretary that my business would not take longer than that, and I remember looking at my watch and commenting to her as I went out that it had been fifteen minutes on the dot."

"And then?" Mason asked.

"Then," Mattern said, "I went down to a jewelry store to see about buying a new wrist watch. A chap whom I know works there, and I looked at wrist watches for nearly half an hour."

"He'll remember the occasion?"

"Oh, yes."

"And the time?"

"He certainly will," Mattern said, laughing, "because we were discussing the accuracy of watches. I bet him that my own wrist watch wouldn't vary more than one second in half an hour from his standard chronometer. I was there half an hour, and we checked the second hand."

"That brings you up to two-thirty," Mason said.

"That's right."

"What did you do after two-thirty, Mattern?"

"I had some matters to go over with the accountant who makes out Mr. Tidings' income tax reports. I asked him to meet me at the office at quarter of three. We were there until five."

"And after five?" Mason inquired.

"I invited a young lady to meet me at five-twenty, to go to dinner and a movie."

"The same young lady whom you took to lunch?"

"No, another one."

"Why five-twenty in particular?" Mason asked.

"Well," Mattern said, "it was . . . well, it just happened to be the time that I mentioned, that's all."

"Wasn't that rather early for a dinner date?"

"Yes, perhaps. But I wanted to get in to the show in time for the first picture."

"This young woman works?"

"No, she doesn't."

Mason said, "Well, let's go back to Tuesday morning."

"I came to the office at nine o'clock," Mattern said. "Mr. Tidings came in about nine-fifteen. We handled some correspondence until ten-thirty, then we discussed details in connection with the closing of the Western Prospecting deal, and you called up. That started Tidings sputtering about what a busybody Mrs. Tump was, and we discussed that for several minutes. Then Tidings went out, and I went over to close that Western Prospecting deal."

"See anyone except Tidings on Tuesday morning?" Mason asked.

"The brokers. Then there was Mrs. Tump shortly after eleven."

"I mean before that."

Mattern thought for a moment, then slowly shook his head. "No," he said. "I don't think anyone came to the office."

"Immediately after noon," Mason said, "your time seems to have been pretty well checked."

"Yes, sir. There's not more than twenty minutes at any one time, and it would have been a physical impossibility for anyone to get out to that bungalow where the body was found and back to the center of town within a twenty-minute period."

Mason said, "That's rather significant, don't you think, Carl?"

"What do you mean?" Mattern asked in surprise.

Mason said, "You haven't any alibi until around eleven o'clock on Tuesday morning. From then on, you have a perfect alibi covering every minute of the day, and the interesting thing is that in virtually every instance you made certain that the time would impress itself upon your witnesses."

"What do you mean?"

Mason stared at him steadily. "I mean, Carl," he said, "that you were *trying* to give yourself an alibi, that you were taking every precaution to see that every minute of your time was accounted for. . . . Take for instance your comments with the secretary of the building manager on the length of time your conference had taken. . . . The discussion about time at the jewelry store. . . . The appointment with the tax accountant, and last of all that five-twenty dinner date."

"Why, I . . . I don't know what you're talking about, Mr. Mason."

"Oh, yes, you do," Mason said gently. "You must have known he was dead before you went over to the broker's, Carl."

For a long moment, there was tense silence in the apartment. A cheap alarm clock ticked audibly on the dresser. Mattern's eyes, wide and protruding behind the dark-rimmed spectacles, showed consternation.

Mason said, "I don't think you killed him, Carl, but I do know that you were interested in that stock transaction. You knew that he was dead before it was time to go over to the broker's office, and you knew that you had to make it appear Tidings was alive at the time that agreement was concluded.

"You were shrewd enough to realize that if you did make it

appear he was alive at noon on Tuesday, the authorities would be forced to fix the time of death as almost immediately after noon, and so you were careful to build up an alibi which would protect you during the afternoon."

Mattern said, "Mr. Mason, I can assure that I did nothing of the sort. I . . ."

"Don't get yourself in bad," Mason said.

"What do you mean?"

"Simply this," Mason observed, crossing his legs, settling comfortably back against the chair, and lighting a cigarette. "I'm a mean fighter, Carl."

"So I've heard."

"In a fight," Mason said, "I try to damage my adversary in every way possible. I hit below the belt."

Mattern nodded.

"I'm representing a person," Mason said, "who is going to be accused of the murder of Albert Tidings."

"And you mean you'd try to pin it on me in order to get that person off?"

Mason struck a match to his cigarette, blew out the flame, and smiled affably at Mattern. "Exactly," he said.

"Do you mean to say you'd frame an innocent man . . ."

"Wait a moment, Carl," Mason interrupted, stopping him with an upraised hand. "Let's leave the innocent man out of it."

"But I *am* innocent."

"That," Mason said, "is nothing for me to decide. That's up to the jury."

"But you have no reason to believe I killed him."

Mason said, "Frankly, Carl, I don't think you did."

"Then why are you accusing me of it?"

"I'm not accusing you of it," Mason said. "I'm simply telling you that you knew he was dead prior to Tuesday noon, that you covered up that death, and then started getting yourself an alibi. But you'll find a jury isn't going to be as charitable as I am."

"You must be crazy!"

Mason said, "*I'm* willing to believe that you're not a murderer, that you shrewdly manipulated things so you could close the sale of that Western Prospecting stock. When you found Tidings was dead, you realized you had to keep his death covered up until you could put through that deal. But what you overlooked, Carl, was that once you started tampering with the facts, a jury would conclude you were guilty of murder."

Mattern blinked his eyes rapidly. "They *couldn't,*" he said.

"Oh, yes, they could, Carl. Let's suppose, for instance, that you had reason to believe Tidings was going to be at that bungalow on Tuesday morning. Suppose you went out with a brief case filled with mail and documents to get instructions, and suppose you found Tidings lying dead on the bed. You slipped quietly out of the house without anyone seeing you. You knew that the news of his death would put a stop to that stock deal, and so you decided to have it appear that he had died shortly after noon on Tuesday. Fortunately, my telephone call gave you an opportunity for a second string to your bow. I had never heard the voice of Albert Tidings. By a bit of vocal manipulation you were able to leave me with the impression that I had talked with Tidings over the telephone.

"You're a very clever young man, Mattern, but you must give me credit for knowing something about the psychology of a juror. I'm telling you, Mattern, plainly and frankly, that a jury probably would convict you of Tidings' murder purely on circumstantial evidence once that chain of facts had been brought to light. The jury would consider that you'd killed him on Tuesday morning. . . . And that would coincide with the findings of the autopsy surgeons."

Mason devoted his attention to watching the smoke drift up from one end of his cigarette, seeming to dismiss Mattern entirely from his mind.

After a few seconds, Mattern said, "But those things can't be proven."

Mason smiled. "Oh, yes, they can," he said. "*I* can prove them." "*You* can?"

"Yes."

"How?"

Mason smiled and said, "I'm not going to disclose my entire hand, Mattern, but remember that you were a bit greedy and a little hasty. Realizing that the stock transaction might be open to question, you were just a little too anxious to get your split from Bolus. Peculiar chap, that Bolus. Rather selfish, I would say. Once the authorities accused him of being your accomplice in the *murder,* he'd move heaven and earth to show that he was your accomplice only on the stock jobbing deal, and that you alone were responsible for Tidings' death."

Mattern shifted his position uncomfortably in the chair.

Mason said, "Thought I'd let you know where I stood, Mattern, that's all. I wanted to be absolutely fair."

"What do you want me to do?" Mattern asked.

"Nothing," Mason said, in some surprise. "Nothing at all. But I just wanted you to know that when it comes time for me to defend my client, I'll be able to make out a pretty good case against you."

Mattern laughed and said, "I can't see what you're getting at, Mr. Mason. By telling me this in advance, you've put yourself entirely in my power. Suppose I should relate this conversation to a jury?"

"No need for you to bother," Mason said. "I'll tell them about it myself. Remember, Mattern, I dropped in to tell you that I had reason to believe you knew Tidings was dead Tuesday morning before that stock transaction was concluded. Among other things, I wanted to hear your voice so I could convince myself that it was you who were talking with me over the telephone Tuesday morning. I'm convinced now."

"A jury wouldn't take *your* evidence very seriously."

"Perhaps not," Mason said. "It would be your word against mine."

"And you're interested in saving your client's neck," Mattern said.

"Just as you're interested in saving your own," Mason reminded him.

"Mine isn't in any danger."

"And," Mason went on, "you'll also remember that one of the reasons for this visit was to ask you if you had any financial interest in that stock sale of the Western Prospecting Company."

"And I assured you that I didn't," Mattern said.

Mason arose, stretched, yawned, and said casually, "Know Colonel Gilliland?"

"No," Mattern said.

"In charge of the income tax evasions detail here," Mason said. "Charming chap. You'll probably get acquainted with him later on."

There was anxiety in Mattern's eyes.

"Friend of mine," Mason went on. "You know, the government has quite a system. If anyone gives 'em a tip on an income tax evasion, the government will investigate, and if they recover a tax on the strength of that tip, they'll pay a reward amounting to a percentage of the tax. You can't fool the government, you know. They can examine the records of banks and the books of corporations. . . . Well, I'll be running along, Mattern."

Mattern said, "Hey, wait a minute. You aren't going to tell this man Gilliland anything about me?"

"Why not?" Mason asked.

"Because— Well, because under the circumstances that would be the hell of a thing to do."

"Why?"

"Haven't I co-operated with you?"

Mason said, "It's all right, Mattern. There's nothing to worry about. If you didn't get any cut out of that fifty thousand, no one can do a thing to you. Of course, Gilliland will go into the books of the Western Prospecting Company, will scrutinize Bolus' income tax statement, check the bank records, look into your bank deposits, and work on a few other angles. He'll make a good job of it."

Mattern said, "Come back here, Mason. Sit down."

Mason raised his eyebrows. "Why?"

Mattern said, "You've got me."

"Got you?" Mason asked. "What do you mean?"

"I got ten grand out of that sale," Mattern blurted.

"That's better," Mason observed, walking over to a chair and seating himself. "Tell me about it."

"There's nothing much to tell," Mattern said meekly. "I felt like a heel all the time, but I needed the money. I just *had* to have it."

"Why?" Mason asked.

"Oh, some bum hunches on horses," Mattern said.

"Did Bolus get in touch with you?"

"No. I got in touch with him. I knew something about the stock. I put the proposition up to him. I was to interest Tidings as trustee in the stock, and get a fifty per cent cut. . . . And it's really a good stock at that, Mr. Mason, a very good speculative buy."

"But you didn't get fifty per cent?" Mason asked.

"No," Mattern said bitterly. "Bolus, the damn crook, chiseled me. After I'd brought the parties together and got the deal so far under way that I couldn't have backed out of it without making everyone suspicious, Bolus told me he'd been under more expense than he'd figured, that he'd have to give some banker a cut, and that I'd have to take ten thousand instead of twenty-five."

"Why give the banker a cut?" Mason asked.

"Some banker that Tidings had asked for a report on the stock developed an itching palm. Anyhow, that's what Bolus said."

"All right," Mason said. "Go ahead. Tell me how you knew Tidings was dead?"

"I tell you I didn't know it."

"Bunk," Mason said.

"Honestly, Mr. Mason, everything else is just as I told you."

Mason said, "Mattern, I'm getting damn tired of your lies. . . . Know what I think I'll do? I think I'll go down to the D.A. and give him a tip on you."

"You've got nothing on me," Mattern said.

"No?" Mason asked with a cold smile.

"Absolutely not."

"In the first place," Mason said, "you needed that ten grand because you'd made a mistake in picking ponies. Is that right?"

"Yes. What of it? Lots of people play the races."

"Uh huh," Mason said. "But you need money in order to play the races."

"Well, I got the money, didn't I?"

"*After* you'd incurred the losses," Mason said. "My best guess, Mattern, is that the original bets were made from money you'd embezzled from Tidings and the trust accounts. The audit of Tidings' books would have left you in quite a spot if it hadn't been for that ten grand."

Mason needed no more than a look at Mattern's dismayed countenance to serve as confirmation of his charge.

"All right," he said. "There you are. You've been embezzling money. Tidings called you on Tuesday morning. He had the dope. He was going to send you to jail. You knew that if you could stall things along for a few hours, that Western Prospecting sale would go through, and you'd have money enough to make restitution. You figured you could juggle the books so that the original embezzlement could be covered. You got desperate and excited and pulled a gun on Tidings. Tidings came for you, and you pulled the trigger."

"That's a lie," Mattern shouted.

"Perhaps it is," Mason observed, "but you'd never make a jury believe it."

"No jury could ever find me guilty of murder. There isn't a shred of evidence."

Mason smiled. "Thanks a lot, Mattern. You've given me a perfect out. I don't need to worry about my client. You're the fall guy. Good night."

Once more Mason arose from his chair.

"Listen," Mattern said desperately. "I'll give you the real low-down, Mr. Mason. I'll tell you how it was. Honestly, I didn't kill him. He'd been dead for a long time when I saw him."

"When was that?"

"About eight-thirty Tuesday morning."

"Where?"

"Right where he was lying. Right on the bed where the body was found."

"What happened?" Mason asked.

Mattern said, "Tidings was trying to get something on his wife. He told me that she was mixed up with some man who had to keep in the background because of what might happen in a divorce action. Tidings said he'd found out about this man and that he was going out to see his wife and call for a showdown. There were some important papers he had to go over, and he promised to be at the office at seven-thirty Tuesday morning to sign them.

"When he hadn't shown up at the office at eight o'clock, I put the papers in a brief case, and drove out to his wife's house. I thought that perhaps they'd effected a reconciliation. He really was crazy about her. The door was unlocked. I went in. There were bloodstains on the floor. I followed the bloodstains to the bedroom. . . . You know what I found."

"What did you do?" Mason asked.

"I beat it," Mattern said. "I was scared stiff. I figured that with his death, his books would be gone over, my embezzlement discovered, and that I'd go to jail. I was good and sore. If he'd only lived a few hours more, I'd have been in the clear. . . . So then I figured that it might be a long while before anyone would find the body, and I might be able to stall things along so I could get that Western Prospecting deal through. I knew that the cashier's check was all made out payable to the brokers.... Well, you know the rest"

"And that was you who talked with me over the telephone that morning?"

"Yes. When you rang up and wanted to talk with Tidings, I didn't know what to do. I didn't want to say he wasn't in the office.... And then I got the idea that saved me from making any admissions. I knew you hadn't heard Tidings' voice. I have a little ability when it comes to controlling my voice. I've done a bit of work in amateur theatricals."

Mason said, "Well, Mattern, you know where this leaves you."

"Where *does* it leave me?"

Mason said, "You're a pushover for the D.A."

"But I'm innocent. Surely you must believe me."

Mason studied him thoughtfully. "Better start helping me look for the real murderer, Mattern. That's your only out."

Mattern impulsively shot out his hand. "You're a square shooter," he said. "I'll do that, Mr. Mason. You can count on me for anything."

The two men shook hands.

10.

A TELEGRAM WAS lying on Mason's desk when he entered the office Friday morning, and Della Street informed him that Mrs. Tump was impatiently awaiting his arrival in the outer office.

Mason opened the telegram. It was signed Adelle Hastings, and read:

HAVE CONTACTED PARTY REFERRED TO. NO CAUSE FOR CONCERN OVER ANY DEVELOPMENTS TO DATE. GO RIGHT AHEAD. EVERYTHING OKAY.

Mason thrust the telegram in his pocket, and said to Della Street, "All right. Let's see what Mrs. Tump wants, and get *her* out of the way."

Della Street ushered Mrs. Tump into the inner office. The woman's grayish-green eyes glittered as she came sailing across the office. Only her lips were smiling.

"Good morning, Mr. Mason," she said.

"How are you this morning, Mrs. Tump?"

"Very well, thank you. What have you found out?"

"Not a great deal," Mason admitted, "but I'm making progress."

"What about that fifty-thousand-dollar stock sale, Mr. Mason?"

Mason said, "I'm going to set that aside."

"Is the stock worth anything?"

Mason indicated a chair, gave Mrs. Tump a cigarette, took one himself, lit up, and said, "That stock which was delivered to Loftus & Cale represented the private holdings of the president of the company. That should answer your question. I'm going to set the transaction aside on the ground that Tidings was dead before the check was delivered for the stock."

She studied him with her glittering, hard eyes. "You can do that?"

"Yes."

"How are you going to prove it?"

"For one thing," Mason said, "I can prove it by the testimony of the autopsy surgeon—I hope."

Mrs. Tump said, "Mr. Mason, I want to talk with you frankly."

"Go ahead."

"I'm not one to mince words."

"Let's have them unminced then," Mason said with a smile.

She said, "Very well, Mr. Mason. When I wanted you to handle Byrl's case, you began stalling for time."

Mason raised his eyebrows in silent interrogation.

"Now, of course, Mr. Mason, when we first came to you, you had no way of knowing that Mr. Tidings was dead."

"Correct," Mason said.

"Now, as I understand it, if you can prove that Mr. Tidings died somewhere before eleven o'clock on Tuesday morning, it will enable Byrl to get fifty thousand dollars back into the trust fund."

"Correct."

"Who will pay that fifty thousand?"

"We'll proceed against Loftus & Cale," Mason said. "They'll have to try and get the money back from Bolus. Because I warned them of what they could expect, they're taking steps to impound the money."

"That's very clever of you, Mr. Mason."

"Thank you."

"Mr. Mason, are you representing Adelle Hastings?"

Mason said, cautiously, "In what connection, Mrs. Tump?"

"In any connection."

"A lawyer has to keep the affairs of his client confidential."

Mrs. Tump said, "You know what I mean. If she should be accused of murdering Tidings, would you be her lawyer?"

Mason studied his cigarette thoughtfully. "That would be hard to say."

"Very well," Mrs. Tump said. "I just want to say one thing, and then I'm through, Mr. Mason. Personally, I think Adelle Hastings is a snob, an arrogant, insulting little snob. She's done a lot to make things disagreeable for Byrl. I hate her because of that. But I know she isn't one who would commit murder. I'll say that for her—although I still hate her.

"Now then, Mr. Mason, suppose she's accused of that murder. She might depend upon an alibi, and she might want to prove that Tidings died after twelve o'clock Tuesday in order to make her alibi good. Now then, if you tried to help her do that, you'd be working directly against Byrl's interests because we want to show that Tidings died *before* eleven o'clock. . . . You understand me, Mr. Mason?"

"Yes."

Mrs. Tump got to her feet. "Very well, Mr. Mason," she said.

"I just wanted to know where you stood. I'm never one to mince words. I don't care whom you represent, but there's one thing on which there must be no misunderstanding: Albert Tidings met his death *before* that stock deal went through. . . . Good morning, Mr. Mason."

Mason glanced across at Della Street as the door closed behind Mrs. Tump. "That," he said, "is that. . . . Get your hat and coat, Della. Bring along a notebook. We're going to call on the woman who holds the other part of that ten-thousand-dollar bill."

"You know who she is?" Della Street asked in surprise.

"I do now," Mason said grimly, "—just about three days too late."

"How did you discover her?"

"By a little head work," Mason said. "And I should have known a lot sooner. Come on. Let's go."

They drove in Mason's car out through the city, swinging to the northward away from the through boulevard.

"Mrs. Tidings?" Della Street asked, as they started climbing up a twisting road.

Mason nodded.

"But she was in Reno. *She* left Monday. She *couldn't* have been at your office Monday night."

Mason said patiently, "*She's* the only one who's tried to make her alibi stretch back of Monday night. All the others presented alibis for Tuesday afternoon."

"Well?" Della Street asked.

"Well," Mason said. "The answer is obvious. She's the only one who *knew* that he was killed Monday night. She couldn't look ahead into the future, and know that Mattern would try to protect his ten thousand dollars by having Tidings alive on Tuesday morning."

"That's all the evidence you have to go on, Chief?" Della Street asked.

"It's enough," Mason said grimly. "The minute she told me about leaving for Reno on Monday noon and driving all night, I should have known."

"And she's the masked woman?"

"Yes."

"Do you suppose she'll deny it?"

"Not now," Mason said. "I'm only hoping that I can get there before Holcomb figures it out."

"You think *he'll* figure it out?"

"Yes."

They drove in silence up the winding road. The house in which the body of Albert Tidings had been found glistened white and clean in the sunlight, giving no evidence of the sinister background of gruesome murder which had attached itself to the cozy bungalow.

"Well," Mason said, "here we go." He opened the car door, slid out to the pavement, and he and Della Street walked up the short space of cement which stretched from the porch to the street.

Mason pressed his thumb against the bell button.

Almost instantly the door was opened by Mrs. Tidings who was dressed for the street. "Why, good morning, Mr. Mason," she said. "I thought I recognized you when you got out of the car."

"Miss Street, Mrs. Tidings," Mason introduced perfunctorily.

"How do you do?" Mrs. Tidings said to Della Street. "Won't you come in?"

They entered the house, and Mrs. Tidings indicated chairs.

"Cigarette?" she asked of Della Street, opening a humidor.

"Thank you," Della said, taking one.

"I have one of my own," Mason said, taking his cigarette case from his pocket.

Mrs. Tidings said, "Things are at sixes and sevens with me. I think you understand how it is. They're having the funeral this afternoon. It was delayed while the experts were trying to uncover some clue which would point to the murderer. . . . You don't know what progress they've made, do you, Mr. Mason?"

"If they're releasing the body this afternoon," Mason said, "it's certain that they've completed their tests."

"Yes. I surmised as much, but I don't know what they've found."

"They haven't told you?"

"Not a word.

"Of course," Mrs. Tidings repeated, "I'm upset. We'd separated, but it was a shock to me . . . . I hated him."

Mason said, "I appreciate your position, Mrs. Tidings. By the way, I came to get the other half of that ten-thousand-dollar bill."

"Why, Mr. Mason, what do you mean?"

Mason looked at his wrist watch. "Minutes may mean the difference between a good defense and a verdict of first-degree murder. If you want to waste time arguing about it, go ahead. It's your funeral. . . . And I don't mean the remark figuratively."

"You seem rather certain of your ground, Mr. Mason."

"I am. When you and Peltham came to my office, I noticed two things. The first was that Peltham had laid careful plans to get in touch with me at any hour of the day or night, just in case he ever wanted a lawyer. The second was that a lot of things in connection with your visit showed extreme haste and lack of

preparation: the fact, for instance, that Peltham gave me a fictitious name which wasn't listed in the telephone directory. Also
there was your mask."

She kept her eyes veiled. "What about the mask?"

"It was a black mask with a silver tinsel trimming," Mason
said. "It had been part of a masquerade costume, something
which had been stored away as a souvenir."

"I don't see what that proves," she said.

"Simply this," Mason said. "Peltham had made careful preparations to see me in case something happened. When that something did happen, he had to act fast. He decided to protect you by
keeping your identity a secret even from me. That meant a mask.
Now people don't just carry masks around with them, and you
don't find them hanging on lamp posts late at night. But you *had*
one, probably tucked away in some bureau drawer, *at home*. That
means that whatever happened that made it imperative for the
woman Peltham was protecting to see me, happened right in her
home or reasonably close. I should have known the answer the
minute I discovered Tidings' body *here*."

She looked at him for a moment in silence, studying the gran-
ite-hard lines of his face. Then, without a word, she opened her
purse, took out a small envelope, tore it open, and from that envelope extracted the other portion of the ten-thousand-dollar bill
which she handed to Mr. Mason.

There was some surprise on Della Street's face, but Mason
didn't so much as flicker an eyelash.

"When did you know he was dead?"

"Why, when I returned from Reno of course."

Mason said nothing, but once more looked at his wrist watch,
an eloquent reminder of the passing of time.

She said, "Honestly, Mr. Mason, I'm telling the truth."

Mason said, "You were in love with Peltham. He wanted to protect you. You came to my office shortly after midnight. You did everything possible to keep me from learning your real identity as well as the nature of the case on which I was to be employed. You subsequently claimed that you had left for Reno late Monday afternoon. Apparently, you were actually in Reno Tuesday morning.

"Considering all of those various circumstances in their proper light, it means that the body of Albert Tidings was lying right here, in that bedroom, at the very moment you were calling on me at my office. . . . Now then, did *you* kill him or did Peltham?"

"Neither."

"But you knew he was dead?"

She hesitated for several seconds, then said, almost inaudibly, "Yes."

"And you were the ones who put him into that room and on that bed?"

"Yes."

"Who killed him?"

"Honestly, Mr. Mason, I don't know."

"Better tell me what you do know," Mason said.

She said, "I'm going to be frank with you, Mr. Mason."

"Do," Mason said, and then added significantly, "for a change."

She said, "I wanted a divorce. I am very much in love with Bob. Bob had reason to believe that Albert was dipping into the Hastings Memorial Trust Fund. He was working with Adelle Hastings, trying to straighten things out. He wanted her to demand an audit of the books. Under the circumstances, if my attachment for Robert had been discovered, it would have made very serious complications all around. You can understand that, Mr. Mason."

Mason said tonelessly, "I can understand that."

Della Street slipped a shorthand notebook from her purse. Mason said, "Don't do it, Della. I don't want any of this recorded anywhere. . . . Go ahead, Mrs. Tidings."

She said, "Albert had been trying to effect a reconciliation. I told him that it was impossible. Bob and I had been to a show. We were driving home. We found Albert's car parked down near the circle at the end of the road. It was raining hard. Albert was in the car, slumped down in the seat to one side of the steering wheel. He had been shot and was unconscious. We stopped our car. Bob and I got out in the rain and tried to see how seriously Albert was injured. There was still a faint pulse. He had been shot in the chest. We realized that we couldn't do anything in the space there was inside the car. I told Bob he'd have to help me get Albert into the house, and then I'd telephone for a doctor and the police.

"Together, we got him out of the car and half carried, half dragged him into the house. We put him on the bed. I ran to the telephone, and was just on the point of putting through the call when Bob called to me. He said, 'It's too late now, Nadine. He's dead.'

"I ran back to the bed. There was no question about it. I suppose that in moving him, we'd started the hemorrhage—making it more severe. Anyway, he was dead. There wasn't the faintest pulse."

"What did you do?" Mason asked.

"Bob told me that I couldn't be dragged into it, that he would skip out and keep in hiding, that this would tend to direct suspicion to him, that it would be better for me to put my car in a garage somewhere and take a plane to Reno where I had friends. I could claim that I'd driven up there. By leaving the house door open and unlocked, it would make it appear he'd broken in in my absence.

"We talked things over and decided that here in the house it might be quite a while before the body was discovered, that I might be able to build up an alibi that would hold water. It would help my alibi to have the time of death appear to be as late as possible. There was mud on his shoes, mud stains on the counterpane of the bed. We realized that these might help fix the time of murder. So we took off his shoes and topcoat, pulled the mud-stained counterpane out from under him, and wrapped them up in a bundle."

"What became of them?" Mason asked.

"I don't know. Bob took them. He said he'd take care of them."

"Then what did you do?"

"Then I drove Bob's car, and Bob drove Albert's car. He wanted the car discovered as far away from the house as possible. We parked the car and then telephoned you. Bob said you could protect me if anyone could, but he pointed out that if my alibi in Reno held up, I wouldn't have any need for an attorney, that if they didn't discover Albert's body for four or five days, no one could tell exactly when he'd died, and that if I could get a lucky break, I might be able to keep absolutely out of it.

"We'd managed things very circumspectly. No one in the world had any idea that Bob and I were . . . were . . . that we cared for each other."

Mason said, "You overlooked one thing."

"What's that?"

"On the California line near Topaz Lake there's a state quarantine checking station. They check the cars that go through, particularly the cars that come into the state. They keep a record of license numbers. . . . You went to Reno by plane?"

"Yes."

"And stored your car?"

"Yes."

"Where?"

"In a small garage where I sometimes keep it."

"Do they know you?"

She smiled and said, "Not as Mrs. Tidings."

"Under another name?"

"Yes."

"Mrs. Peltham?"

"No, not Mrs. Peltham. Mrs. Hushman."

"Who's *Mr.* Hushman?" Mason asked.

She lowered her eyes, then after a moment said, "Mr. Peltham."

There was the sound of a car being driven rapidly past the house. The tires screamed a protest as the machine was whisked around the turntable. Della Street, getting up from the chair in which she was sitting, crossed over to the window to look out.

"A police car," she said to Mason.

Mason's eyes narrowed. "Mrs. Tidings," he said, "I want you to promise me one thing. Make absolutely no statements. Refuse to answer any questions."

"But surely, Mr. Mason, you don't think . . ."

From the window, Della Street said, "Sergeant Holcomb and an officer are getting out. They're coming toward the house."

"Will you promise me?" Mason asked.

"Yes."

"Remember, your life depends on keeping that promise."

"But, Mr. Mason, they can't touch me, regardless of how I went to Reno. I certainly *was* there by five o'clock Tuesday morning, and the testimony of Albert's secretary shows that he was alive and well until noon on Tuesday."

"Did you," Mason asked, as steps sounded on the porch, "know that Mattern was going to do that?"

"No, of course not. It was just a lucky break for us."

Mason said, "Well, there's one thing wrong with that. It isn't the truth. Any time you go to court relying on something that isn't the truth, your whole defense may collapse under you. I don't handle my cases that way. I find out the truth, and build up my defense on a solid foundation. . . . Now then, *if* you killed him, I want you to tell me."

"I didn't kill him."

The doorbell rang steadily and insistently.

"If you're lying to me," Mason said, "heaven help you."

"Mr. Mason, I'm telling you the absolute, honest truth. I've lied to you before. Now I'm telling you the truth."

The doorbell continued ringing, and was supplemented by the pounding of imperative knuckles on the panels of the door.

"If you didn't kill him," Mason asked, "who did?"

"Honestly, Mr. Mason, I haven't the faintest idea. It must have been someone over that trust fund. Sometimes I've suspected . . ."

The door groaned against pressure as the officers pushed their shoulders against it.

Mason said, "All right. Go open the door."

Mrs. Tidings crossed over and opened the door.

Sergeant Holcomb came pushing his way into the room. He looked at Perry Mason and Della Street.

"You two!" he said, in a voice that showed his anger. "What are you doing here?"

"Talking with my client," Mason said.

Sergeant Holcomb said, "You knew I was coming. How did you know it?"

Mason shook his head.

"You're retained by Mrs. Tidings?"

"Yes."

"For what did she retain you?"

"To handle her business."

"What's the nature of that business?"

Mason smiled. "Really, Sergeant, an attorney doesn't discuss the affairs of his client."

Sergeant Holcomb whirled to Mrs. Tidings, "All right, Mrs. Tidings," he said. "We're going to have some answers to some questions here and now. The records show that you didn't drive your car to Reno. During the time that you were in Reno, your car was parked in a garage on East Central Avenue. They know you there as Mrs. Robert Hushman. They have seen your purported husband, Mr. Hushman. The garage men have identified photographs of Robert Peltham as being photographs of Robert Hushman. They've identified photographs of you. . . . Now then, what have you to say to that?"

Mason said, "I can answer that question."

"I don't want *you* to," Sergeant Holcomb said. "I want an answer from *her*."

She said, "I have nothing to say."

Mason nodded. "I have instructed her not to answer *any* questions."

"If she doesn't answer that question," Sergeant Holcomb

said, "she's going to headquarters. She's going to have a chat with the D.A. If she doesn't give an explanation of certain facts at that time, she's going to be charged with first-degree murder."

Mason carefully ground out the end of his cigarette. "Put your hat on, Mrs. Tidings," he said.

11.

BACK IN the automobile, driving toward Mason's office, Della Street said, "Why didn't you tell Mrs. Tidings about the news?"

"You mean about Peltham's coat being found in his automobile?"

"Yes."

Mason said, "I'll let Holcomb do that."

"That will be an awful shock to her, Chief. . . . Shouldn't you have tipped her off that you had reason to believe it was a plant, and not to get all excited about it?"

"No," Mason said.

"Why, Chief?"

Mason said, "I originally intended that little plant to trap Adelle Hastings. I wanted to smoke Peltham out into the open, and I figured that someone would do some talking if it appeared that Peltham was dead."

"That's just the danger," Della Street pointed out. "If Mrs. Tidings thinks Peltham is dead, she might say something."

"Let her say it," Mason said. "If Peltham's hiding behind her skirts, it's time he was pushed out into the open."

"Do you think he is?"

Mason said, "I don't know. Get this, Della. Lots of lawyers go into court with a case founded on false testimony. Sometimes they make it stick. Sometimes they don't. Personally, I've never dared to take the risk. Truth is the most powerful weapon a man can use, and if you practice law the way we do, it's the only weapon powerful enough to use.

"A lawyer doing the things that I have done and relying on anything less powerful than truth would be disbarred in a month. This case bothers me. . . . It baffles me. I can't figure exactly what happened, yet I *have* to know what happened.

"I *think* I know now what happened, but I haven't enough truth to forge a sufficiently powerful weapon with which to fight. . . . However, let's quit worrying about it right now. I think things are going to work out. Let's go see Adelle Hastings."

They found Adelle Hastings at her apartment. Beyond a certain hardness of facial expression, there was no sign of emotion.

Mason, studying her with shrewd, appraising eyes, noticed that hard, frozen mask behind which she concealed her feelings.

Mason said, "Miss Street, my secretary, Miss Hastings."

Adelle Hastings acknowledged the introduction with a polite cordiality which gave everything that formality demanded, but went not a step beyond.

"Won't you come in?" she asked.

Mason said, "I hardly expected to find you here. I understood you were working."

"I'm not working today," she said, and offered no other explanation. "Won't you sit down?"

When they were seated, she suddenly turned to Perry Mason. For a moment the mask dropped from her face. Her eyes were glittering. "Why," she asked, "did you send that telegram?"

"Because I wanted the information," Mason said.

She indicated the morning paper. "One might almost have suspected that it was a trap," she said.

"A trap?" Mason asked, as though he failed to follow her reasoning.

She clamped her lips tightly shut.

"Of course," Mason went on, "now that you mention it, it is rather strange that you were able to get the message from a man who had been seriously if not fatally wounded and transmit that message to me."

She blinked her eyes rapidly, fighting back tears.

"Can you," Mason asked, "tell me exactly what time you communicated with Mr. Peltham last night?"

"No."

"The police," Mason pointed out, "will be very much interested. I'm afraid that now, Miss Hastings, you'll have to take us into your confidence."

"Have . . . have the police found him? The body?"

"I don't know," Mason said. "The police don't always feel particularly friendly toward me. I have to depend on the newspapers for information, just as you do."

The fingers of her left hand sought those of her right, twisted nervously. There was no other evidence of emotion.

Mason said, "Obviously, in the interests of all concerned, it's vital that the body should be found."

She remained motionless and silent.

"The police," Mason went on, "have ways of being very insistent and at times very disagreeable. I take it you understand that."

"Are you," she asked, "threatening me?"

Mason met her eyes. "Yes," he said.

"I don't frighten easily," she said.

Mason took a cigarette case from his pocket. "Mind if I smoke?" he asked.

She bit her lip then, a swift flicker of facial motion which betrayed for a moment her nerve tension, but she smiled graciously and said, "Pardon me for not offering cigarettes, Mr. Mason. I have some here . . ."

"No, thank you. I prefer my own. Would you care to have one of mine?"

She took a cigarette from his case. Della Street also took one, and Mason held matches to their cigarettes, then settled back comfortably in the chair. "I'm waiting," he said.

"For what?"

"Your complete statement."

"I'm not going to give it to you."

"That," Mason said, "will be most unfortunate."

She opened her mouth, hesitated, and then suddenly burst into a torrent of words. "Must you always dominate everyone with whom you come in contact? Can't you leave anyone a shred of self-respect or self-volition? My first experience with you was so humiliating that I could cry about it, but now . . . Well, I'm not going to have that first experience repeated."

Mason said, calmly, "Let's face the facts, Miss Hastings. Your dealings with men have been confined to social affairs where women are extended polite courtesy. I deal with problems of life and death. I have neither the time nor the patience for polite courtesies."

"And so?" she asked.

"And so," Mason said, "I am going to learn what contacts you had with Robert Peltham, what your arrangements were, how you received messages from him, and to what extent you were given carte blanche."

"What makes you think he gave me carte blanche?"

"Obviously," Mason said, "one does not get messages from a dead man."

"You think that he is dead then?"

Mason said, "The circumstantial evidence uncovered by the police would point that way."

"He was alive and well at nine o'clock last night."

"You know that?"

"Yes."

"You talked with him?"

"Yes."

"Over the telephone?"

"I don't care to answer that question."

Mason said to Della Street, "I think you'd better call Sergeant Holcomb of the Homicide Squad, Della, and tell him we have a witness who knows something about Robert Peltham."

"You can't do that," Adelle Hastings said.

"Why not?"

"It wouldn't be fair. Mr. Peltham retained you."

"Not to protect him," Mason said, "to protect a woman."

"Who was the woman?"

Mason said, "Mr. Peltham took steps to conceal her identity from me."

She said, "I know now what you were referring to when you talked with me before—intimating that I had something to give you."

"Do you indeed?" Mason said, his voice showing only polite interest.

Della Street said, "Do you wish me to put through that call now, Chief?"

"Please," he said.

Della Street asked Adelle Hastings, in her most polite manner, "May I use the phone?"

"You may not," Miss Hastings said. "I'm not going to have the police brought into this."

Mason said, without looking around, "You'll find a telephone at the drugstore on the corner, Della. You have a dime?"

"Yes."

She arose, put her cigarette in an ash tray, said, "Excuse me, please," and opened the door.

It was not until she had stepped out into the corridor and was about to close the door behind her that Adelle Hastings called, "Stop," in a voice that was harsh with strain.

Della Street stopped.

"Come back," Adelle Hastings said. "I'll tell Mr. Mason what he wishes to know."

Della Street stepped back into the apartment, closed the door, and stood with her back against it, her hands still holding the doorknob. Adelle Hastings tried unsuccessfully to blink back tears. She said to Mason, "Don't you ever give an adversary an opportunity to save her face?"

Mason said, "I'm sorry, Miss Hastings. I deal in results. I care little for methods."

"So I've observed," she said. "I think, Mr. Mason, I could learn to hate you with *very* little effort."

Mason's tone was detached and impersonal. "Many people hate me."

"I'll tell the truth," Adelle Hastings said wearily. "I'm cornered.

I have to. Robert Peltham came to me nearly two weeks ago. He told me he was satisfied there was something wrong with the administration of the trust fund. I didn't believe him at first, but he called my attention to certain significant facts. He said that for personal reasons it was impossible for him to take the initiative. He suggested that I do so."

"You did?"

"I made some preliminary investigation."

"And then?"

"Then," she said, "last Monday night—Tuesday morning to be exact—at about three o'clock in the morning, Mr. Peltham called me on the telephone. He said he had to see me at once on a matter of the greatest importance."

"At that time, you'd taken steps to see that there was to be a complete investigation?"

"Yes."

"And what happened?" Mason asked.

She said, "Peltham told me that Albert Tidings had been murdered, that the circumstances surrounding the killing were such that he would be accused of the murder. He seemed very much upset."

"Did he mention anything to you about a woman?" Mason asked.

"Not directly, but I gathered that he hadn't been alone at the time of the shooting."

"Did he admit to you that he had shot Tidings?"

"No."

"What else?" Mason asked.

She said, "Peltham told me that it might be some time before Tidings' body was discovered, that under no circumstances must

I ever admit to a soul that I had any intimation that he was dead, that I must go ahead just as though Tidings were alive, that I must continue to push things, that it was vital to him that it be definitely established there was a shortage in Tidings' accounts before the public knew of the murder."

"Did he say why?"

"No."

"What did you tell him?"

"I told him that I'd do it. He'd been fair with me, very truthful, and very candid. I trusted him."

"Did he say anything else?"

"He told me to see that my time could be accounted for—in case that should become necessary."

"In other words, he expected that *you* might be accused of the murder."

"I don't know. He didn't say. He only told me that, and I didn't ask him why."

"But you knew why, didn't you?"

She hesitated a moment, then faced him defiantly, and said, "Yes."

"That's better," Mason said. "Now then, you arranged to keep in communication with Peltham?"

"Yes."

"How?"

She said, "Mr. Peltham didn't actually leave town. He went to a little hotel and registered under the name of Bilback. I kept in communication with him."

"By telephone?"

"Both by telephone and in person."

"What happened last night?"

She said, "I went to see him."

"He was in his room?"

"Yes."

Mason glanced at Della Street. "And did you," he asked, "call him after you read the paper this morning?"

"Yes, of course."

"With what result?"

She said, "I was advised that Mr. Bilback hadn't been seen this morning—that he wasn't in his room."

Mason said, "You've gone to a lot of trouble in this case keeping me groping in the dark."

She smiled. "I was trying to protect Mr. Peltham," she said. "Under the circumstances, you can appreciate my position."

"That was your only reason?"

"Why, yes, of course."

Mason said, "On Monday night Mr. Tidings had an appointment with a woman, a woman who was in a position to cause him a great deal of trouble. When he left his office, he was in a hurry to keep that appointment."

Her face was a studied mask.

Mason said, "Suppose you tell us about that appointment, Miss Hastings."

"I don't know what you mean."

Mason said, "I'm warning you, and I'm warning you for the last time."

She blinked tears back from her eyes.

Mason consulted his wrist watch. "You have exactly thirty seconds," he said.

She waited for ten seconds, then said, in a voice that was choked with emotion, "I saw him."

"Where?" Mason asked.

There was another interval of silence, then at length she said, "Here."

"Not here," Mason said. "On the turntable out by Mrs. Tidings' bungalow. He asked you to meet him there. He didn't want to be seen coming to your apartment. You'd already accused him of being short in the trust accounts. He said that if you'd meet him there, he'd explain everything."

She shook her head in tight-lipped silence.

"Where," Mason asked, "did you meet him?"

"Here."

Once more Mason crooked his elbow so that he could consult his wrist watch. "Thirty seconds," he said.

The room became uncomfortably silent. At the end of twenty-five seconds, Adelle Hastings stirred and inhaled a quick breath, as though getting ready to speak. Then she clamped her lips again into dogged silence.

Mason got to his feet. "Come, Della," he said, and held the door open to let her precede him into the corridor. Then he turned to face the motionless form of Adelle Hastings sitting mutely on the chair. "Remember," he said, "you had your chance."

He pulled the door shut.

12.

MASON LATCHKEYED the door of his private office and said, "Skip out to the reception room, Della. See who's there, and tell Gertie I'm back but that I don't want to see anyone."

Della Street slipped silently through the door. She returned to find Mason lighting a cigarette.

"What's new, Della?" he asked.

She motioned with her finger on her lips for silence, and tip-toed across to him. In a low voice, she said, "There's someone in the law library."

Mason raised his eyebrows in surprise. "Who?"

"I don't know," she said. "He wouldn't give any name to Gertie, said that he simply must see you, and that he couldn't wait in the reception room. She told him she'd have to have his name, and he pushed his way past her into the law library and told her to go peddle her papers. Gertie was peeved about it, but she said he seemed to be a rather high-class individual, and she didn't want to have him thrown out."

Mason said, "That, Della, will be Robert Peltham."

He strode across the office, jerked open the door to the law library, and said, "Hello, Peltham. Come in."

Peltham, who had been seated at the long table, nervously puffing a cigarette, jumped to his feet and walked rapidly across to where Mason was standing. "What the devil," he asked, "has happened? How could anyone have got my overcoat, my car, and . . ."

Mason said, "It took you long enough to get here."

"What do you mean?"

"I had to see you," Mason said. "I tried to get you in here the easy way. That didn't work. So I tried the hard way."

Peltham stared at him. "You mean that you . . ." His voice trailed away into silence.

Mason said, "This is Della Street, my secretary. I don't have any secrets from her. Come in and sit down. Why didn't you let me talk with you?"

"I didn't think it was wise."

"Why didn't you put your cards on the table the first time you came to the office?"

"I did."

Mason said, sarcastically, "Yes, you certainly did. You and your masked friend. You and your mysterious allusions to what was going to happen. Why the devil didn't you tell me Tidings was dead?"

"Because I didn't know it."

"Bunk," Mason said. "And why didn't you tell me that I was to represent Mrs. Tidings? Then I might have done a decent job of it instead of floundering around."

"You've done nobly," Peltham said.

"That's what *you* think," Mason told him. "Now you listen to me. Time is precious. I want you to do exactly as I tell you to do. . . . You're dead, do you understand?"

"What do you mean?"

"Exactly what I say. You're dead. You've been murdered."

Peltham said impatiently, "Mason, can't you understand? I wanted you to protect Mrs. Tidings. I . . ."

"I am protecting her," Mason said, and then added significantly, "now."

"Weren't you before?"

"How could I? I was chasing will-o'-the-wisps. Why the devil did you say it was okay for me to represent Byrl Gailord?"

"Because it was. I know all about her. Tidings was trustee handling her funds—and a sweet mess he made of it, too. You'll probably find that there's an enormous shortage in her trust accounts."

"How does it happen you know all about her?" Mason asked.

"Through Mrs. Tump. Mrs. Tump has been sort of a godmother to her, rescued her from Russia, and brought her over here, and saw that she had a chance. . . . That is, she did her best. The child was spirited out of the welfare home where she was left for safekeeping and . . ."

"And you thought there wouldn't be anything inconsistent in the representation of Byrl Gailord's interests and of Mrs. Tidings'?"

"That's right."

"And you know Byrl Gailord personally?"

"No, I don't. I only know of her through her godmother."

"Then," Mason said, "you didn't know that Byrl Gailord was a social climber, that she was trying to crash the set that Adelle Hastings travels with, that she's set her cap for a young man in whom Adelle Hastings is interested."

"Byrl Gailord!" Peltham exclaimed.

Mason nodded.

"Why, I can't believe such a thing is possible. Adelle Hastings has never said a word to me about it."

"She," Mason told him, "would be the last person on earth to say a word about it to anyone—particularly to you."

"But your request to represent her was forwarded to me through Adelle."

"All right," Mason said. "We won't argue about it. That's done. That's water that's already gone under the bridge. What's Nadine Tidings to you?"

"What do you think?"

"I'm not thinking," Mason said. "I want to know."

Peltham met his eyes and said tersely, "She's everything in the world to me."

"And Adelle Hastings?"

"What do you mean?"

"What's she to you?"

"Why, nothing. Just a friend, that's all. She's a swell girl, and I've always admired her, but that's all there is to it."

"She knows about your feeling for Mrs. Tidings?"

"Certainly not. No one knows about that. I've gone to the greatest trouble to keep that entirely secret."

"Why?" Mason asked.

"Because of what would have happened. Can't you see? I was on a board of trustees with Tidings. Tidings distrusted me. There was a shortage. Tidings would have yelled 'frame-up,' that I wanted him in prison so I could marry his wife. Nadine wanted a divorce. Tidings had just enough on her so he could drag her name through the mud."

Mason said, "And you were foolish enough to think that any

such crazy scheme as the one you tried would protect Mrs. Tidings?"

"Of course it would. It has, hasn't it?"

"No," Mason said shortly, "it hasn't. Police took Mrs. Tidings into custody an hour or so ago. They're going to charge her with first-degree murder."

Peltham said, "I didn't see how they could connect Nadine with it. Her alibi should have held up."

Mason said, "Let me show you where you made a whole flock of mistakes. . . . People found out about Tidings being dead and where he was. As each person made that discovery, he started protecting himself or herself by building up an alibi."

"Well?" Peltham asked.

Mason said, "The district attorney has all of those alibis in front of him. They're mathematical clues. No one except the murderer of Tidings knows exactly *when* he was killed. Each person thought that he was killed shortly before he or she made the discovery of the body. . . . Therefore, the district attorney only has to check back on the alibis to pick the ones that cover the longest periods, and he knows he's getting warm. Mrs. Tidings started making her alibi date back from Monday afternoon. . . . You can figure what that means."

Peltham frowned.

Mason said, "Here's what the district attorney is going to say in front of a jury. You made love to Nadine Tidings underhandedly, surreptitiously. You had clandestine meetings. You took the name of Hushman and gave her the name of Mrs. Hushman. You . . ."

"Good God!" Peltham exclaimed. "Who knows that?"

"The district attorney," Mason said. "What do you think he is, a damn fool?"

Peltham stared at him in speechless dismay.

Mason said, "Tidings found out about you. He . . ."

"No, he didn't. I swear that he didn't."

"I'm telling you," Mason said, "what the district attorney is going to say to a jury. You were having a secret rendezvous with Nadine Tidings in her house. Albert Tidings was still her lawful husband. You decided to kill him, thereby getting him out of the way as a husband, sealing his lips, protecting Nadine's good name, and your good name, and leaving the way free to marry her."

"I swear that's not true. I swear by all . . ."

"Save it," Mason said. "You don't have to convince me."

"But I want to convince you."

"It won't do any good," Mason told him. "I bought this package. Whatever's in it is mine. I hope Nadine Tidings isn't guilty, but I'm going to represent her whether she's guilty or innocent. It's a bargain I've made, and I keep my bargains. . . . But after this, if anyone ever gets me to go groping around in the dark, you can have me committed to an insane asylum. You baited a trap with a ten-thousand-dollar bill. You probably didn't know it was a trap at the time, and I didn't. But the trap has sprung. I'm caught, and you're caught. Nadine Tidings is caught. . . . We've got to get out. The first thing is to let the district attorney believe that you're dead—and let the murderer of Albert Tidings believe that you're dead."

"Why?"

"Can't you see?"

"No."

"All right," Mason said. "You don't have to see. I've got you dead, and all I want you to do is to *stay* dead."

Mason turned to Della Street. "Della," he said, "this man is dead. Take him out and bury him where *I'll know where he is.*"

"Where," she asked, "do you want him taken—and when?"

Mason said, "You've got to get him out of this office building. Once out, you can use your ingenuity. You . . ."

The telephone on Mason's desk rang. Mason frowned irritably at the interruption, but Della Street picked the receiver off the hook, and said, "Don't ring us, Gertie, unless it's something . . . Oh, it is?"

She looked up at Mason. "Paul Drake on the line," she said. "He says it's important."

Mason picked up the receiver.

Drake said, "I haven't time to talk, Perry. This is a hot-tip. You're getting the double cross."

"How do you mean?"

"Your own clients," Drake said, "are giving you the double cross. They're going to drag all of us up to the D.A.'s office. They . . . Here they come now, Perry."

Mason heard the receiver slam up at the other end on the line.

Mason whirled to Della Street. "They're in the building. You'll have to sneak Peltham out of this office while they're getting me. . . . You and Peltham stand by that door to the corridor. When you hear the officers coming in, you slip out into the corridor. I'll hold them here. Let's hope they're not watching the entrance to the building. They . . ."

Mason heard a commotion in the outer office, heard Gertie's voice raised in shrill protest. "You can't go in there. Mr. Mason can't be disturbed. You . . ."

Mason nodded to Della Street. She grabbed Peltham's arm, rushed him to the door of the corridor, and held it open.

The door leading to the outer office opened an inch and then was slammed closed. From the other side of the panels came the noise of a struggle.

Mason nodded to Della Street. "Now," he said.

She and Peltham slipped out into the corridor. Della Street closed the door silently behind her.

The door from the reception room jerked open. Sergeant Holcomb said, "You little hell-cat, get away from there," and wrestled Gertie's ample figure away from the door. A plain-clothes man grabbed her shoulders, spun her around, and the two men pushed their way into the office.

Mason, sitting at his desk, apparently engrossed in studying a law book, looked up, frowning at the interruption. "What the devil's the meaning of this?" he asked.

Sergeant Holcomb said triumphantly, "It means that you've skated on thin ice once too often. Now, you've broken through."

"What are you talking about?"

"I have my instructions, Mason. You can either come with me to the district attorney's office to answer questions now, or you can go to jail."

"What sort of blackmail is that?" Mason asked, indignantly pushing back his chair and getting to his feet.

"There's no blackmail about it," Holcomb said. "As far as I'm concerned, I'm hoping you say 'no.' I want to arrest you and throw you into the can right now. The D.A. has you dead to rights, but just because you're a lawyer, he says you're going to have a chance to explain—if you want it."

Mason paused, frowning at Sergeant Holcomb, making a

mental calculation of the time it would take Della Street to get Robert Peltham down in the elevator and out through the back entrance to the alley.

"Have you," he asked, "got a warrant?"

There was no mistaking the triumph on Sergeant Holcomb's face. "That," he said, "was exactly what I was hoping you'd say. . . . No, Mr. Mason, I haven't a warrant, but I'm going to get one in just ten seconds. The skids are all greased."

He strode across to the telephone, picked up the receiver, and said, "Get me the D.A.'s office."

Mason shrugged his shoulders. "All right," he said. "I'll go with you to the district attorney's office."

"It's too late for that now," Sergeant Holcomb said.

Mason's voice was cold. "I think not," he said. "I have never refused to accompany you. I simply asked you if you had a warrant for my arrest."

Sergeant Holcomb dropped the receiver. "All right, Mason," he said. "Let's get started."

Mason delayed as long as he dared getting his hat and coat. Then he said, "I'll have to call my receptionist and tell her I'm going to be out."

Sergeant Holcomb said, "Make it snappy."

Mason called Gertie to the private office. She was still panting from her struggles, and she glared with hostility at the officers.

"Gertie, I'm being taken to the office of the district attorney for questioning. I want you to make some notes on things that are to be done in cases that are pending."

"Make it snappy," Sergeant Holcomb said.

Mason said, "In the case of Smith versus Smith, arrange for the taking of a deposition."

For a moment there was a frown of perplexity on Gertie's forehead; then with the realization that Della Street was not in the office and the knowledge that the files held no case of Smith versus Smith, she said, with a flash of comprehension, "Yes, Mr. Mason. Is there anything else?"

"Yes. In the case of Jones versus Raglund, my time is up for the filing of an answer and cross-complaint tomorrow. In the event I don't return and am unable to file the answer and cross-complaint, arrange to get a stipulation extending my time."

"Yes, Mr. Mason. And suppose I can't get a stipulation?"

"Then you'll have to get a court order," Mason said.

"Just how will I go about doing that?"

Sergeant Holcomb said, "Come on. You'll have a chance to telephone her after the D.A. gets done with you."

"This is an important matter," Mason said. "I can't let the case go by default."

"Well, you can telephone her. Come on. We haven't got all day. The D.A. is waiting."

Mason said to Gertie, "Simply explain the circumstances to the presiding judge. Now in the case of Hortense versus Wiltfong, you'll have to give back the retainer. Explain to Mr. Hortense that I'm going to be unable to handle his case. That's not to be done unless I fail to return by five o'clock, or . . ."

Sergeant Holcomb moved toward Mason. "My God, you don't have to dictate memoranda covering your whole practice. . . . Say, what are you doing, sparring for time?"

Mason said, "That's all, Gertie. . . . Come on, *gentlemen.*"

13.

PERRY MASON followed Sergeant Holcomb into the district attorney's outer office. The plain-clothes officer brought up the rear.

Mason saw Paul Drake seated beside a man who was obviously a police detective.

"Hello, Paul," Mason said, affecting surprise. "What's the idea?"

Drake got to his feet. "So far no one's told me."

Sergeant Holcomb said, "Come on, Mason. The D.A.'s waiting."

Drake shot forward his hand impulsively. "Perry," he said, "no matter what they say, I want you to know that I'm for you. No one can ever make me believe there's anything crooked about the way you do things."

"Thanks," Mason said, gripping Paul's hand and feeling, as he did so, a folded piece of paper which Drake had surreptitiously slipped into his palm.

"Come on," Holcomb said impatiently, standing in a double doorway which led to an inner suite of offices.

The detective who had been seated next to Drake intervened.

"You two guys don't need to go into a huddle," he said. "Break away."

Mason turned away, casually slipping his right hand into his trousers pocket.

"This way," Holcomb said.

Beyond the double doorway, a long corridor stretched past doors bearing the names of deputies. At the far end of the corridor, a mahogany door was inscribed simply with the words, "Hamilton Burger, District Attorney."

"He's expecting us," Sergeant Holcomb said, and opened the door to walk in. Mason followed, and the plain-clothes man, apparently having done his duty by having herded the lawyer thus far, turned to stand with his back to the wall near the doorway.

The automatic door check clicked the door shut.

Mason saw Hamilton Burger seated behind his desk, a barrel-chested, thick-necked individual who gave the impression of having great physical strength and a bulldog mental tenacity.

"How do you do, Mason," he said. "Sit down over here in this chair."

Mason nodded and glanced around at the office. A man, who was evidently a shorthand reporter, sat at a little table, a notebook opened in front of him. The page of the notebook which was visible was half filled with shorthand characters, evidently notes taken of a conversation with some other witness. Carl Mattern sat back against the wall looking very self-righteous. Mrs. Tump, seated beside him, glowered belligerently at Mason, and beside her, Byrl Gailord, who had evidently been crying, raised her eyes to regard Mason with hurt dignity. There were dark smudges where the mascara had been dissolved by her tears and smeared by her soggy handkerchief.

"All right," Mason said. "What is it?"

Hamilton Burger said, "I have sufficient information to justify a warrant for your arrest. Because you are an attorney and so far have had what officially amounts to good standing, I've decided to give you an opportunity to explain your actions."

"Thank you," Mason said with acid politeness.

"I may say," Burger went on, "that while you are in good standing at present, that has been due, in my opinion, largely to luck. I have long warned you that your methods would eventually get you into trouble."

"I think we can dispense with any lectures," Mason said. "My methods are my own, and my ethics are my own. I'm responsible for both. If you have anything to say, say it."

Hamilton Burger said, "Sit down in this chair, Mason."

Mason took the chair which was nearest to the district attorney's desk, separated by only a few feet from that of the shorthand reporter.

"I warn you, Mason, that this interview is to be reported, and that anything you say may be used against you. You don't need to make any statements unless you want to. If you do make them, they are to be deemed free and voluntary statements, made without coercion or promises."

"Forget the formula," Mason said. "Let's get down to brass tracks. I know all the preliminaries."

Burger nodded to Mattern. "Mr. Mattern," he said, "I want you to tell Mr. Mason exactly what you've told me. You can condense it to simply hit the high spots."

Mattern said, "What's the use? He knows it all."

"Nevertheless," Burger said, "I want you to repeat it."

Mattern raised his eyes to stare steadily at Mason, a stare of cold accusation. He said, in a strong, well-modulated voice, "I was Mr. Tidings' secretary. Last Tuesday morning Mr. Mason called at my office."

"What time?" Mason asked.

"Shortly before nine o'clock," Mattern said.

Hamilton Burger said, "Kindly don't interrupt the statement of the witness, Mr. Mason. Your opportunity for a defense will come later. I simply want you to be advised of the information which has been placed in my hands. This is not the time to cross-examine witnesses."

"If you want to accuse me of anything," Mason said, "and expect me to answer that accusation, I'm going to know the details. Go ahead, Mattern."

Burger frowned with annoyance.

Mattern, still with his eyes fixed steadily on Mason, said in the same level voice, "Mr. Mason told me that Mr. Tidings had met with an accident. He didn't say what sort of an accident. He said that Mr. Tidings, according to his information, was dead, that he was representing Byrl Gailord, that Byrl Gailord was the beneficiary under a trust which Mr. Tidings was administering, that he understood Tidings had intended to make a purchase of a large block of stock in the Western Prospecting Company, that it was very much to the advantage of his client to have the deal go through, that he thought the stock was a good investment for her, and that he was interested in having the amount involved—fifty thousand dollars—earmarked by having it appear that at least that much of Tidings' funds were held in the Gailord trust."

"Did he say anything about it being to the interests of other clients to have it appear that Tidings' death should be assumed by the police to have occurred at a time subsequent to that at which the death had actually occurred?" Hamilton Burger asked.

"Not in so many words," Mattern said, frowning as though searching his recollection. "I think I've already told you exactly what he said, as nearly as I can remember, Mr. Burger."

"Well, tell it to me again," Burger said.

"He said that there were reasons which he wouldn't go into which would make it very much to the advantage of his clients to have it appear that the time of death did not occur until after noon on Tuesday."

"Did he say client or clients?" Burger asked.

"Clients. I remember that very distinctly," Mattern said.

"But he didn't say specifically whether by clients he referred to Miss Gailord and some other client?"

"No, he didn't. But I do remember that he used the word clients—in the plural."

"Very well," Burger said. "Go ahead."

Mason faced the hostility of Mrs. Tump's eyes, the silent accusation of Byrl Gailord, and casually took a cigarette case from his pocket. He selected a cigarette and made a search of his pockets for matches. In the course of the search, he managed to extract from his right-hand trousers pocket the folded note which Drake had given him. He snapped a match into flame, and lit the cigarette. As Mattern resumed his statement, Mason made a surreptitious study of the message Drake had slipped him. It had been printed in ink upon a narrow strip of paper. The words were simple and to the point: "Freel is registered in St. Germaine Hotel under name Herkimer Smith, Shreveport, Louisiana."

Mason shifted the match to his left hand, dropped it into an ash tray; his right hand casually dropped into the side pocket of his coat and deposited Drake's printed message.

Mattern went on steadily. "Mr. Mason told me that under the law of agency I would have no authority to conclude the deal if Tidings were dead, that his clients wanted the purchase consummated, that it would be better for all concerned to have it appear that the transaction had been completed before Tidings died. He said that if I'd co-operate with him, he'd give me ten thousand dollars when the purchase had been completed."

"Did you agree to co-operate with him?" Burger asked.

"I objected at first," Mattern said. "Naturally the information came as a shock to me, and I was astonished to think that a man in Mr. Mason's position would make such a proposition to me."

"And did you communicate your reluctance to Mr. Mason?"

"I did. I told him that I couldn't do it."

"And what did Mason say?"

"Mason pointed out to me that Tidings was dead, and there was nothing I could do that would restore him to life, that it would be much better for all concerned, particularly his clients . . ."

"And he used the word in that connection and in the plural?" Burger asked.

"That's right, he did. Yes, sir."

"Go ahead."

". . . that it would be much better for his clients if it was made to appear that Mr. Tidings had met his death after noon of that day. He asked me if it wasn't true that Mr. Tidings had secured a cashier's check in an amount of fifty thousand dollars which was to be delivered for the purchase price of the stock. I told him that this was true. So then Mr. Mason suggested that he would call me later on, on the telephone, that I was to tell his secretary that Mr. Tidings was available and would talk with Mr. Mason. Mason said that he'd come on the line, and I could carry on a conversation, and he would pretend that it was Tidings on the other end of the line, that I was also to advise any other person who called that Mr. Tidings was in his office but was engaged in a conference and couldn't be disturbed, that I was to go ahead with the stock purchase just as though Tidings were there, and that I was to swear that Tidings had accompanied me down in the elevator; and then, to clinch matters after the purchase had been completed, I was to swear that Tidings had called up and asked me if everything had gone through according to schedule."

"And he promised you ten thousand dollars for this?" Burger asked.

"Yes, sir."

"Was that ten thousand dollars paid?"

"Yes, sir."

"How?"

"In fifty- and hundred-dollar bills."

"What did you do with that money?"

"I deposited it in a bank."

"The bank where you carry your regular account?"

"No, sir. It was another bank. I went to a bank where I wasn't known. I told them that I wished to open an account and made the deposit under a fictitious name."

"What name?"

"Anthony Blake."

"Did you tell anyone about this?"

"No, sir. . . . Not until I told you early this morning."

Burger glanced at Mason. "All right, Mason," he said, "what have you to say to this?"

"I want to ask him a couple of questions," Mason said.

"I don't think this is the time or the place," Burger said. "This isn't a trial. I'm merely putting my cards on the table showing you the information which I have at hand."

Mason ignored the comment and said to Mattern, "I suppose, Mattern, the district attorney found out about that fictitious account and asked you to explain it."

"He did nothing of the sort," Mattern said indignantly. "No one knew anything about that account. My conscience started bothering me, and I finally came to the district attorney and explained all the circumstances to him."

Mason turned to Hamilton Burger. "You can see what happened," he said. "Mattern knew that Tidings was dead. He confessed to me that he'd discovered that fact early Tuesday morning. Bolus, who's president of the Western Prospecting Company, was planning on unloading his stock. He'd offered Mattern a ten-thousand-dollar bonus when the deal went through. I pointed out to Mattern that with the facilities at your command, you'd be able to trace that payment through the bank. He knew he was trapped, so he concocted this story."

"That's a lie," Mattern said.

The district attorney said, "You can't make anything like that stick, Mason. I've talked with Emery Bolus, the president of the Western Prospecting Company. It's true that the sale was of private stock. I believe it was the stock held by Bolus, who wished to unload, but Bolus knows nothing whatever of any ten-thousand-dollar payment and had no inkling that Tidings was dead at the time the transaction was completed. You can't escape the consequences of your act by trying to drag others into it."

"And," Mason went on calmly, "Bolus has consulted an attorney. Bolus learned that under the law of agency the sale would have been invalid in the event it appeared Tidings had died—*unless* it should appear that *I* had consented to the sale as attorney for Byrl Gailord, which would have made Mattern an agent for the beneficiary instead of the trustee. Under those circumstances, Bolus could insist that the sale was valid. This story has been concocted in order to bolster up that sale. The stock is probably valueless. Bolus has agreed to give Mattern another five or ten thousand to tell this story. It gives Mattern an out, accounts for his actions, and will leave Bolus still holding the money."

"That," Burger said coldly, "is an ingenious attempt to distort the facts, but unfortunately for you, the evidence doesn't corroborate it."

Mason said, "All right. I'll go at it from another angle. How about you, Mrs. Tump? You are the one who employed me to represent the interests of Byrl Gailord. You know when you came to me. When was it?"

"I called on you," she said, "on Tuesday morning. I guess it was around ten o'clock. But you knew that I was going to call on you and that you were going to represent Byrl."

"How in Heaven's name did I know that?" Mason asked. "I'm not a mind reader."

"You knew it through Robert Peltham," she said. "You've been in touch with Robert Peltham ever since this case started. Do you deny that Robert Peltham called on you and employed you to represent his interests Monday night?"

"What makes you think that happened?" Mason asked.

"He told me . . ."

"Don't answer that question," Burger interrupted. "We're not here to give Mr. Mason an unlimited opportunity to fish for information and then work out a story which will hold water."

"What *is* the purpose of this interview?" Mason asked.

"Simply to give you an outline of the circumstances which make me feel that it's my duty to have a warrant issued for your arrest on a charge of criminal conspiracy and on a charge of being an accessory after the fact."

"Accessory to what?" Mason asked.

"To the murder of Albert Tidings."

"I see," Mason commented calmly, "and whom am I supposed to be aiding and abetting?"

"Robert Peltham."

"Oh," Mason said, "so *he's* the murderer now, is he?"

"You know he is."

"And how do I know it?"

"He told you so shortly after midnight on Monday night—or to be exact, the time was Tuesday morning. You met him at your office, and he retained you. You arranged for an alibi for Peltham and his mistress. In order to make that alibi good, you wanted it to appear that Tidings was still alive on Tuesday morning, that he met his death sometime after noon on Tuesday. Everything that you have done, Mason, supports that conclusion. The circumstantial evidence is strongly against you, and in view of the statement of Mattern, who is a direct witness, I feel it my duty to institute criminal proceedings against you unless you can convince me that you are innocent."

"And how can I convince you?" Mason asked. "I can't ask

questions of the witnesses. I can't even find out what evidence you hold. My hands are tied."

"Not if you're innocent," Burger said. "You don't need to cross-examine witnesses in order to find out what cards I hold in my hand. You can make a simple, direct statement of your connection with the case."

"I can't do that," Mason said.

"Why not?"

"Because it would betray the confidences of a client."

"Do you deny that Robert Peltham called on you sometime between midnight and one o'clock on Tuesday morning?"

Mason said, "I'm not going to give you any information whatever concerning the activities of any client."

"Under the circumstances," Burger said, "I consider the interview closed. I have evidence which proves conclusively that Peltham was in love with Tidings' wife, that Tidings refused to grant a divorce, and that while the affair had been kept successfully from his knowledge for some little time, he had finally learned about it and sought to trap the participants. It was while he was so engaged that he met his death."

"When?"

"At eleven-fifteen Monday night."

Mason spent several seconds staring at the smoke which eddied upward from the tip of his half-smoked cigarette. "At eleven-fifteen," he said musingly.

"That's right."

"Someone hear the shot?" Mason asked.

For a moment it seemed as though Burger was about to reply to the question, then he picked up the telephone on his desk and inquired, "Is Miss Adelle Hastings in the office? . . . Very well. I want to see her next. . . . And Paul Drake . . . Very well, have him wait. I'll see Miss Hastings next."

Mason said musingly, "Eleven-fifteen. . . . That isn't the way I understand it. That time of death doesn't coincide with the facts as I've worked them out"

"What time," Burger asked, "do *you* consider that death took place?"

"About nine-thirty," Mason said without hesitation.

"On Monday night?"

"That's right."

Burger said, "I am not committing myself finally on that point as yet, Mr. Mason. There's one more witness whom I must interview personally before I make a definite commitment."

"That witness heard the shot?" Mason asked.

"That witness," Burger said with cold finality, "saw the deed committed. He recognized Robert Peltham as the murderer. He actually saw the murder. I've talked with him over the telephone. I haven't his signed statement as yet."

Mason stretched forth his long legs, crossed the ankles, and stared down at the toes of his shoes. "Well," he said, "there's nothing I can add."

"You might tell me how you fix the time of death as being around nine-thirty."

Mason shook his head.

"Very well," Burger announced in the voice of one terminating an interview, "I shall instruct my men to issue a complaint on which a warrant for arrest will be issued, Mason. I'm sorry, but I've repeatedly warned you that your methods were going to get you into trouble."

"I'll be eligible for bail?" Mason asked.

"I shall charge you with being an accessory after the fact on first-degree murder."

Mason said, "You haven't that complaint ready now?"

"It will be ready within the next hour."

"Until that time I'm not under arrest?"

Burger said, "I don't intend to arrest you without a warrant."

Mason arose from the chair, tossed his cigarette into the ash tray, and said, "Thank you very much for your consideration in giving me an opportunity to present my side of the case."

"I'm sorry that you couldn't make a more satisfactory explanation."

"So am I," Mason said.

Mrs. Tump said bitterly, "Well, I don't know where that leaves *us*. You certainly can't hold Byrl to any such bargain as that. *She* doesn't want that stock."

"I'm afraid that will have to be thrashed out in a civil court, Mrs. Tump," Burger said.

Mrs. Tump glared at Mason. "To think that I accepted *you* as an honest lawyer," she said scornfully.

Mason bowed. "My regrets, Mrs. Tump."

Byrl Gailord said sobbingly, "It seems as though everyone were conspiring against me. Now my money is put into a worthless stock—as much of it as hasn't been embezzled."

"Are you certain the stock is worthless?" Mason asked.

"Of course it is," she said.

Mason said, "Well, I have matters to wind up."

Without so much as a backward glance, he walked to the door and out into the corridor.

Carl Mattern watched him go, his eyes steady, his face expressionless.

14.

FROM A DRUGSTORE on the corner, Mason telephoned his office.

"Hello, Gertie," he said. "Guess who this is?"

"Uh huh," she said.

"The office being covered?"

"Uh huh."

"No one listening on the line?"

"No."

"Okay," Mason said. "Pretend I'm your boy friend, and you're making a date."

"I can't tonight," she said. "I think I'm going to have to work. There's been a bunch of stuff at the office I can't understand. The boss is in some sort of a jam, and the place is lousy with detectives. They get in my hair. . . . What's that? . . . Well, I'm just talking to a boy friend. Haven't I got a right to tell him why I can't make a date? . . . Baloney, Mister. You mind your business, and I'll mind mine. . . . Hello, Stew, I guess I'm not supposed to talk. Anyhow, I can't make it tonight."

Mason said, "Della Street had a body to bury. Heard anything from her?"

"Uh huh."

"An address?"

"Uh huh."

Mason said, "Go down the hall to the rest-room, and then duck out to a telephone where you won't be heard. Ring her and tell her to grab a portable typewriter and meet me at the St. Germaine Hotel just as soon as a taxicab can get her there. Got that straight?"

Gertie said, "Well, I'll do it just this once, but don't think you can pull that line on me all the time. You're always having cousins come in from the country that need to be entertained. What did you try to date *me* up for if you knew *she* was coming? . . . It's getting so that every time I check back on you, you're chasing around to night spots with some dizzy blonde, and she always turns out to be a cousin or a sister-in-law. If you ask me, you've got too much of a family—all blondes."

Mason chuckled and said into the telephone, "Well, you have to admit, Gertie, that it's always a new one. You shouldn't get peeved as long as I'm playing the field."

Mason heard a man's voice at the other end of the line saying something to Gertie and then her voice in the transmitter saying, "Now you listen to me, Stew. Maybe this is on the level, and maybe it ain't. I'm broadminded, but I'm getting fed up with this. Now you just give me a ring about five minutes to five, and if I don't have to work tonight, I'm going to go right along and crab your party. If that gal ain't your cousin, I'm going to get a nice double handful of blonde hair. . . . And don't think you can kid me."

"All right, sweetheart," Mason said, "good-by," and distinctly heard a masculine voice say at the other end of the line, "You just let me talk with that boy friend of yours, sister. I want to get his address."

Mason slipped the receiver back onto the hook, stepped out to the curb, waited for a taxi, and gave the address of the St. Germaine Hotel.

He had to wait ten minutes before Della Street put in an appearance.

"Made it as fast as I could, Chief," she said. "How serious is it?"

"Plenty," he said. "They've framed me."

"Who?"

"Mattern."

"That shrimp!"

"He's worked up a good story," Mason said.

"By himself?"

"No. Some lawyer concocted it, and Bolus is back of it. They've lost ten grand, but they still have forty thousand to fight for, and Bolus doesn't intend to let that go without a struggle."

"Where do you come in on that?"

"I'm the sheep," he said, "that's being led to the slaughter."

"What do we do here?"

Mason said, "We pay our respects to a man by the name of Herkimer Smith, who's registered as being from Shreveport, Louisiana, and we don't let him know we're coming."

"Okay. You want to find out his room?"

"Yes."

Della Street extended her hand. "Gimme."

Mason gave her a dime, and she walked over to the telephone booth. Mason stood by the open door while she dialed the number of the hotel switchboard and said to the operator, "This is the

Credit Department of the Ville de Paris. We have a c.o.d. to send to your hotel to a Mr. Herkimer Smith of Shreveport, Louisiana. It's a c.o.d. so all we're interested in is checking on the registration. . . . If you will, please."

After a moment, she said, "Thank you," hung up the receiver, and said, "Okay, Chief. He's in 409."

Mason touched Della Street's arm, signaling for her to leave the telephone booth. He pulled another coin from his pocket and dialed the number of the Drake Detective Agency. "Mason talking," he said. "I want an operative who looks tough and is tough. I want him in a hurry. Send him to the St. Germaine Hotel. Have him go up to Room 409 and walk in without knocking. I'll be there. Have him hold up two fingers so I'll know he's your man. He isn't to say anything until I give him the lead. Got that?"

He received an okay from Drake's secretary, hung up the telephone, and said to Della Street, "Let's go."

They walked silently to the elevator, went to the fourth floor, and Mason stood for a moment getting the run of the numbers on the doors before piloting Della Street down the corridor to the right. They paused in front of Room 409, and Mason knocked.

The thin, reedy voice of Arthmont A. Freel, from the other side of the door, asked in high-pitched nervousness, "Who is it?"

Della Street said sweetly, "Chambermaid with towels."

The door was unlocked from the inside. Mason placed his shoulder against it. As Freel turned the knob, Mason pushed the door back. He and Della Street entered the room, to confront the frightened eyes of Freel.

Mason said, "Hello, sucker. How does it feel to be elected to the gas chamber? See if there's anyone in the bathroom, Della. Go over by that table and sit down when you've looked."

Mason walked over to the closet, jerked the door open and looked inside. He carefully closed the door of the hotel bedroom, walked over to a comfortable chair, and sat down. Della Street completed her inspection of the bathroom, and drew up a chair to the wicker table near the window. She calmly set up her portable typewriter and fed two sheets of plain paper, sandwiched with a sheet of carbon paper, into the machine. Having done that, she sat back with her hands folded in her lap.

Freel stared at her uneasily for a moment, then shifted his eyes to the lawyer.

"Well," Mason said, "I'm sorry they made you the goat. Personally, I don't think you're guilty, but you always were a sucker. You were half-smart, and you stuck your neck out just far enough so they could hang the murder rap on it."

"What are you talking about?" Freel demanded.

Mason selected a cigarette, tapped it gently on the edge of the cigarette case, snapped a match into flame, lit up, and sucked in a deep, appreciative drag on the cigarette.

"It really is too bad, Freel. You never were one to understand the fine points of the game." Mason paused to inhale another deep drag of smoke, shook his head mournfully, and added, "Too bad."

"I don't know what you're talking about," Freel said.

"I'll say you don't," Mason said with a chuckle. "You don't know what anyone's talking about. That's the trouble with you, Freel. You sit in on a game you don't understand, and when someone tells you to stick your chips in the center of the table, you shove in the whole stack. . . . Now it's just too bad."

"You can't rattle me," Freel said. "You did it once, but you can't do it again."

Mason said, "You'll pardon me if I take a rather detached interest in the thing from the standpoint of legal technique. Personally, I think some shrewd lawyer figured the play."

"You're crazy," Freel said.

Mason smiled. "Don't say it so scornfully, Freel. Within thirty days, *your* only defense will be insanity. You'll have a bunch of doctors calling on you, and you'll be sweating blood, trying to make them think you're crazy. So don't mention insanity so lightly.

"You see, Freel, there are a flock of alibis in this case. Some of them are nice alibis. The alibis stay put, but the time of the murder doesn't: it keeps jumping around.

"Now you're a nice little guy, but you have too much of an appetite—for money. You're money hungry, money crazy. You're getting along in years and you can't get jobs now—not the clerical jobs you're fitted to handle. That bothered you. You wanted money so you could have security. That's a laugh, Freel. Security—for *you!*"

Freel started twisting his fingers, worried eyes regarding Mason apprehensively, but he said nothing.

Mason smoked leisurely, regarding Freel as one might look at an interesting specimen in an aquarium. Over at the table, Della Street sat motionless, keeping herself in the background, effacing her presence from Freel's consciousness.

"So," Mason said, "you were offered money to swear that you'd seen the murder committed. You were told that Peltham was dead, that he could never deny your accusation. And so you agreed to take the money and swear that you'd seen Peltham, and seen him fire the shot. What you overlooked was the fact that the murderer never had any intention of really pinning that crime on Peltham. You haven't got it yet, Freel. You probably won't get it for about a week. But you've been elected to a reserved seat in the state's lethal gas chamber, and it's been done so nicely that the operation will be virtually painless.

"For about a week you'll be the state's star witness, then Peltham will show up with his alibi, and there you'll be—right out in the open with your neck stuck way, way out. The district attorney will come down on you like a ton of brick."

"Peltham's dead," Freel said sullenly.

Mason laughed and said, "You *think* he's dead. That overcoat business was a gag. He was playing that in order to cover his escape. A woman he was sweet on was due to be put on the spot in connection with that murder, and he didn't want to be examined. He took a powder so he wouldn't have to testify concerning his relations with her. That's all."

Freel squirmed uneasily. "I haven't said anything to anyone."

Mason said, "Oh, yes, you have. You've made your crack to the D.A., and he's given the newspapermen an interview on the strength of it. The D.A. isn't going to back up on a thing like that."

"You're stringing me again," Freel said.

"Think so?" Mason asked. "Well, think again. Get this, you poor dumb dope, and let it sink into that thick skull of yours. Albert Tidings was killed while he was sitting in his automobile sometime after it started to rain Monday night. He didn't die instantly. He was found unconscious in his machine shortly after eleven o'clock. He was taken to Mrs. Tidings' house, put into bed, and died almost instantly. There was a thirty-two caliber revolver in his hip pocket. He hadn't fired that gun. Apparently, he'd made no effort to pull it. There was fresh lipstick on the handkerchief in his overcoat pocket.

"Tidings had learned about Peltham and his wife. If Peltham had approached the automobile in which Tidings was seated, Tidings would have pulled his gun. There wouldn't have been any lipstick on his handkerchief. If you'll just get the cobwebs out of your brain and try to concentrate for a minute on that lipstick, you'll find out a lot. Who kissed him, his wife? She hated him. No, Freel, there was only one woman whom he would have kissed who would have kissed him. He kissed that woman and then got shot. Figure it out for yourself."

Freel twisted his fingers in an agony of apprehension. His bony knuckles cracked and in the silence of the room the sound seemed distorted, magnified.

Mason stretched his arms above his head and yawned. "Oh, well," he said, "it's all in the game. We live our little lives and they seem important to us. Ho-hum. . . . Guess I must be getting sleepy. The state will take your name away and give you a number. Then they'll present you with a nice suit of clothes, slide you into the lethal gas chamber, and leave you for fifteen minutes. When you come out, you'll have a tag pinned on the lapel of your coat and be delivered to the undertaker as part of the day's routine. I suppose it seems important to us, Freel, but it really doesn't make much difference. We're just cogs in a machine."

Freel licked his lips, tried twice to swallow. He said nothing.

"Well," Mason said, "God knows you're responsible for what happened, Freel. You know why Tidings didn't shoot his gun along at the last. He shot the ammunition you'd given him instead. You're really responsible for what happened and it is only fair you should pay the price."

Mason looked at his watch, then brought his eyes to hard focus on Freel. "Three minutes from now," he said, "I'm going to walk out of this room. When I close the door, it'll be too late for you to do anything to save that neck of yours. I'm your only hope, Freel."

Freel leaned forward and said, in the manner of one who is unduly anxious to impress his audience, "You can't pin it on me, Mason, you can't do it. I tell you I'm in the clear."

Mason laughed. "In the clear . . . you . . . that's a hot one. You damn fool, you have admitted that you were on the ground when the crime was committed."

"Honestly, Mr. Mason, I . . ."

Mason, looking at his wrist watch, motioned Freel to silence.

Abruptly the door opened. A man who seemed to be all chest and jaw steam-rollered his way into the room, kicking the door shut behind him. He held up two fingers to Mason.

Mason jumped up from his chair, moved over to grasp the intruder's hand cordially. "Well, well, Captain," he said, "it's been a long time since I've seen you. I wasn't expecting you. I thought Sergeant Holcomb of Homicide would show up to make the arrest. I see you decided to come yourself."

"Yeah," the visitor said in a deep, booming voice, "I came myself."

Mason, talking rapidly, said, "Now listen, Captain, this little guy is a rabbit. He's a rat. He's a poor, shrivelled-up, chicken-feed blackmailer. But I don't like to see this murder rap hung on him. I think he's about ready to tell the truth. If he tells the truth, I'm going to try and save his neck. If he tells the whole truth, they won't give him first-degree murder. It's his only chance. There's my secretary over there with her typewriter all ready to take down what he says. Captain, let's do the square thing . . . let's be human . . . let's give this guy a break. Give him sixty seconds. Won't you do that for me?"

The private detective blinked his eyes. In a deep, rumbling voice he said, "Sixty seconds—for you."

Mason turned to Freel. "All right, sucker, make up your mind."

Freel, who had evidently been thinking while Mason and the operative were talking, said in a high-pitched, whining voice, "All right, I'll confess. And if I confess you'll try to save my neck?"

Mason nodded.

"You promise?"

Again there was a nod.

Freel took a soiled handkerchief from his hip pocket and wiped his forehead. "What do I do?" he asked.

Mason indicated Della Street with a nod of his head. "Start talking to her," he said, "and sign your name to it when she gets it written."

Freel looked across at Della Street. "It all started," he said, "when I tried to blackmail Albert Tidings. First I wanted to sell him information and then . . ."

Della Street's hands poised over the keyboard for a moment then crashed down on the keys as the portable typewriter exploded into staccato noise. As Freel paused in his statement, Mason said, "When that's finished, Della, get him to sign it. Have the Captain sign as witness. Put the paper in an envelope, beat it over to *The Clarion,* and hand it to the editor personally. Take Freel along with you."

Della Street nodded, then, with her hands held over the keyboard, glanced expectantly at Freel.

Mason said in a low voice to the private detective, "If he gets rusty, break him in two. If he tries to beat it, collar him and hold him."

"How shall I hold him?" the operative asked.

Mason looked at him scornfully. "You have two hands—aren't they enough?"

He pushed past the operative to the door, stepped out in the corridor, and pulled the door shut. He stood for a moment listening. Five seconds after the door had closed he heard the type bars on Della Street's machine clack into rapid action.

Grinning, Mason started walking down the corridor.

15.

IN HIS PRIVATE office, tilted back in the swivel chair, his feet resting on a corner of the desk, Mason grinned up at Sergeant Holcomb.

"This time," Holcomb said grimly, "I have a warrant."

"I don't think the D.A. wants you to serve it, Sergeant."

"Take another think."

Mason said, "That was an interesting case, Sergeant. Two or three things about it were puzzling but after all it wasn't as complicated as it seemed. *The Clarion's* getting out an extra I understand. You'll probably enjoy reading it."

"Nuts," Holcomb said.

Mason went on calmly, "Freel gave *The Clarion* a complete confession. Della Street delivered it personally and Freel along with it."

Holcomb's eyes showed both interest and suspicion. "What is this, a run-around?"

"Nope, the low-down. Better watch your step, Sergeant, or you'll be pounding pavements."

"I have a warrant," Holcomb said.

"So you have."

"Get your hat."

Mason, holding his hands up in front of him as though holding an imaginary newspaper, pretended to read. "So rapidly did *The Clarion* work in breaking the case that the police were still baffled. Even after the Extra Edition hit the street, one of the more amusing sidelights was the spectacle of Sergeant Holcomb of the Homicide Squad, with the dogged persistence of an unimaginative police officer, serving a warrant on a well-known attorney just as *Clarion* newsboys were selling the extras which gave the true facts of the case. Sergeant Holcomb, however, dutifully plodding along in the line of duty, escorted the grinning Perry Mason into Headquarters, pushing aside as he did so newsboys who were shouting the name of the real murderer."

Mason went through the pantomime of folding a newspaper and putting it down on the desk.

Sergeant Holcomb said, "You can't stall along that way."

"I'm not trying to stall, Sergeant. I'm trying to give you a break."

"Yes, you always did like me."

"No kidding, Holcomb, you're not a bad sort . . . you're obstinate and pig-headed and a little dumb, but you have the courage of your convictions, loyalty to your work and absolute honesty. Why don't you get aboard the bandwagon?"

"Doing what, for instance?" Holcomb asked. "Not that you're selling me anything, Mason."

"The lipstick on Tidings' face, for instance," Mason commented. "That was an interesting angle, Sergeant. There were several women in the case but only one of them would have kissed Tidings. Only one of them could have approached Tidings out there on that lonely road without having him reach for his gun."

"What do you mean, lonely road?" Sergeant Holcomb asked.

"You know what I mean. Tidings wanted to get something on his wife. He was waiting out there near her house. A car drove up. Tidings knew the people in that car. They had been following him. They stopped the car and got out. Tidings kissed the woman."

Sergeant Holcomb was thinking with knitted brow and furrowed forehead. "Who?" he asked.

"Byrl Gailord," Mason said.

"How do you figure?"

"Byrl Gailord wanted money. Mrs. Tump wanted money. Tidings liked Byrl: he hated Mrs. Tump. He wouldn't see Byrl while Mrs. Tump was with her so Mrs. Tump waited and followed Tidings when he left the office. They followed him to Adelle Hastings' apartment but didn't have a chance to talk with him. They followed him out to where he was waiting for his wife and did have a chance.

"Byrl kissed him, made a fuss over him, and then Mrs. Tump came pushing up and made her demands, and threatened to bring him into court. Tidings laughed at her. He told her the minute she made a move he'd show that Byrl was the illegitimate daughter of Mrs. Tump's daughter, that the Russian nobility business was a fake. And that was when Mrs. Tump shot him."

"A nice bed-time story," Sergeant Holcomb said.

"No, it's logic," Mason insisted. "I found a roll of money in the mattress of Freel's bed. Freel hadn't made that dough out of Mrs. Tump. She was too smart to pay in advance. The only other person who could have played Santa Claus was Tidings. I figured Freel had sold out to Tidings and I knew Tidings wouldn't buy expensive ammunition without using it.

"I knew that Mrs. Tump would never hire a lawyer if she thought there was any possibility of getting a settlement without a lawyer. She didn't hire me to negotiate a settlement but to give herself an alibi. One would hardly be expected to hire a lawyer to interview a dead man. It was a clever move but the trouble was I knew Mrs. Tump would never offer to pay a fee while there was any chance of chiseling a settlement without a fee.

"You police, incidentally, overlooked a bet. Your laboratory could analyze that lipstick and analyze the lipstick used by the women in the case."

Sergeant Holcomb seemed thoughtful. "We could have done that—can do it yet—but that isn't going to keep me from serving this warrant on you, no matter how much you talk."

Mason got to his feet, stood broad-shouldered, eyes locking with those of Sergeant Holcomb. "Get this," he said. "As far as I'm concerned I don't give a damn what you do. If you're foolish enough to drag me down to Headquarters while *The Clarion* is putting the news on the street, it won't hurt *me* any. You'll be the one who gets all the laughs. No, Sergeant, the reason I'm telling you this is because I'm trying to give you a break. Beat it up to *The Clarion* office, tell them you have doped the whole thing out, grab Freel as a material witness—and you'll get your picture in the paper."

Sergeant Holcomb said, "I am going to serve that warrant."

"Go ahead. You'll have your picture in the paper in any event. How would you prefer to have the caption read? Sergeant Holcomb Who Solves Murder Mystery in *Clarion's* Office, or Sergeant Holcomb Arresting Prominent Lawyer, While *Clarion* Newsboys, Seen in Lower Left-Hand Corner, Are Selling Newspapers Giving True Facts in Case to the Public?"

"How do I know this isn't a stall so you can beat it?" Sergeant Holcomb asked.

Mason looked up at him and laughed. "I should run away from a law practice that keeps me in the high income-tax brackets. For another thing, figure it out for yourself. Somebody kissed him, somebody shot him—and beat it. Then Mrs. Tidings and Peltham came along, found him dying, took him up to Mrs. Tidings' house, and started to telephone for an ambulance. Tidings died and they tried to cover up. It's the only theory that . . ."

The door opened. Della Street came bustling into the office.

"Okay?" Mason asked.

"Okay," she said. "It was just exactly as you figured. Mrs. Tump bribed him to pin the crime on Peltham. Freel had sold Tidings the information about Byrl Gailord just as you'd suspected."

"Can he prove Mrs. Tump committed the crime?"

"No, only that Mrs. Tump bribed him to pin it on Peltham."

Mason grinned across at Sergeant Holcomb. "Even better than I thought, Sergeant," he said. "*The Clarion* won't dare to accuse Mrs. Tump of the murder in so many words. They can only publish Freel's confession and accuse her of bribery. You know if I were you, Sergeant, I think I'd go to work on Byrl Gailord. I doubt if she had any idea Mrs. Tump was going to shoot him, but after the crime was committed she agreed to stand by her grandmother. I think a shrewd officer who went to work fast, before *The Clarion* hit the streets, could . . ."

Sergeant Holcomb spun on his heel, took two quick steps toward the door, then stopped and came back. Abruptly he pushed a hand out at the surprised lawyer.

"All right, Mason," he said, "I don't like your methods. Some day I'm going to throw you in the can, but I do appreciate good detective work when I see it and I'm enough of a cop to pull for a guy who solves crimes, even if I don't like the way he goes about it."

Surprised, Mason shook hands.

Sergeant Holcomb said, "Don't think for a minute this gives you any right to cut corners on your next case."

"What does it give me?" Mason asked, his eyes twinkling.

"My thanks for handing me a tip on a silver platter and for bringing a murderer to justice. Any cop worth his salt will respect a man who can do that."

Mason clapped Sergeant Holcomb on the shoulder. "Spoken like a man, Sergeant. Go to it."

Once more Sergeant Holcomb strode across the office. Just before he jerked the door closed, he turned back to say to Mason, "I still don't like your methods."

"I understand," Mason said.

Sergeant Holcomb's glittering eyes held the lawyer. "And I don't think," he went on, "that I like you."

The door slammed.

Mason turned to grin at Della Street. "That," he announced, "is that."

"Why," she asked, "did you give Holcomb a break like that?"

"Because I think he's the one to corner Byrl Gailord and make her tell the truth."

Della Street regarded him steadily. "And because you wanted to give him a break."

"Well, perhaps," Mason admitted.

"He hates your guts, Chief."

"I know he does, but he's a fighter and I like fighters. How are things going over at *The Clarion?*"

"Like a house afire. Sergeant Holcomb can't see Freel—they have him sewed up."

Mason grinned. "He can get a lot of advertising trying," he said, "and they'll put Freel back into circulation after the extra hits the streets."

The telephone rang. Della Street picked up the receiver, said hello, and then, cupping her hand over the mouthpiece, turned to Perry Mason. "Adelle Hastings wants to know if there is anything she can do."

Mason said, "Tell her to meet us at the Haystack Cocktail Lounge in fifteen minutes. I want to see her face when she reads that newspaper."

With her hand still cupped over the receiver, Della Street in the manner of a secretary who has been trying to deal in details, said, "If we get there in fifteen minutes do you think we'll still be there when *The Clarion* comes out?"

"The way I feel," Mason said, grinning, "we're going to be there all afternoon."

Della Street removed her hand from the mouthpiece. "Hello, Miss Hastings," she said.

THE END

DISCUSSION QUESTIONS

- Were you able to predict any part of the solution to the case?

- Aside from the solution, did anything about the book surprise you? If so, what?

- Did any aspects of the plot date the story? If so, which ones?

- Would the story be different if it were set in the present day? If so, how?

- What role did the setting play in the narrative?

- What did you make of the relationship between Perry Mason, Della Street, and Paul Drake?

- If you were in Perry Mason's place, is there anything you would have done differently?

- Can you think of any contemporary mystery authors that seem to be influenced or inspired by Erle Stanley Gardner's writing?

- For those familiar with adaptations of the Perry Mason series, how do the characters in the novels compare to what you've seen elsewhere?

- Otto Penzler notes in the introduction that Erle Stanley Gardner wrote hardboiled pulp fiction before creating the Perry Mason character. Did you notice any remnants of this earlier style in *The Case of the Baited Hook*?

AMERICAN MYSTERY CLASSICS

from

PENZLER PUBLISHERS